The Legend o

B

Yearning

MARGIT SANDEMO

Translated from the Swedish
by Gregory Herring and Angela Cook

Tagman

The Legend of the Ice People

Yearning

The original Norwegian version was published in 1982 under the title
Sagan om Isfolket 4: Lengsel by Bladkompaniet, Oslo, Norway

First published in Great Britain in paperback in October 2008
by Tagman Worldwide Ltd in The Tagman Press imprint.

Tagman Worldwide Ltd
Media House
Burrel Road, St Ives, Huntingdon,
Cambridgeshire, PE27 3LE
Tel: 0845 644 4186
Fax: 0845 644 4187
www.tagmanpress.co.uk
email: editorial@tagmanpress.co.uk

ISBN: Paperback 978-1-903571-81-1
A CIP catalogue record for this book is available from the British Library

Text & Cover Design: Richard Legg
Translation: Gregory Herring and Angela Cook

Printed by CLE Print Ltd, St Ives, Cambs, PE27 3LE, UK

Tagman www.tagmanpress.co.uk

This first English translation of *The Legend of the Ice People*
is dedicated with love and gratitude to the memory
of my dear late husband Asbjorn Sandemo,
who made my life a fairy tale

THE ICE PEOPLE
Descendants of Tengel the Evil

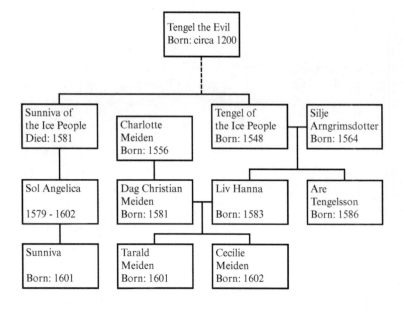

Tengel the Evil
Born: circa 1200

Sunniva of
the Ice People
Died: 1581

Charlotte
Meiden
Born: 1556

Tengel of
the Ice People
Born: 1548

Silje
Arngrimsdotter
Born: 1564

Sol Angelica
1579 - 1602

Dag Christian
Meiden
Born: 1581

Liv Hanna
Born: 1583

Are
Tengelsson
Born: 1586

Sunniva
Born: 1601

Tarald
Meiden
Born: 1601

Cecilie
Meiden
Born: 1602

Chapter 1

As time marched on, everything happened exactly as Sol had predicted. In the very year that she went to her death, a new baby girl was born into the family to take her place – she might even be described as a second Sol. This was the firstborn daughter of Liv and Dag, baptised Cecilie, a name which evoked those of both her grandmothers, Charlotte and Silje. But despite reminding them of Sol in so many ways, Cecilie had not inherited the cold-heartedness and deep sense of torment that had characterised Sol's life.

At the same time, on a farmstead at Eikeby, not far from where this newborn baby girl was awakening to life, a far less fortunate and deformed child was also growing up. The Eikeby farmstead was one of many that made up the Gråstensholm estate. In itself, it was a continuous source of worry to its landlord, Baron Dag Meiden and his mother Charlotte. They did their best to help the impoverished tenant family to avoid starvation, but their task was made more difficult by the fact that the old crofter who lived there had decided to take literally the words of the Old Testament that commanded mankind 'to go forth and multiply'. In fact he seemed to be trying to do it all single-handedly.

His youngest children were still small when his eldest son married and took on the daily work of the farm. He also showed himself to be very much his father's son in his determination to populate the world as fast as possible. By the year 1607, the son had produced fifteen children of his own, all of whom struggled for food. They had to battle for possession of every platter against their aunts and uncles, many of whom were not very much older than themselves.

One of these fifteen children was named Yrja. She was a young girl who had caused Tengel much trouble at her birth by trying to make her entrance feet first. It was an arrival that was to prove symbolic and typical of her young life: almost everything she put her hand to in her early years seemed to go amiss.

She had been an unlucky infant whose weary, exhausted mother was incapable of producing enough breast milk to feed her. Nor were her childhood years much better, because Yrja was always left the last scraps on the table. As a result her body had not developed properly. It was said that she had suffered from rickets, the condition that would come to be known centuries later as the 'English sickness'. All the neighbours said this was connected with the fact that, while her mother was pregnant with Yrja, she had met a crippled man on the road and this had undoubtedly caused the illness. In addition, Yrja's mother looked upon her as an encumbrance. She already had several other young offspring to care for and felt Yrja contributed little or nothing to the family and was consequently worthless.

Her father was still obliged to perform some extra duties for the Gråstensholm estate as part of his tenure and one day as he was leaving for the manor, in sheer frustration his wife told him to take the girl with him.

'At least I'll have one less to look after,' she shrieked. 'For one day at any rate!'

Irritated, the farmer told her that it was impossible to take a child out labouring with him.

'Then tie her to a tree while you work!' the wife replied. 'It's my big washday and I just can't look after all these little ones – and the older ones will be helping with the wash.'

In this way it was decided that Yrja should go with him. She was then six years old and it was already clear that she had inherited her father's heavy peasant shape and face. Whenever her mother looked at her, she felt she was staring at a mutilated and uncultivated thistle.

The landlord's children, Tarald and Cecilie, together with their cousin Sunniva, were playing at Gråstensholm Manor when they first saw the young peasant girl tethered to a tree a short distance from the barn. She was standing, head bowed and kicking her toe idly in the dirt, casting furtive glances at the children as they played. The look on her face and her behaviour both shouted out desperately: 'What fun they're having! If only I could join in!' Yrja had often heard her aunts and uncles talk about past children's parties at Gråstensholm. *They* had all been invited – but that had been when Master Dag was a child.

On realising that Yrja was tied to the tree, Cecilie stopped playing and stared. Although she was the youngest, she was the dominant one of the three. 'She can play with us, can't she?' she asked the others.

Tarald and Sunniva looked quizzically at Yrja. They could see clearly that she had not been endowed with any great physical beauty, heavily built, undernourished and deformed as she was. But just as the roots of a pine tree

3

can often bite fast into an exposed craggy outcrop and still find the nourishment to grow strong and tower over its neighbours, Yrja had somehow, despite all the odds, managed to thrive. She was indeed a tall, uncultivated thistle.

'Yes, why not?' chirped Tarald at last. 'Let's ask.'

Together they ran over to the tree. But they stopped a few yards away from her. They could see that Yrja's toe was now digging frantically in the dirt in embarrassment.

'Hello,' said Tarald. 'What's your name?'

Without looking up she whispered something inaudible.

'What did you say?' asked Cecilie, taking a step closer.

The girl before them swallowed hard again and tried to speak, but the words were clearly sticking in her throat. Overcome by her shyness, she covered her face with her arm. Then at last she managed to say, 'Yrja.'

'Yrja?' repeated Cecilie. 'Was that what you said?'

She nodded but could not meet their gaze.

'Yrja?' repeated Sunniva incredulously. 'Surely nobody's called that!'

The tethered girl looked as though she wanted the earth to swallow her up.

'You can't say that!' said Cecilie scornfully to Sunniva. 'You don't know every name in the world!'

'Do you want to come and play with us?' asked Tarald.

Yrja raised her head to look at him and in that instant knew that she would die for him were he ever to ask. Then she lowered her eyes again without answering.

'We shall ask your father,' announced Cecilie. 'He's the Eikeby crofter, isn't he?'

Yrja nodded vigorously. Father will say 'no', of course, she thought – but still they asked me anyway. They *really* asked!

The three ran over to the barn, where her father and some other workers were repairing the entrance ramp, and only then did Yrja dare hazard another glance at them. The boy was handsome, with dark hair and eyebrows like sea birds in flight, she thought, remembering the way they swayed upwards at their centres. One of the two girls was very pretty and as graceful as a china vase that Yrja had once seen in another crofter's cottage. The other girl, the youngest, was a bundle of energy who had already dirtied her fine dress despite the early hour. They were all standing eagerly around her father now and she could see he was not going to be easily persuaded. At that moment a lady came towards the barnyard – a gentle, fine lady who Yrja recognised. It was the mistress from Linden Allée and all three children rushed over to her at once.

'Grandma! Grandma, can Yrja play with us?' they chorused. 'Please tell her father that she may – he doesn't believe us.'

Hearing the urgency in their voices, Silje gave them a warm smile. 'Of course she may. I shall speak to her father. But isn't that the little girl who … Yes, I'm sure it is!' She waved the Eikeby crofter to join her and they all walked over to the tethered child.

'Now children,' said Silje, 'I want you to know that young Yrja was born the morning after you, Tarald. My husband Tengel helped to bring both of you into the world almost at the same time. He rode back and forth between Eikeby and Gråstensholm all through the day and night. There is only about seven hours' difference in your ages. And you, Sunniva, were born five days after them.'

'What about me, then?' asked Cecilie, the alert and attentive one. She was offended at seemingly being left out. 'Why aren't I in this secret gang?'

'Dear Cecilie,' laughed Silje, 'you know very well that you are only five years old. You have been reminding me for several weeks that your birthday is coming soon. But one year is not a great difference. And besides there is something else that binds you to them – you are the image of Sol, Sunniva's mother. She had darker hair than you – and was perhaps just a little more beautiful. Never have I seen a more beautiful girl.'

Tarald nodded. 'I have seen her portrait at Linden Allée.'

'Oh, that does not do her justice at all,' said Silje, aware that Sunniva needed to have a picture in her heart of an outstanding mother. 'Sol sparkled with so much life and vitality that it took your breath away.'

'Sol was my Mama,' said Sunniva proudly. 'But am I not as beautiful as she was?'

Silje looked at her for a moment. 'You are not really like her at all, Sunniva. You have blond hair and blue eyes. And you are as delicate as a butterfly. And you have your own very special beauty – of that you can be sure.'

None of the children had ever heard any account of Sol's fate: how she was due to be burned at the stake as a witch after murdering Sunniva's father, Heming the Bailiff-killer, with a pitchfork. Or how Tengel had managed to send her poison on her last night in prison in order to spare her the agony and torment of the fire. All they knew was that she had died soon after the birth of Sunniva.

At times Sunniva had asked about her father, only to be told that he was dead and that she had inherited his fine and handsome looks. Nobody ever spoke of how he had met his macabre end. And nobody ever uttered even part of his despised name out loud.

'Tarald, untie Yrja now,' said Silje kindly. 'And then when you have finished playing, invite her to eat with us.'

In this way Yrja was introduced to Gråstensholm, and from then on she often spent her days there. The four children, so close in years, stuck together through thick and thin. It seemed in many ways as though the three Gråstensholm children somehow *needed* Yrja with them for some unspecified and unknown reason.

It has to be said that they divided up the workload a little unevenly and it was Yrja who was always given the boring, less glamorous roles in all their games, like running errands, standing watch and other menial tasks. Sunniva could do nothing she was assigned – she was hopeless, the others decided – while Tarald and Cecilie waged a continuous battle over who was in charge. This was a battle Cecilie consistently won, since she always refused to be beaten by an older sibling.

The adults could not conceal their surprise at how completely Yrja had been integrated into the group. Liv conjectured that perhaps they needed somebody to impress – a phenomenon not unknown either to children or adults. From Yrja's point of view and that of her family, this new lifestyle brought great improvements for her. She was well fed at Gråstensholm, sometimes getting extra helpings, and she began to grow and become stronger. After a few months Silje decided to take Yrja under her wing, moving her into her service at Linden Allée. Yrja would come a few days each week to help Silje with lighter tasks in the studio and around the house. Everyone was pleased with the arrangement, especially because Silje would now and again reward the girl with a treat – an item of clothing or a small coin.

Amazingly, Sunniva was also keen to help her grandmother, at least in the studio where exciting things happened. So the two girls took turns to assist Silje, who was now not as agile as she had once been. This arrangement worked superbly – not least because Silje could send them away the moment she felt it was becoming tedious to have little girls fussing around in the room.

It had been several years since Sunniva moved up to Gråstensholm to be brought up alongside Dag and Liv's two children. Silje had found early on that she now lacked the energy to look after young children at home and Liv had gladly offered to care for the orphaned girl.

Silje had concerns for her youngest son, Are, who showed no sign of ever wanting to wed. All he ever thought about was the farm – its livestock, the harvest, the house and forests. This worried Silje and she fretted and nagged at him. She wanted more grandchildren and the farm needed a capable housewife. But when the moment finally arrived, the 'proposal' took on a ludicrous aspect.

It happened during Yrja's first year at Linden Allée, on a day when all the grandchildren were spending time with their grandparents, playing noisy games of hide-and-seek. For some reason they were distracted and for a little while they forgot all about Yrja, who had hidden herself in the barn. She sat as quiet as a little mouse in the calving stall and wondered why nobody came to find her.

Then yes, she heard a noise. Somebody was coming. But these were heavier footfalls than those of a child – so she drew back deeper into the shadows. Peeping through a crack in the stall's wooden partition, she saw it was Klaus, the stable lad at Gråstensholm, who had come down to Linden Allée in pursuit of his duties. He came into the barn and stood looking around for an old bridle – but he didn't notice Yrja's presence. Suddenly another of Sol's protégés also entered the building on an errand of her own. It was Meta, who over the years had been of immeasurable help to the family.

Klaus had never been very gifted. For many years he had mourned Sol, overcome with bitterness at her loss. He had been devoted to her, but then without warning he had taken a liking to the diminutive Meta, who had hair the colour of ripened corn. Now, meeting her so unexpectedly like this alone in the barn, he suddenly found he could not control his inner urges any longer.

Proudly he grabbed hold of Meta and wrenching at his own clothes, asked abruptly if she would like to see his manhood unclothed. Meta had no such desire and her screams began to pierce Yrja's eardrums. In panic the little girl started creeping on all fours towards the door and on the threshold she was almost run down by Meta. The older girl ran out ahead and met Silje, who was coming towards them on her way to the barn. Meta's face had turned a sickly green colour and she hurried into the gap between two of the farm buildings and vomited violently. In the heat of the moment, nobody noticed the inconspicuous little Yrja.

'My dear Meta,' said Silje in an alarmed voice, 'what is wrong? Are you ill?'

The girl turned to face Silje, teeth chattering, and shook her head. 'It was Klaus ... He unfastened his trousers and ... I was very frightened!' She turned away suddenly and began to retch again.

'Oh, my goodness!' gasped Silje in a horrified voice and ran into the barn.

Klaus was still standing in the same place with an embarrassed grin on his face. He had however refastened his clothing again.

'You must not do things like that, Klaus!' said Silje in a calm and determined tone. 'Especially not to Meta!'

Unseen inside the shadowy doorway, Yrja stood listening, but still nobody noticed her presence.

'But I like her,' replied Klaus sheepishly.

'Forget such thoughts,' snapped Silje. 'You must understand that Meta was terribly frightened and injured once by a band of soldiers who all exposed themselves to her as you just did – yes, and they did much worse things besides! So when you acted in a similar way just now, she remembered that awful day and was so shaken that she became sick. Have you understood?'

Klaus was downcast. 'But Sol liked it. And now I want to lie with Meta.'

Silje was both taken aback and deeply exasperated by this announcement. 'Never! Now you listen to me, young lad! You can forget all about Meta! Besides, have you not noticed that there is a girl here on the farm who always tries to catch your eye?'

'Tries to catch my eye …'

'Who likes you!'

'Me? Somebody likes me?'

Silje was making things up as fast as she could go – she had never acted as a matchmaker before. But she was determined to save Meta from the attentions of a man completely unsuitable for her.

'Who is it, Mistress Silje?'

'Rosa! Rosa with the red cheeks and the friendly smile. Have you not noticed her working in our kitchen?'

It was torture watching the workings of Klaus's mind as he tried to think. He had obviously not noticed the chubby scullery maid with the stocky legs who worked for Silje. Like Klaus, Rosa was also a simple soul with no family and too many summers behind her to be a temptation to most of the young single men. She was certainly five years older than Klaus, Silje reckoned, but nonetheless was a good-hearted lass and while Silje hadn't the vaguest idea what Rosa thought of Klaus, she had every reason to believe that the maiden would be grateful for the attentions of almost any man.

As a result of this impulsive intervention, Silje sought out Rosa later in the day, as she was cleaning some saucepans in the scullery. Taking her aside, she asked quietly: 'Have you ever noticed that you have an admirer, Rosa?'

The well-rounded maid blushed, her cheeks turning bright crimson. 'An admirer – me? No, Mistress, you mustn't jest so! Who is it?'

'Klaus, the stable lad who sometimes comes here from the big house.' Silje paused, giving the maid time to reflect. Sure enough, immediately after Silje's mention of the scullery maid's name to Klaus in the barn, he had found a reason to linger outside the kitchen window to find out more about Rosa and catch a glimpse of her. Now, if Meta kept quiet about Klaus's little indiscretion – and she probably would – and he too kept his secret, then Rosa would never know he had tried to shame another girl.

'Mmm … yes, well, Mistress, I suppose I did see him outside the kitchen window earlier. But I would not have thought such a big, strapping handsome lad as him would be …'

'He's not very bright, you know, Rosa,' interrupted Silje. 'But he is kind.'

'I'm not so bright neither! I see – Klaus, eh? Did he say if he'd soon be coming back here again?'

'Not in so many words, Rosa. But he often has to come down here on errands.'

Rosa was silent for a moment, mulling something over. 'Then would I be allowed to offer him some spiced buns, Mistress? I would take the stale ones, of course.'

Silje smiled. 'You shall give him the *best* our house can offer, Rosa. He is worth it, I should say – even if he is a bit empty-headed!'

You should be ashamed of yourself, Silje thought, as she went into the large parlour, chuckling to herself. What have you started now?

As soon as Silje had left the kitchen, Rosa grabbed hold of Yrja to keep her from following her mistress. 'Yrja, you go up to Gråstensholm a lot, don't you?'

'Yeah.'

'Couldn't you take a message to that Klaus – he's the handsomest on the whole farm, you can't miss him – and say that if he comes down here I'll see he gets well fed ... a real treat? Say – oh, say its because he cured Master Tengel's lame horse so well last winter.'

Yrja nodded and promised to pass on the message. She knew who Klaus was all right, but to say he was the 'handsomest' at Gråstensholm – well no, that was something she couldn't understand! Rosa's eyes followed Yrja's little twisted body as she went in search of her revered Mistress Silje. Rosa could hardly wait until Klaus had an opportunity to visit her. Imagine! Such a fine-looking man!

Quietly, Yrja entered the parlour at the precise moment that Silje was about to get her second surprise that day. Master Tengel – big, broody and frightening to behold – was walking over to them. Yrja knew that behind his terrible appearance there lay nothing but goodness and decency. She also knew that next year would see him turn sixty. Yet he looked so much younger than her own father, who still had some way to go before his fiftieth year.

'What is going on, Silje?' asked Tengel. 'I have just heard that Meta has walked out and left us! She has gone to a family in Tönsberg that has been asking her to work for them as a scullery maid. She said that either she or Klaus must leave and because she is worth less to us, then she would be the one to go.'

Are came in just in time to hear Tengel's last few words and he immediately looked alarmed. 'What did you just say about Meta leaving us? I hope she hasn't. We cannot manage without her!'

'We shall have to if the girl does not want to stay with us,' said Tengel. 'Anyway, you are always complaining about her work. So I don't understand what is causing you to feel all this upset.'

'When did she leave?' yelled Are, ignoring Tengel's question. 'And by what means?'

'She set off walking, carrying a small bundle, about an hour since, I think – maybe two.'

Are was incensed. 'I shall ride after her – straightaway!'

Silje followed him into the hallway. 'Are, please be careful! Do not forget what Meta once suffered. That is also the reason for her leaving today.'

Are turned pale. 'Klaus?'

'He did nothing to her – merely showed himself. But it awakened bad memories for her.'

'I shall tear him apart with my own two hands!'

'No!' said Silje forcefully. 'I have taken care of Klaus. She will have nothing to fear from him any more.'

'Are you sure?'

'You may be certain of it. He has other interests now.'

Are simply nodded. He realised immediately that there was no harm in Klaus – his transgression was due solely to his foolishness. Shortly afterwards Yrja heard the sound of hooves galloping down the allée and she knew Are was riding out to find Meta and bring her home.

Yrja never found out what Are did after he had rode out of the yard. In truth, she did not understand what all the fuss had been about anyway. Klaus had been guilty of something unpleasant in the barn – but whatever it was, she had not been able to see from where she had been hiding. Nor would Silje and Tengel ever know the full truth of Are's bid to save Meta. Although they would know the outcome soon enough, they were never to learn exactly what took place and Are staunchly refused to reveal anything about the matter.

They could not know that Are had ridden like the wind along the road to Tönsberg, his mind in turmoil, full of regret for the years he had lost. Before very long, to his great relief, he caught up with Meta before she reached her destination and slowed his horse a little to gather his thoughts. 'Dear me,' he thought, 'she looks so tiny and pitiable.'

Her appearance in fact reminded him of that day seven years ago, when Sol had come home with this wretched lost individual. How angry he had been then at the sound of her Skåne dialect and how unpleasant he had been to her. Feeling deeply conscience-stricken, he rode up beside her and jumped from the horse. Meta turned to look up at him, wide-eyed and frightened, her eyelids swollen from all her bouts of sobbing.

'Why Meta?' he asked, in a tone that was a shade too harsh. 'Why are you running away like this?'

Immediately her chin began to quiver again and he realised that he had started badly.

'We cannot be without you at Linden Allée, Meta, you must realise that!' He was almost shouting at her and she turned away from him once more.

'What I really mean is that *I* cannot be without you, Meta!'

She swung round to face him again, with a shocked expression. 'You, Master? But you have always disliked me.'

'*Have* I?' he asked aggressively. 'Well, perhaps at first I did – but have I done so these past years?'

Meta paused to reflect. 'No,' she said, a little surprised. 'It just seemed like it.'

'You imagined it,' said Are. 'For have we not worked well together, you and I? We have, haven't we?'

'Yes,' she whispered, head bowed.

Are stood remembering the little shadow who followed him everywhere, in the open countryside, in the yard and in the outbuildings. And now she was about to disappear!

Without pausing for breath, he suddenly blurted out, as though it were one long word, 'Metawillyoumarryme?'

Are had never seen such a perplexed expression on anybody's face as he saw then. He was both taken aback and surprised at his own outburst.

'Me?' she said softly. 'But I am no more than a farmyard maid!'

'You are much more than that. It was not until you were gone that I understood how much you meant – to me!'

Tears fell from her half-closed eyes. Are watched, not knowing where his courage had come from or where he had found the words. Girls and 'things like that' had not been part of his life until that moment. He had no experience to tell him how to act, and perhaps for that reason he sounded brusque.

'Don't you want to, then?' he asked quietly.

'I cannot,' she whispered.

'Because of what had happened all that time ago?'

Her head nodded rapidly.

'But …' Are paused, agonising over how to express himself. 'But you do like me, don't you Meta? Just a little bit?'

15

In a muffled squeaky voice she replied, 'I like you a lot, Master.'

'So if … you know what … hadn't happened, would you have said, "Yes"?'

'Master, I am not worthy of you.'

'Don't say that!'

His words came out in a rush and again he thought: 'Oh, no! I was too harsh with her again.' This was not going very well at all. Why was there nobody here to help him get out of this dilemma? The country road was deserted as far as the eye could see – besides, he didn't really want anyone to witness this divine mess he had created.

'My own parents were not always so well respected,' he said at last, speaking slowly and more quietly. 'There was a time when they were outcasts themselves, a bit like you. And only Aunt Charlotte saved us all from starvation. What do you say to that?'

'I don't know what to say, Master.'

'Please call me Are.'

'A … Are,' she repeated breathlessly, unaccustomed to addressing him by name.

'Listen to me, Meta,' he said, placing his hands gently on her shoulders. 'If you have no wish … to share a bed with me, then you will not have to. I am not a … passionate person.'

Did that sound foolish, he asked himself? He was sure it did, but he dared not use other words. 'If only you will marry me … and let me … surround you with my love, that will be enough.'

Now she will certainly laugh at me, he thought desperately. But no, strangely enough she was not laughing. Taking a deep breath, he continued in a firm voice, 'But although I have said that, I … er … would dearly like to have a child ... or two. I'm sure you understand – Mother nags me continually about it.'

Meta bowed her head so that he saw only the blond hair on her neck. 'I am not without feelings,' she whispered. 'It is just that when certain things happen – like they did today – I go numb inside.'

'Do you compare me with Klaus?'

Meta was aghast at the thought, as she lifted her head to look up at this tall, powerful young man with black hair and classic prominent cheekbones. It was his unassuming earnest manner that she trusted and which made her feel safe – and she wanted to stay close to him.

'No! Oh, no! I would never do that!' she exclaimed.

Gently he pulled her close and kissed her forehead. He was not moved to do anything more. He was pleased to have achieved that much at least. Meta trembled, but remained pressed close against him.

'Think about it,' he whispered, his voice faltering from the emotion he was feeling. 'At least come back home. Mother seems to have "dealt" with Klaus, so that you will have nothing more to fear from him.'

Silje was, of course, privy to none of this. All she, and a wide-eyed Yrja, knew was that Are came riding back into the yard with Meta sitting in front of him, beaming happily. They had ridden slowly back, deeply engrossed in conversation.

'We are to be wed, Mother!' he cried from a distance, as though trying to prevent any objections. 'It is all settled.'

But there were no objections at all. On the contrary, both Tengel and Silje, together with his whole family were very happy for them. Nobody questioned the wisdom or otherwise of the move and everybody seemed to understand the inevitability of it.

And what was to be made of Klaus? It was only a few days after Silje had conspired to bring him and Rosa together that she caught sight of them secretly making their way towards the barn. Silje chuckled softly – Rosa would certainly not be afraid to see what Klaus was so proud to show her.

'Are they going to thresh corn?' asked Yrja, a little confused.

'I suppose you could say that,' laughed Silje.

* * * *

After talking things over, Tengel and Charlotte decided to give Klaus a smallholding that had been standing empty for some years and Klaus made an honest woman of Rosa just in time to avoid a scandal. They had two children before Rosa's childbearing years were behind her – two children who, while they made no epoch-breaking discoveries, were blessed with far greater intellect than both their parents.

Nor was Meta about to disappoint the family. She produced three boys in quick succession, proving that she was not lacking in passion for her Are – not in the slightest!

Although little Yrja loved everyone in the family, she placed Silje high above all the others. She was, however, unable to understand her own parents. She still lived at home, yet each morning her mother would ask, 'Are you not up at Lindallé today?'

Whenever Yrja answered, 'Sunniva is helping Mistress Silje today,' her mother would become irritated and wonder why 'that spoilt child' had to stick her nose in everywhere.

At home, before working at Linden Allée, Yrja had always been too weak to care for and carry her small brothers and sisters. Now that she was stronger and healthier, she had asked many times if she could do work around the home. But her parents always refused to hear of it.

'Mind your back, lifting heavy things,' they said, seemingly full of consideration, but still insisting that she look after Are and Meta's three young sons.

Yrja could not understand this at all. She could not see that she was the most important source of income for the family. Every small thing she was given at Linden Allée – and sometimes at Gråstensholm – was of no value in her eyes and she handed these all to her parents. They, of course, were frightened she would injure herself and that they would lose all the good things Yrja provided – food, clothes and above all the coin that Mistress Silje regularly pressed upon her.

For her part, all that mattered to Yrja was being at Linden Allée. As the time she spent there lengthened, the signs of low self-esteem, poor confidence and hunger that she had suffered at the hands of her parents began to disappear. She seemed somehow to absorb knowledge from Tengel and Silje, just by being around them. From Meta, she learned housekeeping skills and from all three she learned some growing self-confidence. Very quietly and unobtrusively her own personality continued to grow and develop, but because she was so quiet and shy, at first no one took any notice.

Chapter 2

A young woman came walking steadily up the avenue of linden trees towards the farm. Her gait was regular, but not particularly elegant, because lack of nourishment while she was still a child had left the bones in her body noticeably deformed and twisted. She had now reached an age when she was conscious of her unfortunate condition and, despite her wearing long skirts, it was apparent to any onlooker from the way she walked that she was badly bow-legged.

Visitors to her parent's home had often entertained themselves by trying to guess out loud what her uncovered legs might look like. She had never responded with witty or sharp replies to these taunts – that was not in her nature. Her pleasant face was always set in a friendly bright expression and her eyes shone with warm-heartedness for everyone. Her stamina was incredible and she seemed not to know the meaning of the word 'no' when anybody asked for help. Neither did it seem bother her that she had a body that was cumbersome and ungainly, or that her face was less than elfin-like.

Yrja was now nineteen years of age – the 'uncultivated thistle' had grown up. At this moment, on a late August day, she was about to celebrate her birthday together with Tarald and Sunniva. Silje had decided to combine the three birthdays into one great celebration and all the children would be coming.

Sunniva, of course, had always been delicate and graceful, but now she was also so elfin-like! Yrja admired her enormously and, in lonely moments of reflection, she had often wished that she too was as nimble and had the same fragile beauty. It never occurred to her that she herself possessed a charm that was less easy to define, that even a thistle bears beautiful flowers.

She would also be seeing Cecilie today – the forthright and happy Cecilie Meiden, whose personality at best held all the world's confidence and humour. The things she dared to say sometimes! The thought of them made Yrja chuckle. Cecilie, the 'crazy one', was a year younger than the others and, perhaps because of this, sometimes made a play of feeling inferior, complaining that she was being treated unfairly. Yet no one knew better than she did how to assert herself. Cecilie indeed was strong – very strong – in spirit.

Suddenly as she walked towards the house, Yrja felt herself blush. Tarald, she realised afresh, would be there – and she dared not whisper the thought out loud. Barely two months had passed since she discovered that she had fallen in love with the young heir to Gråstensholm – but no one must ever find out. Not ever! For who was she? Yrja, an ugly uncouth nobody from a poor smallholding – and she was well aware that often, behind her back, she was called 'the Thistle'.

Yrja in fact, expected only that she would become an old maid. This was something her parents had prepared her for, and she had come to accept the idea. But was it not a brutal act of the good God in heaven to give her a heart that would not obey these rules?

She was walking now along the top part of the avenue. She knew there was a story about the first eight trees that told how they had each been planted in honour of some individual living on the estate and that, when that person died, so also did the tree. Two trees so far had fallen and been replaced with new saplings. One had been planted for the old dowager Baroness Meiden, who Yrja had never known, and one other for Sunniva's beautiful mother, Sol. Both had been dead for a long time and strong new lindens now stood in their place. Passing one of the oldest trees, Yrja noticed sadly that it was looking a little withered – but she did not know the name of the man or woman to whom it was attached.

Dag Meiden, the Public Notary himself, had a tree here, as did his kind and loving wife, Liv. They were Tarald and Cecilie's parents and both were highly respected and loved by all who knew them. As she was absently pursuing these thoughts, Yrja found she had reached the end of the avenue. For a moment she halted and stood still in the yard. Did she look tidy and elegant? Nothing ever fitted her twisted body properly. The freshly laundered wide-sleeved blouse, however, had the clean smell of sun and fresh air, her hair was freshly washed and combed, and she had brushed from her dark skirt the sheep's wool and cat hairs that covered everything in her parent's cottage at Eikeby. Nobody would have dreamed of describing her as conventionally beautiful; but she had done her very best with what she had.

* * * *

Silje sat at the window, looking out into the yard, where Are's three boys were playing. They were all three such very different characters. As she watched, the middle one, Trond, was standing on top of the large boulder that was the centrepiece of the farmyard. He had the agility of a small lizard and was now shouting his victory, playing at being king and teasing the others below him. Silje was sure that Trond would one day hold a position of authority; he certainly had drive and leadership in him.

Brand, the youngest, was well built and dependable, just like his father in so many ways. He kept trying to grapple his way up the stony surface of the boulder, but slipped back down every time. The oldest had been named Torgeir, although everyone called him Tarjei. He was not taking part in the 'battle' with his younger brothers. He had the sharpest mind of them all and was incredibly astute. At that very moment he looked as if he was solving one of the great mysteries of the world.

Silje's gaze wandered dreamily back and forth among the boys. Tarjei was Tengel's favourite and she remembered how the lad had grown and how, through him, Tengel had seemed gradually to have discovered an unaccustomed serenity – as though a long, long wait was finally over. Her dreamy reminiscences, however, were brought to an end when Meta walked out to the yard and shouted at the boys, scolding them for climbing on the boulder. Were they not supposed to be going to a birthday celebration? Were they wearing their best clothes? Would she have to be ashamed of them in front of the baronial Meidens? Indoors at once, the rascals!

Silje smiled, thinking back to when Meta had taken over as housewife at Linden Allée. It must be all of thirteen or fourteen years ago now, surely? Yes, because Tarjei was born between Yuletide of that same year and the New Year, and he would soon be thirteen. How funny that one could keep track of the years by recalling the ages of the children on different occasions – yet it certainly made things easier to remember.

On the other hand, it was also an unwelcome reminder that one was growing older as well. It was through the children that one realised how quickly the years were passing, thought Silje with a twinge of sadness. Then she quickly shrugged off the thought.

So now Meta was in charge of the farmhouse while Tengel and Silje had effectively been 'retired to the dower house'. It had not really happened that way, of course. They had both been very happy to hand over the household responsibilities and do a bit less. Are, energetic and hardworking as ever, had added more rooms to the house, doubling its length to make it large enough for his growing family. Tengel and Silje remained in the older part that to them had once seemed so huge, but which now looked worn and tiny by comparison. Nonetheless, Silje still adored it – and judging by the time they spent there, so did everyone else in the family.

How history repeats itself, she thought. She had also arrived at Linden Allée like Meta: lost, an outcast and with nothing to her name. A blacksmith's daughter, she had been of such lowly birth as to be seemingly worthless. Yet poor Meta had started even further down the social ladder; she had been born to a mother who had been one of society's most pitiable and downtrodden people. In spite of this, Meta had proven herself to be a worthy housekeeper, something Silje could not deny. Meta was gifted and determined to live her life to the best of her ability, and she had such boundless energy that one was sometimes left quite breathless.

Silje, still sitting comfortably at the window, gave a satisfied sigh. She now had six grandchildren – she counted Sunniva among them, even though they were not related by blood. It was sad that she had not been able to care for the precious young girl herself, but Dag and Liv had brought her up well. A grown woman now, she often stayed overnight at Linden Allée and still assisted Silje in her studio from time to time.

Counting them off on her fingers, Silje spoke their names softly to herself: there was Sunniva, Sol's daughter; Tarald and Cecilie, Liv and Dag's fortunate children; and then there were Are's three boys, Tarjei, Trond and Brand. Tarald's personality, it had to be said, had still not developed, but that would come with age and wisdom, and she was sure he would turn out to be a fine boy. In fact they were indeed fine grandchildren, every single one of them.

And yes, she thought, raising her gaze to look out through the window again, there was Yrja, just entering the yard – another young girl who came from a very humble background. Silje was pleased as always to see her, but she could not help thinking as she looked at her: 'That poor hopeless child – is there nobody who could at least help her to put up her hair properly?' Her clothes were not at all fashionable and they sat so badly on the awkward figure. The mother obviously cared nothing for the appearance of her daughter and gave her no real assistance with herself. As she watched, Yrja met Sunniva in the middle of the yard. What a contrast they presented, she reflected. What an incredible difference there was between them! Yrja was a heavy shapeless lump, rocking from side to side, when compared to the graceful slender Sunniva.

Silje stretched out and straightened her aching leg. Lately it had been troubling her, but Tengel had said that it was a touch of gout and it was nothing to be concerned about. She hoped he was right. At that moment somebody entered the room behind her and she didn't need to turn to know that it was Tengel. But she turned anyway, because she still always liked to look at him.

His hair and beard had turned grey – the colour of ice on a cloudy day – but he still stood straight and tall. He was now seventy-two years old and he bore every one of his years with true dignity. Crooked sinews and blue veins, the legacy of hard work throughout his long life, were visible on the hands that he placed lovingly around her shoulders. Silje closed her eyes briefly, warming as ever to his touch. But she knew, although she was not permitted to say it, that he was tired. Indeed he was very tired, even though he would not admit it to himself. He had tried to stop seeing patients and most people respected his wishes. There were only a few now who continued to ask for his healing powers when they were in great pain or need and when all else had failed.

After bending to kiss her hair gently in greeting, Tengel glanced out into the yard. For a moment or two, in silence, they watched Are's three boys, who had managed to scamper roguishly outside again.

'When will the birthday party begin?' he asked.

'Not for an hour yet – they will be able to dirty themselves properly long before then!'

Tengel grinned: 'Then I should like to call on Tarjei first.'

Silje nodded. She understood just how much the highly intelligent boy meant to him. Tengel loved all six of his grandchildren, but Tarjei held a very special place in his heart. This was the child Tengel had waited for, hoped for, through so many anxious years across two generations, and she knew that he was convinced that Tarjei would become his luminary and his triumph.

When his grandfather went down and beckoned, Tarjei immediately accompanied him into what could be called the infirmary or sickroom. He was a most unusual boy. He had something of Tengel and Are's high cheekbones and the same thick black hair; but there was another kind of glow too, in the slanted eyes.

Are had never been very clever when it came to reading and writing, but his thirteen-year-old son appeared to have inherited the collective sharp intellect of Tengel, Silje, Liv and Sol. He would hardly have inherited much from Meta, for while she was kind and capable of understanding everyday things, as well as being hardworking and tenacious, she did not set her sights very high. Indeed she was often frightened by her son's brilliant mind. However, far more important than anything else, Tarjei had Tengel's unswerving determination to do only good in this life.

'Tarjei,' Tengel began, 'you have heard the legend of the Ice People, haven't you? You've heard us speak of Tengel the Evil, who swore a pact with the Devil 400 years ago and how that placed a heavy burden upon his descendants – but likewise gave them knowledge and powers far beyond those of other men.'

The lad nodded calmly. In contrast to the other children, he did not always want to rush out and continue playing games as soon as the opportunity arose. He was interested in many things and, sensing this was an important moment, he listened very attentively to his grandfather.

'You might not yet know how much pain has been brought upon us by his legacy,' continued Tengel, 'but it has not been without virtue as well. And we are pledged also to hold on to the good it has brought us. Here before you, Tarjei, is my collection of healing herbs and objects – and these are Sol's. She called them her "treasures". They are things that she inherited from Hanna – and Hanna was one of the earlier true inheritors of the powers.'

Tarjei nodded again without speaking.

'I had thought to speak with you about all this on your birthday in four months' time,' added Tengel thoughtfully. 'But I believe it's right to begin now.' He paused again to choose his words with the utmost care. 'There is so much you have to learn and nobody knows how much time we may have. I am healthy and strong at present but, as you know, I am no longer a young man. From this day I wish you to be my apprentice. All this will be yours, and it will fall to you to pass it on in your turn. You are *not* one of those unfortunate ones who have inherited the evil qualities of the first Tengel. But I know you are the only one of my kin who is able to be guardian of all this – for I am sure there is still something of that unfathomable spark within you.'

'I understand, Grandfather,' said the boy quietly. 'I am ready to start learning.'

'Good, good!' exclaimed Tengel. 'That's wonderful. I know instinctively you are too sensible to misuse the items that I am bequeathing to you. They have unimaginable power and many who have held these objects in their hands have used them unwisely – for they have also had the evil of the first Tengel within them. This was indeed what he intended – that these things should be used in the service of the Evil One himself. You do not have evil within you – and when you reach the age I am now, you will choose someone new from the among Ice People's kin to carry the knowledge forward. But be at pains to choose your successor with care! Do not forget that there is danger in everything that you see here.'

'I shall be careful, Grandfather.'

'What do you want to be when you are older, Tarjei?'

'I want to study – study many things!'

'And so you shall.'

'I should prefer to be a pupil with one of the great men of science, like the astronomer Tycho Brahe – except he is dead. Or I would like to study with Kepler, who knew both astronomy and astrology – or Johannes Rudbeckius, who translated the Bible. But I know how difficult all that might be.'

'We shall do what we can for you, my boy. But now, come on, we must greet all our guests. We shall speak more about this tomorrow.'

Tarjei remained standing in the doorway for a moment, a faraway expression glistening in his brown eyes. 'Grandfather,' he said quietly, 'even though it is not my birthday quite yet, I think that this is the very finest gift I could ever be given.'

A broad happy smile lit up Tengel's lined face. 'Then I look forward very much to a longer talk tomorrow.'

'As do I, Grandfather. As do I.'

When they rejoined the main party, they found that everyone from Gråstensholm had come to the birthday celebrations. As the crowd of guests grew, a happy and contagious buzz of excitement and good humour filled the house and the yard. Yrja was overjoyed when she saw the dark-haired Tarald arrive with his sister Cecilie. Although she remained largely quiet and unobtrusive, Yrja found she was rarely able to take her eyes off him.

Cecilie immediately became the centre of attraction. Like her mother, Liv, Cecilie had auburn hair, although it was of a slightly deeper hue. While not so strikingly beautiful as Liv perhaps, she had a sparkling loveliness and zest for life that was all her own. With her neat trim figure, she made sure that she always dressed in the very latest fashion; she was also ready to stand her ground forcefully in the unlikely event that someone chose to argue with her.

With all these outstanding attributes, it was perhaps not surprising that the broken hearts of many a young man lay in her wake. In short, she was the image of Sol in every way, except that she was untainted by the dark shadows of past generations. When they saw Cecilie, many of the older family members could not help experiencing a slight inner twinge of mental pain and loss, as they thought of Sol. The name, image and memory of Sol still lived on vividly in all their hearts – and would always do so.

Naturally Liv and Dag were also there; Dag himself bore the look of a distinguished advocate, still youthful despite his thinning hair. Liv had grown into her role as his wife and had become the strong, pivotal figure at Gråstensholm, always remaining firmly in control of the estate while he was away on official duties. They were now both reaching forty.

With them stood Charlotte and her husband, Jacob Skille, his arm supporting her. Charlotte had shrunk in stature and bent forward at the waist like an old woman. Yet her kind-heartedness still shone in her eyes and she always seemed happy when together with her Jacob.

For his part, Jacob was more than content with life at Gråstensholm and it was he who really managed the estate in practical terms, day to day. In the full knowledge that his stepson, Dag, would inherit everything one day, Jacob was happy to enjoy sitting in front of the fire in the evenings and play cards or draughts with Charlotte. By virtue of his marriage to Charlotte, for as long as he lived he would bear the title of Lord of the Manor – and that was an outcome of greater good fortune than any poor dragoon could ever have dreamed.

These then were the main members of this large and happy family, who had gathered together on this occasion for a particularly joyful celebration in the mansion's great hall.

* * * *

The year was 1620. In far-off Bohemia the rumbling sounds of war were beginning to reverberate, as fighting between Protestants and Catholics had already broken out. Eventually the ugly tendrils of conflict would reach out and touch Norway as well, peaceful and small though it was. Even the parish of Gråstensholm would not escape the war's shadow.

However, none of this marred Silje's thoughts at that moment as she looked around at her family – a family that had grown to a considerable size over the years. Ah, and what good years they had been, she thought as she sat presiding over them all at the table. Wonderful years! Was it possible for anyone to be happier than she was?

Yrja on the other hand was not feeling quite so contented, for no matter how hard she tried, it was impossible to attract Tarald's attention. Sadly for her, it was all too obvious where his interest lay. The lovely Sunniva hardly looked up from the table at all, not daring to glance at Tarald, her second cousin. In her state of yearning, Yrja could not fail to sense the tension and connection between them and she felt as though, unnoticed and in silence, her heart was being crushed. What more could I expect, she asked herself grimly? But if only it didn't hurt so!

It was without doubt a very pleasant and enjoyable birthday party. There were rapid-fire exchanges between the ethereal Cecilie and Tarjei, the young prodigy. Now there, reflected Yrja, is an example of two people in harmony. Trond was fretting and flitting around the pair, babbling away, but failing to equal them in wit and humour. Meantime the four members of the older generation were enjoying a murmured discussion, the kind that would lead everywhere, and nowhere. Are's other son, the portly, sluggish Brand, was steadily munching his way through a whole plate of cakes until Meta stepped in and rapped his knuckles. Dag, Liv and Are were engrossed in discussing the merits, or otherwise, of a legal conflict affecting some of their neighbours.

Among them all, only Yrja felt she did not belong. Despite being one of the birthday children and always being treated as one of the family, she felt a deep sense of dislocation and unease. Her loneliness, of course, was the result of nothing more than the desperation gnawing at her foolish heart – a heart that would not be swayed by common sense nor accept that its downfall in love was perhaps preordained.

She imagined she saw all her imperfections reflected in the eyes of everyone around her – her crooked shoulders, the lack of a discernible waist, gnarled and knotted hands. Those same hands were now unpleasantly hot and sweaty – her nose would be bright red too, she thought bitterly. It often turned that colour whenever she found herself in company. Her nose and her chin were always a source of embarrassment to her – as well as those distressingly unattractive blemishes on her cheeks that always reminded people of a thistle-head.

Yet it was impossible for her to feel jealous of Sunniva,

with her fine and delicately sculpted figure. Always so vulnerable herself, Sunniva brought out the best in everyone about her. This was especially the case with the kind-hearted Yrja. Who could imagine being left motherless as an infant – and in such terrible circumstances too? The whispered stories that had reached her ears back at home in Eikeby had hinted at awful goings-on. But she had never heard the truth. Perhaps that was because nobody in the parish or beyond could really be sure what had happened.

Suddenly Tengel rose to speak and his physique and presence was still so impressive that as soon as he stood up, the chattering and merriment in the hall immediately ceased. He looked around at the assembled gathering of family and neighbours with a stern gaze that was nevertheless filled with great affection too, wherever it fell.

'Now that we are all gathered here together, there's something I would like us to discuss seriously,' he said in a thoughtful tone. 'It is something I have thought about for a long time: the need for us to take a proper family name.'

'That has been in my thoughts as well,' said Are. 'I am simply Are Tengelsson – not much of an inheritance to give one's sons, Tarjei Aresson, Trond and Bran Aresson.'

Tengel nodded his agreement. 'Yes, you all understand, I think, that we have become two families? Dag and Liv, and their children Tarald and Cecilie, they all carry the noble name of Meiden. But what of the rest of us? *I* am Tengel of the Ice People, but that is a clan name that ought never be spoken outside our kin …' Tengel broke off suddenly looking fondly at the simple farm girl from Eikeby. 'Yrja is this very boring for you?'

Yrja shook her head furiously. She was both grateful for his concern and embarrassed that she had suddenly become the centre of attention. 'I shall never myself speak of the Ice People,' she assured him. 'Never.'

'Good, good. You all know that most people are given their names after the names of their farms – just like Yrja here!' He turned to her again. 'You are called Yrja Mattiasdotter Eikeby – Yrja, daughter of Mattias from Eikeby – is that not so?'

'Yes.'

'But you see, we cannot call ourselves Linden Allée. It sounds so … well … it does not sound like a name. Besides, there is nobody in the parish who would know us by that name. I have dwelt upon this for a long time, but nothing has come to me. So now I ask for your suggestions.'

After a few moments of silence, a murmuring of various proposals began to rise from around the tables. One or two were quick off the mark, but Cecilie and Tarjei were unable to resist treating this as an opportunity to have fun. Very soon many wild and wonderful ideas were being yelled out.

'I say "Lindane",' announced Charlotte.

'Or why not "Iceane"?' asked Silje. 'Then something from the Ice People will be there.'

Cecilie countered with, 'But could we not use the name "Icelindane"?'

This was the start of a cannonade of suggestions from Tarjei, Trond and Cecilie.

'Let's make it "Iceallée",' called one. 'No, "Lindice",' shouted another. 'I think "Icylindens" is better,' suggested a third voice. 'What about "Lindicles"?' called another.

'No, I've got an idea,' said Cecilie, 'We'll start with what people call us. We shall be "Up-there-where-that-strange-doctor-lives".'

Tarjei quickly added: 'And-his-impudent-offspring.'

'That's enough now,' ordered Tengel, laughing as loud as anybody else. 'Let's try to be serious for a moment.'

Yrja was speechless. All these youngsters around her were speaking with such disregard for good manners and yet Herr Tengel had just laughed! That could never happen in her home. They might be nothing more than a small farming family at Eikeby, but Lord have mercy on anyone who dared to speak at table – or even worse take part in conversations with one's elders! What was more, she knew that it was the same at all the farms round in the area. Strict rules, beatings and the fear of God were the order of the day everywhere.

Yes, she could not help but envy this unusual family. Why, even the distinguished Baroness Charlotte was not objecting to the informal behaviour at table. And they celebrated birthdays as well! This was something almost unheard of. Her family only observed the religious high days and holy days, such as Yule, Easter, Whitsun, Michaelmas, Pentecost, Epiphany and the Assumption of Mary. These sonorous events always involved devout prayer, church services and solemn obedience. There was certainly never any levity.

After due consideration and more serious discussion of suggestions, Tarald came up with a simple suggestion: Lind. The family was divided between those who agreed with this and those who preferred Lindane.

'Lind of the Ice People,' Charlotte mused. 'That sounds very noble.'

'We shall wait before deciding,' said Tengel. 'Lind or Lindane – which of these do we feel more comfortable with? The name is more for the benefit of Are and Meta and their lads, Tarjei, Trond and Brand, although it will serve you, Sunniva, for as long as you remain unwed. In many ways I wanted this to be decided because you, Sunniva, have no family name other than Solsdotter – daughter of Sol – and it is uncommon to take a mother's name.'

The girl looked down at the table with an apologetic smile and said nothing.

'Sol had no proper name either,' continued Tengel. 'She was called simply Sol Angelica of the Ice People.'

'But she did have a proper father, didn't she?'

'Yes, she did, but I never found out what his Christian name was,' responded Tengel. 'Now, if we have all eaten our fill then I suggest we leave the table.'

* * * *

Later that evening, while undressing in her room, Silje said to Tengel: 'What a splendid birthday feast!' She sighed. 'Everyone seemed very pleased – did you not think so?'

'Yes,' he mumbled. He was seated on the edge of the bed, cleaning between his feet with the wetted corner of a cloth. As usual Silje pretended not to notice. It was too late to teach this old dog any new tricks.

'And so nice that Yrja was invited as well,' she added. 'She enjoyed being included and receiving all the small gifts. But I did think she seemed a little preoccupied today.'

'Hmmm,' Tengel was hardly paying attention.

'Do you know what I think, Tengel?'

'No!'

'I think Sunniva and Tarald have eyes for each other.'

Tengel let his foot fall from his hands. 'That cannot be tolerated!' he said sternly.

Silje stood with her skirts pulled up half over her head.

'And why not?' she asked, her head peeping out from beneath her clothes. 'I think they look wonderfully romantic, the pair of them.'

'But do you not understand? They are kin of the Ice People – both of them!'

Silje, who had managed to find her way out of her skirt, now crawled along the full length of the bed and snuggled under the covers.

'Yes, but think again, Tengel! I'm sure the evil legacy is dying out. You and Sol were the last ones – and both of you had mostly good in your hearts. I am sure it slowly weakens and disappears. Mark my words.'

'No, Silje, we cannot treat it so lightly. Tarald is my grandchild – and I am afflicted. Sunniva is Sol's daughter *and* my sister's grandchild! It must not be. It would be a disastrous match!'

'There then,' said Silje serenely, as she placed her arm so that he could rest his head upon it. 'Surely they are allowed just a little romance? No one has said that they should marry and bring children into the world.'

'And if they really fall in love, would you be able to deny them? Perhaps we should send one of them away?'

'It cannot be Sunniva, that's certain,' answered Silje. 'She will not be able to manage on her own in the world.'

'And I do not believe Liv or Charlotte would ever let Tarald go. He is still too weak and immature. Oh well, we shall have to wait and see.'

Silje was determined to make her point. 'Anyway, I think you are wrong. The evil lineage has faded and died. Look at us – we have had two children and both are very normal. Sol gave birth to a normal daughter. Now we have six grandchildren – if we include Sunniva – and not one of them has been tainted!'

'Hmmm,' Tengel gave a lengthy sigh, 'that is something I'm not too sure about.'

Silje half sat up in bed. 'What do you mean by that?'

'I do not know, Silje, but I *have* seen something. It is something that worries me a lot. A glimpse of the yellow cat-like eyes once or twice …'

'What are you saying? Who is it?'

'No, I cannot tell you that when I am so uncertain. But sometimes it can break out, just as it can lie unseen.'

Silje sank back onto her bolster and stared up at the ceiling. The roof needs repairing, she thought distractedly. She had noticed telltale dark streaks of damp along two of the timbers in the corner. It needed to be done soon. But who was it who had the cat-like eyes? Which of the six could it be? Who had a yellow gleam … No, she couldn't seem to think who it might be.

Silje tried to think of something else, but her thoughts kept returning to the subject, against her will. Might it be Sunniva? But she was meek, quiet and thoughtful. Like a little dormouse, she tried not to draw attention to herself, despite her blossoming loveliness. Tarald, then? He was as beautiful as a young god, although he still lacked confidence and his behaviour could as yet be unpredictable. He combined the finely sculpted features of the Meiden family with the dark eyes of the Ice People. Tarald had vague ideas of himself as a future landowner and precious little else. To that end he had sometimes sought advice from Jacob Skille and Are, both of whom he got along with splendidly.

Yes, Silje thought, Tarald was probably best suited to farming. She had unpleasant memories of the difficult years they had all spent working hard, running the timber merchant's business in Oslo. Dag and Liv had finally sold up because it took too much of their time to manage and Tarald showed neither interest nor ability to take it on. Dag's time was taken up by his official duties as an advocate; Are had plenty to keep him busy on Linden Allée; Liv had been occupied bringing up the children. More to the point, nobody in the family was experienced in trade – the taxes and charges, the tithes to the Crown – all of this infuriated every one of them. When at last they had been free of what Cecilie called 'that whole heap of trouble', there was a collective sigh of relief. But they had received a tidy sum for the business nonetheless, so they had no right to complain.

But, no, now she'd got sidetracked again. Where was she? Oh, yes. Was it possibly Tarald? No, that was unthinkable. He definitely lacked the spirit. Cecilie on the other hand did not – yet she was even less likely. True, she could be spiteful, but only in frivolous comments when she had the opportunity to demonstrate her sense of irony and clever use of words. Nothing vicious came from her heart, for Cecilie would never deliberately hurt anybody. Why, when she was so richly talented in all manner of things, would she need to avail herself of the black arts? No, thought Silje, I have never seen any such tendencies in her.

That left only the three young lads and any idea that it was one of them was simply ridiculous. Why, Tengel had only just had a life-changing conversation with Tarjei and he would hardly have done that if he had doubts about the boy. And surely not the fleet-footed, twelve-year-old Trond? He was always happy running errands for Silje – for which he was invariably rewarded with a tasty treat. And he still greatly enjoyed childish games, something he would probably continue to do for a good many years.

Still harder to accept was the thought of Brand as an

evil yellow-eyed creature. It was Brand who was passionate about caring for animals – he had been known to bring home a solitary half-dead bumblebee for Silje to nurse back to life. He would also stand behind her as she painted, watching her silently for hours at a time. This, if the truth be told, she found quite unnerving, but she didn't have the heart to send him on his way. The pair of them shared this love of all nature's creatures and that was why Brand held a special place in her heart.

No, she told herself, Tengel could suspect whomever he wished, but she for one was certain that none of her grandchildren had those characteristics that were so hated and feared. For almost twenty years they had lived without experiencing the frightening power of that vile legacy. Silje, however, knew something – something that Tengel believed he had managed to keep secret from everyone. She knew that the older he became, the harder it was for him to control the wickedness that had raged within him throughout his life. For as long as he was youthful and strong, he had been a consummately good person. But only now could she begin to understand at what cost.

From time to time, when he was very tired and overworked, she had seen on his face the sort of expressions that scared her. Given the choice she would rather not have seen them. Yet because Tengel had no wish to harm anyone, she could see instinctively that his struggle became harder with every year that passed. This, Silje believed, was the reason for his overwhelming fatigue. Still mulling over these disturbing thoughts, Silje turned over to find a more comfortable position in the bed.

Noticing this, Tengel looked at her enquiringly. 'How does your leg feel this evening, my dearest love?' he asked solicitously.

'Not too bad. My knee aches as usual.'

Tengel put his hand carefully on her knee and she immediately felt its healing warmth. Worry and anxiety had turned his eyes as black as coal, but Silje couldn't see this.

'You still have great power in you, Tengel – I can feel it,' she murmured in a sleepy voice. 'The touch of your hand is as wonderful as ever!'

Chapter 3

A few days later, an unexpected and very welcome event took place. An elegant coach arrived unannounced at Gråstensholm – and it had the very latest type of chassis on which the carriage itself was suspended from leather straps, thereby giving passengers a much smoother ride. Boys and stable-lads all swarmed like flies onto the drive, gazing in wonder at this unbelievably modern vehicle and arguing excitedly amongst themselves about how it worked.

It drew to a halt and a man in his mid-twenties alighted, assisted by his manservant. After glancing about himself with an air of authority, he walked to the front steps of the house, where Charlotte and her daughter, Liv, received him. He was shown into the house and immediately introduced himself in immaculate Danish.

'I do not know whether or not my name is known to you, but I am Albrekt Strahlenhelm.'

'Strahlenhelm?' Charlotte asked excitedly. 'My son Dag stayed with your family, I believe, when he was living in Copenhagen!'

'Exactly so. Might I be so fortunate as to make his acquaintance?'

'Oh, Liv, run and fetch Dag! I think he is in his office. My, this is simply too exciting! I shall arrange for refreshment at once.'

'Thank you. The journey has indeed been a dusty one.'

The young count availed himself of the opportunity to wash off some of the grime from the journey, and shortly afterwards Dag arrived.

'Do you remember me?' asked their guest, as soon as the introductions had been concluded. 'I was that little boy who had disappeared, only to be found by your sister in a singularly unusual manner.'

'But of course I do,' said Dag. 'How wonderful to see you again! How is it with your parents?'

'Excellent, thank you! It is they who have sent me here. I was coming to Norway on other matters, but I have a very special commission for you.'

In due course, when he had eaten from a fine selection of dishes and enjoyed some of the best wine in the Meiden household, he began to explain.

'My parents have never forgotten your sister. She was the best governess they ever had, although for myself I have only a faded memory of her. Nonetheless, the Court is searching high and low to find the perfect nursemaid and governess for King Christian's children in his marriage with Kirsten Munk. You were, of course, aware that he had entered into a morganatic marriage with her? It seems they are having great difficulty in finding anyone. They sought my parents' advice, and as I was to travel to Norway, they bade me come here to ask whether your sister would be able to accept this honourable duty. Naturally we realise that she may be married and ...'

For a moment his hosts lowered their eyes and did not speak. Even after all this time they still felt a deep sorrow at the manner of Sol's passing. Also she was still much missed by everybody on the estate.

'I'm sorry,' said Dag, raising his eyes again at last. 'But my sister has been dead these past eighteen years.'

'Oh! It saddens me so much to hear that!' replied Albrekt. 'My father would have been so pleased to do something to repay her – it has troubled him for so long that he was able to do so little at the time. I trust that her death was in no way connected with that little misunderstanding in Copenhagen?'

'No, not at all. But my sister was fated to die young, I believe, Count Strahlenhelm. To live in this world was not her destiny.'

A silence fell as memories flooded back for each of them. The young count seemed visibly saddened by what he had heard. At last Charlotte also looked up.

'I'm sitting here and wondering,' she said, 'because we have someone who is Sol's double ...'

'No, Mama, we cannot send our young daughter off to Copenhagen all on her own,' protested Dag.

'Can we not? Did you not make that journey once? What about Sol, who travelled alone? Count Strahlenhelm, my grandchild Cecilie is eighteen years old and the very image of Sol. Yet she has a different and more steadfast character. I do not believe that King Christian's children would be better cared for. She is a worldly-wise young lady, very fond of children and, unlike Sol, she is a kind person through and through.'

'But surely Sol was the kindest person one could ever imagine,' said the Count, taken aback.

'Oh, she was in general terms yes,' retorted Dag dryly. 'But she also had her moments.'

They were interrupted by the sound of the outside door

being opened and young voices quickly grew louder in the entrance hall.

'Cecilie! Tarald!' called Charlotte. 'Come here children and present yourselves! We have a guest – Count Strahlenhelm.'

'A count?' A girl's surprised voice could be clearly heard from the hallway. 'Are you sure he's a real count?'

'Cecilie!' reprimanded Charlotte, appalled. 'Please remember your manners.'

As the two youngsters entered the room, Count Strahlenhelm got to his feet. A distinct look of admiration appeared on his face when he saw the slender attractive figure of Cecilie.

'As God is my witness, Miss Cecilie, when I look at you I can almost see my governess again! Young though I was, I am reminded of someone forever beautiful and gracious.' He bowed low and kissed her hand. Despite never having experienced anything like this before, Cecilie responded to the gesture with consummate flair and refinement.

'Children,' Charlotte said quietly, 'Count Strahlenhelm came here to ask Sol to be nursemaid and governess to the children of King Christian. Now, Cecilie, I have suggested that you should go instead, but your parents object.'

'And so do I – very much!' said Tarald. 'She is only eighteen years old.'

'Nineteen, before long,' corrected Cecilie quickly, although there were still some months to go. 'And I am mature for my age.'

'Really?' retorted Tarald.

'Well …' said Charlotte thoughtfully, 'then why not Sunniva?'

'No!' Tarald's reply came like a bolt of lightning and was equally firm. 'Not Sunniva – not under any circumstances!'

'But why not?' inquired Charlotte.

Cecilie could see her chance of an exciting journey abroad was threatened, so she quickly answered, 'Sunniva has too little initiative – she is not resolute enough. She will not defend herself from any unkindness done to her by others – or by fate. She takes it all with a gentle, grateful smile.'

'Now you are being spiteful,' hissed Tarald.

'Not at all,' responded Cecilie. 'I am merely stating the facts.'

After listening carefully to everything that was said, it was Liv who finally decided the matter. 'I agree that we should not send Sunniva. She would never perform the duties in an acceptable fashion. Looking after the children of royalty is not something to be taken lightly – and I believe that it requires someone special, with a firm hand. There is a fine line to be taken between deferential respect for the little ones and the need to put them in their place when they've gone too far. Sunniva could never manage that. She would sit and weep if any of the children told her to keep her worthless fingers off their little royal personages.'

Cecilie nodded assertively. 'I could not agree more.'

'You are perfectly correct, Baroness,' said the Count.

This form of address startled Liv. After twenty years she had still not grown accustomed to being called 'Baroness' or even 'Ladyship'. But she kept her composure and managed not to betray her surprise.

'It appears to me,' continued Count Strahlenhelm, 'as though young Mistress Cecilie would be the perfect choice for the role, in the absence of Mistress Sol. And I feel certain my parents will agree with me. The Court bade my father give his good counsel and he naturally attaches great honour to being able to please the King by finding a suitable governess.'

'But why look for one in Norway?' asked Liv. 'Are there not plenty of girls in Denmark?'

The Count gave a discreet cough. 'There are indeed – and many of them would wish to care for the children. However the children's maids have not lasted long at the castle. I have to tell you that Kirsten Munk is not the easiest of people to have dealings with. Added to which she has encouraged her little daughters to exploit their noble status. Both the mother and her daughters are so horribly conscious of rank and it was for that reason that my father immediately thought of Mistress Sol – he always used to say that she was a girl with a tough hide. Furthermore they will want somebody with learning and Mistress Sol was well educated.'

'As of course is Cecilie,' said Charlotte with pride. 'It has been my duty to educate all our children.'

'Excellent! You appreciate also that the King is pleased to be mindful of his second kingdom, Norway. A Norwegian woman serving him at Court would suit him well. I feel sure Mistress Cecilie would be the right person, were she to consider accepting this honourable position.'

'Why, yes, of course I will!' said Cecilie eagerly. 'I think it would be a wonderful opportunity.'

'Think hard before you agree,' cautioned Dag, the memory of what had happened to Sol in Copenhagen making him wary of letting his own daughter go there.

'Dag,' said Charlotte and Liv with one voice, 'Let her go!'

'But she cannot travel alone,' he replied, taken aback by their onslaught.

'No, you are quite right, she cannot do that,' agreed Count Strahlenhelm. 'But she may travel back with us, if she wishes. My wife waits for me in Oslo – unfortunately her constitution was not well suited to the voyage. We return to Denmark in three weeks' time. Will that be agreeable?'

After a brief pause for reflection, they all decided that it was. Dag was the only one to have doubts and he sighed quietly to himself. He cared so greatly for his forthright young daughter and wished only to give her his fatherly protection. Cecilie, on the other hand, could not help herself in letting out a very girlish squeal of delight and expectation.

* * * *

All too quickly those last days of summer hurried by. Autumn began to turn the leaves from green to early shades of gold on the estate's trees, but the sunshine continued to be bright and crisp. The air too remained soft and balmy for several weeks.

One morning Silje's bad leg was bothering her so much that she stayed in bed all day. Yrja, as large and ungainly as ever, came and took care of her, eagerly attending to Silje's smallest request. When she decided to paint a watercolour of the inside of her room, Yrja gladly fetched all the materials for her.

'Yrja, my little one,' said Silje at last. 'Why don't you arrange your hair differently?'

The girl was pleased at being called little. It was not a form of address that she heard very often. But she already knew that her hair always stood out, like windblown straw.

'What could I do with it, Mistress Silje? I truly do not know.'

'Come, sit here on the bed and I shall try to show you! Do you have a comb?'

Yrja handed her one. It was clean and unbroken, something that Silje appreciated. But then Yrja was generally a clean tidy girl, whose even-tempered good humour and quiet confidence found favour with Silje. She was far more anxious when Sunniva was looking after her. As she combed out the long light-brown hair, Silje felt even more strongly the affection she had always had for the Eikeby farm girl.

'You've been roaming around this house for quite a few years now, Yrja, haven't you?' she said with a warm smile. 'I can still see the four of you – Sunniva and Tarald, you and little Cecilie – playing ball and riding hobbyhorses. And out in the avenue Cecilie always came last in the races and always got so angry about it. I used to watch and see that you let her beat you from time to time.'

'Oh, that didn't happen very often,' said Yrja, smiling. 'I didn't need to.' She was trying not to show that the comb was pulling her hair. 'Miss Cecilie could usually take care of herself – like that time when they were going to race all the way from Gråstensholm to here. I can't run very well, so I didn't join in, but anyway Cecilie was bound to lose because she was the smallest. But she would never accept defeat. So once behind the hill over yonder, she pretended to fall down a pile of stones and hurt herself. She deliberately tore her skirt before she came tottering into the yard here. Never have I seen anybody limping with so much pain. At once she became the heroine; nobody cared who had won the race. I saw it all – every last thing – because I wasn't in the race.'

Silje chuckled. 'Typical of her! Yes, Cecilie will be able to look after herself. It is not so with Sunniva. I have tried to give the girl self-confidence, but she is such an anxious soul. It's a comfort that she has you and Tarald. He looks after her so well.'

Yrja said nothing, but a definite expression of sadness showed on her face at the mention of Tarald's name. Seeing this, Silje realised that she had stumbled upon a little heartache. Dear, kind-hearted Yrja! Yet she was so lacking in physical virtues – something with which Tarald was unfortunately far too concerned. Silje glanced at the girl's hands, resting on her knees. They were shaped like the blades of oars and they somehow went with her broad angular face. Yet still her eyes shone with warmth – if only one took time to look into them! Returning her attention to the combing, Silje started to talk about other things.

'Take the looking-glass from the table over there. Now watch, and see what I do.'

Yrja did as she was told and held the mirror up, so that she could see Silje's hands moving.

'I shall part your hair in the centre and comb it up from your forehead. Then braid it properly over your ears.'

'But then my hopeless face will be even bigger, won't it?'

'Quite the opposite – it will look smaller with flatter, straight hair. I will plait two tight pigtails …'

It all took time, and while she worked, Silje asked Yrja about her home. It was a cheerless tale of a life of hard work and being frequently scolded, and seemed to offer nothing to be happy about. At a time when infant deaths in the parish were so frequent, however, the family at Eikeby appeared to be exceptionally robust, suffering instead from an overcrowded home. Yrja did not have any space to call her own, poor thing! And it soon became clear that she looked forward to her days at Linden Allée like a breath of fresh air.

In the past when Yrja had first started helping at the house, Silje had been a little ashamed at sometimes giving a coin or some other small treat to the girl. She was after all a playmate of her family's children. But now she could see that she had done the right thing, for although Yrja did not say so in as many words, it was obvious that her parents regarded these gifts as a secure income. More to the point, they would never have allowed their daughter to waste her time at Linden Allée if there had been nothing in it for them. They saw the arrangement as a form of service, as Yrja being a hired maid for Mistress Silje, and could never have understood the fine friendship she had developed with the whole family. Had they known, they would doubtless have taken her away.

Understanding this fully for the first time, a feeling of guilt came over Silje. She vowed to herself, there and then, to pay Yrja more regularly. She had not realised that those few coins had meant so much, but then there were a lot of mouths to feed at Eikeby. It now seemed hardly surprising that the poor girl had suffered from rickets as a child.

Silje suddenly felt it was all so terribly sad for such a clever girl, who would have made a wonderful wife and mother for anyone. Now, though, her father had married off his daughters one by one – and each time he chose his sons-in-law himself. He had also decided that Yrja should be the one to stay at home and take care of her parents, as they grew old. It was a simple decision for there was little chance that a suitor would volunteer himself.

Most men were fearful of girls who had suffered from rickets, because they had difficulty bearing children. When they said 'children' they always meant sons. When asked how many children he had, it was customary for a man to answer for example: 'Well, I have four children.' Then after a long pause he would add: 'And three daughters.'

Whenever Yrja spoke of her future, she always had a gloomy look in her eyes; the idea of caring for her nagging and demanding parents was not an appealing one.

'There! Now take a peep in the looking-glass,' said Silje at length, changing the subject. 'I shall put plaits on top of your head and you shall have a string of pearls in your hair – or like this, across your forehead. Now for some face powder – please fetch some from the drawer over there! Yes, that one. Your nose shines like a beacon, Yrja, and that won't do. And by the way, where is Sunniva today?'

'I … er, saw her with Tarald walking across the pastures.'

'Going where?' asked Silje, more harshly than she had intended.

'I don't know, Mistress Silje. They were just walking slowly along.'

My God, I hope Tengel doesn't see them, thought Silje. I shall have to talk to one of them myself.

'There now! What do you think of that?' asked Silje aloud. 'Doesn't that look better?'

Yrja stared solemnly at her reflection for a long moment. 'Oh, I look so fine,' she breathed.

'You are a beautiful young lady,' said Silje warmly, even though this was a considerable exaggeration. Yet, even in her misfortune, Yrja did have an indefinable but distinct attractiveness. 'You may keep the string of pearls – they are not real ones.'

'Thank you,' gasped Yrja, her eyes brimming with tears. 'Thank you, dearest Mistress Silje!'

At that moment Sunniva came into the room, together with Tarald.

'Good day, Grandmama,' said Sunniva, bright-eyed. 'How are you feeling?'

'Quite well, thank you. And where have you been?'

'Just out walking,' answered Sunniva. It was a suspiciously vague reply, but she did not elaborate further.

In his turn, Tarald greeted his grandmother with a warm embrace, as Sunniva stood by smiling. Yrja waited quietly for someone to notice her new, elegant appearance, but she was rewarded with nothing more than an indifferent aside from Tarald.

'Ah, so you're with Grandmama. That's nice.'

Yrja's blossoming feeling of joy slowly died within her. Silje could willingly have slapped the two youngsters, but she knew that their minds were busy with other thoughts. Sunniva in fact seemed more sure of herself than usual. She laughed and looked shyly at Tarald, listening fascinated as he told what they had seen on their walk. At last it was Sunniva who noticed the change in Yrja.

'Why, Yrja,' she giggled excitedly. 'Have you been dressing up?'

The simple farm girl said nothing, but cast an unhappy glance at Silje.

'I have been combing and dressing Yrja's hair,' said Silje quietly. 'I think she looks very pretty indeed.'

Thank the Lord that Tarald had it in him to see how disheartened Yrja had become. He was not usually the most observant of people, but now he at least had the wit to make amends.

'I think Yrja looks pretty too,' he agreed turning to look at her. 'The different style of your hair becomes you very well.'

Sunniva was confused – she had never intended to hurt Yrja, but she had not been as observant as was her custom.

'I do as well – of course,' she added swiftly. 'I simply didn't recognise you, Yrja. Come, let's go to the kitchen, I'm hungry!'

'May I go?' Yrja asked Silje.

'Yes, you run along. I shall manage by myself.'

'I'll be back shortly. Do you want anything from the kitchen, Mistress Silje?'

'Yes,' she answered hesitantly. 'Yes, please – a honey cake.'

Yes, she thought, I'm entitled to a treat. She was now fifty-six and, ever since Sol had teased her about becoming matronly, she had bravely kept away from her beloved honey cakes. But there was little purpose in worrying about her figure today – and besides she needed some kind of pleasure to compensate for her painful leg.

Silje no longer painted quite as much as before and for a time she had taken up her weaving again. But the physical effort soon proved too much for her and small watercolours were all she produced nowadays, like the one she was painting just then. Somehow it seemed to her that almost every undertaking became an obstacle that grew into an enormous mountain right in front of her. She also spent a lot of time taking in the seams of her clothes, which of late often seemed to be too large for her. So, in fact, under all the circumstances, a honey cake would be very welcome indeed.

Silje knew that Tengel's days at that time were also very busy. He was tutoring young Tarjei in experiments, using the Ice People's ancient herbs and rituals, and always took him on visits to the sick whenever he went. Sometimes the brilliant mind of this young man left Tengel speechless. Although he used to think of himself as clever, he saw that Tarjei was leagues ahead of him. The boy analysed the plants' toxins, trying to find out exactly what caused their effects and why. On one occasion he had experimented on himself with a concoction of different herbal narcotics – the result being that Tengel was forced to use all his powers to revive him.

Eventually the lad woke up and let out a yell of delight. 'Now I've found that out! We cannot use those herbs – they are not congenial.'

Tengel, in a rage brought on by his concern for the lad, asked: 'And did you really need to use such drastic methods, just to discover that?'

Yet they enjoyed one another's company greatly, Silje reflected. She recalled the serious, brooding expressions that inevitably appeared on their faces whenever Tarjei wanted something explained. Invariably Tengel, who had never had to ask 'why' in his whole life, endeavoured to frame an answer that would satisfy Tarjei.

In the end it was Sunniva who brought Silje her honey cake and when she appeared, bearing the cakes on a plate, she was chuckling to herself exuberantly.

'Cook wanted me to scour the pantry, but I'd rather talk to you Grandmama. So I got Yrja to do it instead.'

'You shouldn't have done that. Yrja was already doing something for me.'

Sunniva's eyes widened disconsolately.

'Don't you want to talk to me, Grandmama? Would you prefer Yrja?'

'No, of course not, my dear. I only meant that … Oh, it's of no matter! What did you want to say to me?'

Sunniva had picked up the looking-glass on the table and was admiring herself in it. Clearly satisfied by what she saw, she put the mirror down again, smiled at Silje and sighed deeply.

'I am so happy, Grandmama, I could burst!'

'I'm very pleased for you,' replied Silje tentatively, feeling slightly uneasy with the course of the conversation. 'Is Tarald still in the kitchen?'

'No, he had to go back to Gråstensholm …'

Before Sunniva had the opportunity to reveal any undesirable confidences, Silje quickly interrupted: 'Sunniva, my little one – I don't think you should spend so much time alone with Tarald.'

The girl stared at her in disbelief. 'But why not?'

'You are too closely bound by blood.'

'Second cousins? Is that too close? Second cousins can wed each other, of that I'm sure. Why, even first cousins may marry!'

'That is so, but there is something different about the Ice People.'

'Hah! All those old legends! That's just talk!'

'No, Sunniva, it is not! Do you think that Grandpapa Tengel looks like normal folk?'

'No, he does look strange of course – but he's still the best person on earth!' Then she whispered silently to herself: 'After Tarald, that is.'

'Sunniva,' said Silje patiently, 'you must try to understand.'

'I do understand – only too well,' said Sunniva sharply and, covering her face with her hands, she burst into a flood of tears. 'Cecilie is to travel to Denmark – because you all like her so much,' she said between sobs. 'And Tarjei and Grandpapa are always together. Aunt Charlotte worships Tarald, and so do his parents. You, Grandmama, would prefer Yrja to help you. Nobody likes me at all – I'm just a mistake that somebody has to care for. I know that you did not want me when I was a babe and gave me away to Liv and Dag instead. Do you want to rob me now of the only person who is fond of me?'

Silje was shocked. Whatever could Sunniva be thinking? How was it possible that this girl believed nobody wanted her or loved her?

'My dear Sunniva,' she said, placing her hand on the girl's arm. 'I let Dag and Liv bring you up, because I no longer had the energy to care for a child properly. Shall I tell you something? When my four children were small – your mother, Dag, Liv and Are – I was most likely the worst mother and housekeeper anywhere in Norway. But I loved them all, just as I love you and all my other grandchildren. Yet the Lord alone knows how often I was impatient and short-tempered with them! Dag will tell you how buckets and cleaning cloths flew across the room when I was in a fury – and that I would run off into the woods sometimes in frustration when the children bickered with each other too much. He'll remember that I threw away their oatmeal and that they had to wear clothes so badly sewn together that the neighbours would laugh – and this all happened when I was young and hearty! When a person grows older it becomes harder to deal with too much noise and all the work that a small child makes. Liv was born to motherhood – I never was.'

Sunniva had stopped crying and the tears in her big sad eyes had been replaced with a look of astonishment. Very slowly her expression began to change to one of hope and optimism.

'I can well believe that you feel forgotten sometimes,' continued Silje, 'with no mother or father. But you have to understand that everyone on the two farms loves you – indeed they adore you, for the open-hearted soul you are.'

A trembling smile spread across the girl's sweet face. That Sunniva was an insecure individual there was no denying. She was too weak to endure misfortune and she imagined she saw that all around her. She aroused the protective instinct in those about her – soaking up attention like a dry sponge – but she had very little to give in return.

Her features – and that wonderful, beautiful face – reflected nothing of Sol's inner strength.

Silje found herself seeing the traits and flaws that Sunniva had inherited from Heming, such as the need to hide away from adversity, and the talent he had for living off other people and exploiting their goodwill. As a child, she had clung fast to the strong robust Yrja, allowing her to do all the wearisome work and keep Sunniva out of trouble. And yet, on the other hand Sunniva could be a loveable little creature, who wished harm to nobody and was always careful not to be a nuisance.

Pondering these thoughts, Silje placed an arm around Sunniva's shoulders for a few moments. Then, taking a deep breath, she added: 'And when it comes to Tarald, we have no objection to the pair of you being good friends. You can flirt a little, hold hands perhaps – even kiss sometimes – and stay fond of each other. But never may you do more than that. Never, never anything more!'

Sunniva seemed truly shocked that her grandmother could talk in this way. 'But we had not thought of doing otherwise, Grandmama! We really and truly wish to be wed.'

Silje was astounded. Had this girl been taught nothing? Had she no idea of the consequences of such a wish. 'That's out of the question!' she replied at last. She had decided she was at one with Tengel in that regard. 'In that case you must break off the friendship at once!'

'Oh, no!' Sunniva whined, like the wind rushing through a gap in a door. 'Oh no!'

'Well then, have your little romance and let it run its course. It will certainly fade with time.'

'Oh, Grandmama, you are a good person, but you do not understand. Do you do not know what it means to really love someone?'

Silje found it hard to keep a serious expression. She pretended to cough and after a while, with great effort, she said: 'Just promise me this: that you will keep within the bounds of decency! At all times!'

'Yes, Grandmama, that is not hard to promise.'

That I doubt, thought Silje and she related the whole conversation to Tengel later that evening. After listening carefully, he clenched his teeth, thinking hard.

'Sunniva doesn't know what she's saying,' he said at last. 'I shall have to have a serious talk with Tarald.'

'Yes, I wish you would, because it does worry me – and I don't think I dealt with it as well as I should have today.' Silje was silent for a few minutes lost in thought; then she turned to face Tengel again.

'Have you realised that history is repeating itself? Liv and Dag grew up together as brother and sister – and they fell in love. I know all was well because Dag is totally unrelated by blood. And Tarald and Sunniva both grew up under the same roof and now their turn has come. Our home always seems to have been blessed with the right atmosphere for romance.'

'Yes it does. But this time it cannot be permitted. I will talk to Tarald – and Dag as well. He must have his say.'

'Good. And I shall speak to Liv about it.'

* * * *

Yrja was lying in her bed at Eikeby, trying desperately to quieten her sobbing. Swallowing hard, she was making every effort to stifle her telltale intakes of breath. She needed to blow her nose, but how could she, when she was crushed together in a long row of sisters in the wide family bed. Her brothers occupied another bed; while in a third lay her parents, surrounded by the very youngest children.

The married couples and all their children shared beds in the next room. They were her aunts and uncles, her older siblings and their families. Yrja could hear the sound of one couple making love at that very moment and was trying her best to ignore it. She hated having to listen to such intimate behaviour, but it went on all the time. She always thought it was worse when it was her own parents, hearing her mother's plea to be left in peace brushed aside by her father's gruff impatience.

She was in tears, because she could not help herself. It was unusual for her to feel self-pity – she always tried hard to avoid it – but today had just been too much for her. The future that fate had decreed was weighing down on her – in fact it seemed like there was no future at all.

She began thinking again about Tarald; then stopped. No, she told herself sternly, she must not let him enter her thoughts. It would be conceited and wrong, because he was not the one for her. He had already made his choice and it was her destiny to care for her parents in their latter days. Such a prospect was a privilege, she told herself. It was a selfless act and one for which she should be grateful.

Then why was she so despondent? Would she be able to free herself from the terrible feeling that she was suffocating whenever she thought about the future? She felt the tears rising again within her and she could not stop them. A lifetime seemed such a terrible long time …

* * * *

Before Tengel had an opportunity to speak to Tarald or anyone else, two events took place in quick succession. First young Count Strahlenhelm and his wife returned with their large retinue to collect Cecilie and take her with them back to Denmark. Great excitement ensued as final preparations were made and a lengthy farewell took place on the steps of Gråstensholm.

Liv was almost continuously blowing her nose and wiping away her endless tears. In an indistinct voice Dag spoke a thousand words of advice and warning, whilst Charlotte was almost beside herself with joy. To think that one of her own grandchildren was to be in the service of the King's children.

Admittedly they were not the 'right' children: not the ones that could inherit the Crown. They were the children of Kirsten Munk, the King's morganatic wife. But what did that matter? They were legitimate and accepted – by most people, anyway. She knew there were two young girls, and didn't they have a boy as well? She was not sure. But one child had died, or so she thought. She hugged Cecilie over and over again as tears ran down her face, sobs merging with gleeful laughter. Oh! What bliss!

Finally the carriage disappeared from sight beyond the church, with the whole family waving it off. They watched Cecilie's outstretched arm waving back until the carriage was out of sight. After it had gone, there was a deep feeling of anti-climax and everything seemed strangely quiet on the estate.

Sitting at the window in Linden Allée, Silje also watched the carriage draw away. Cecilie had come over to say her goodbyes the night before and this had been a bittersweet moment, because those staying behind knew how much they would miss her.

'A very sweet lass, our Cecilie,' thought Silje. 'Not as dazzlingly beautiful as some of the women of the Ice People, perhaps, but leagues ahead of them all in charisma and fortitude.'

In her heart Silje knew that she would come to miss her spirited granddaughter very much indeed.

* * * *

Just three days later the whole family, including Silje, were sharing supper at Gråstensholm. Silje was able to attend, because her leg was much improved, and she and all the others were enjoying the usual warm family atmosphere. Halfway through the meal, a messenger arrived asking for Tengel. The pastor had sent him, he announced, and Tengel rose at once from the table to speak to the man.

'The pastor?' asked Charlotte in surprise. 'It's not often he sends for Tengel.'

'That's right, he hasn't ever been sick before,' retorted Dag.

Nobody in the parish or the neighbouring areas was frightened by Tengel's grotesque appearance any longer. His unnaturally wide, high shoulders now seemed to cast a protective comforting shadow over the sick people he treated. Yet still the spiritually unyielding man of God had kept his distance – and of course Tengel was not the most enthusiastic of churchgoers.

Nevertheless Tengel rode off immediately, leaving the others to finish their meal without him. Supper, as usual, consisted of many courses and they were still eating when they heard him return, talking animatedly to one of the servants in the entrance hall.

'No,' they heard him say loudly, 'please don't touch me.'

'Back already?' muttered Are. 'That was quick.'

With heavy rapid strides Tengel came into the dining salon.

'Well now,' said Charlotte, 'you'll have time for a little food after all. Why don't you sit down?'

But Tengel remained standing at a distance from them all, just inside the doorway, and Silje knew at once that something was seriously wrong.

'What's the matter, Tengel?' she asked.

Shaking his head in distress, his answer was very brief. 'It's plague!'

Chapter 4

Plague! The sound of that dreaded word echoed ominously around the silent room. All those gathered at that supper table stared at Tengel in horror. Meta's jaw dropped and she gasped, as she drew her two youngest sons closer to her. Out of sight beneath the table Sunniva reached out for Tarald's hand.

In her place Liv whispered to herself, 'Thank the Dear Lord that Cecilie left in time!'

All colour had drained from Silje's face. 'How serious is it, Tengel?' she asked in a hushed voice.

'Two farms at the other end of the parish have it – and one man in the pastor's household. That is where I have just been and I must not touch *anything* here. I have to go out again.'

'No!' exclaimed Silje.

'I must. They have nobody else but me. Besides, the pastor gave thanks to God that his is the only parish hereabouts with somebody who knows medicine,' Tengel gave a wry smile. 'The best in Norway, so he said.'

'What sort of plague is it?' asked Silje, who had seen so many. The word 'plague' itself covered such a wide range of epidemic sicknesses.

'Blood pestilence,' Tengel replied.

Silje and Charlotte groaned quietly. This was bad news. 'Blood pestilence' was the name given to a sickness that caused the whole body to dehydrate rapidly, following severe bouts of bloody diarrhoea – in the same way as dysentery, cholera or typhoid. It invariably caused very many deaths.

With barely a moment's hesitation, Tarjei rose from the table and said: 'I shall come with you, Grandfather.'

'No! By all that's sacred, I forbid you to!'

'But I am not afraid.'

'You must not carry this sickness back here to our home, my boy! And I cannot risk losing you – especially not you, Tarjei! Our legacy goes forward with you. I will not risk *any one* of you, don't you understand?'

'What about us then?' asked Jacob Skille gently. 'Can we risk losing you?'

The others around the table all muttered their agreement.

Tengel was touched, but concealed his feelings with a curt nod. 'Somebody has to care for the suffering!'

'Yes, of course,' agreed Tarjei. 'But it is completely senseless for you to do it on your own, Grandfather. You will not have the strength to carry on for very long and then the parish will be without any relief at all.'

Yrja, who had accompanied Silje and supported her that evening when she walked up to the big house, got to her feet. 'If you will permit, Master Tengel, I too should be exceeding pleased to help you.'

'And bring the pestilence to Eikeby – with so many living there? No! I thank you, both Yrja and Tarjei, but you do not understand what this means. I must segregate myself. I may not see my home again for a long time.'

'Oh, Tengel!' moaned Silje. 'Tengel, you must not do this. Oh, why can I not be with you?'

He gave her a fleeting smile. 'I shall manage well enough – but I cannot drag the youngsters into this.'

Tarjei interrupted. 'Allow me to be segregated together with you, Grandfather. You see, I have a theory.'

'Tarjei, my son!' pleaded Meta, 'don't bring sadness upon us!'

'I really can come with you as well, Tengel,' insisted Yrja. 'I am not afraid, and if I should be smitten by the sickness – well, there are already too many of us at Eikeby.'

Her eyes met Silje's fleetingly, but Yrja avoided her gaze. Mistress Silje, she realised in that moment must know the truth. It showed in her expression. She was obviously understanding and sympathetic – but also powerless to help Yrja, no matter how much she might want to.

'My dearest Yrja,' said Tengel, moved by her generous offer, 'I thank you for those words.'

Sunniva leaned over to be embraced by Tarald. 'I am so afraid! What if we should become sick! I might die! Oh, Tarald!'

He put his arm around her protectively. 'I will take care of you, dearest one,' he whispered.

Tengel cleared his throat and held up his hands to gain their attention. 'From now on you must all stay in your homes!' he said sternly. 'Receive no visitors! Do not venture outside – not even between Gråstensholm and Linden Allée. I shall go home now and collect the things I need – and then it might be some time before you see me again.'

'Tengel,' cried Silje. She tried to get up and go to him, but her knee failed beneath her.

'Do not touch me,' he said quickly. 'But don't worry – you will not be rid of me that easily.'

Tarjei was not about to give up. His strong-featured face with its high wide forehead was full of determination. 'Grandfather! You will never manage under those conditions! I *shall* come with you, whether you wish it or not. Somebody has to look after you as well.'

'I too will come and help you,' said Yrja with equal determination. 'It is a task that needs more than one. And I promise to go nowhere near Eikeby! Will that not suffice?'

'Stubborn children,' muttered Tengel shaking his head distractedly. 'All right! Come on, then! The gods know how much I need you. But do not touch any of the sick. *That* I do forbid!'

Meta rushed over to her son. 'Tarjei, we cannot afford to lose you to some foolish pestilence! You are destined for other things.'

'Don't worry, Mother,' he replied. 'I shall be safe – because I believe I know how. And that is the most important thing, isn't it Grandfather?'

Tengel, who had already learned so much from the agile mind of his grandson, nodded solemnly. 'Yes, it is most important. Now, Trond, will you run to Eikeby and tell them that Yrja will not be home for a while? Good! Well done. And Tarald, make sure that Klaus drives Silje home in a carriage! Sunniva, you must go down to Linden Allée and live with Grandmama until this danger has passed. While Yrja is away, Silje will need your help.'

And with that, the three of them quickly left the room.

Silje had been trying hard to stay calm, but now she could not hold back her tears any longer. 'I have always been so proud of my Tengel,' she sobbed, 'but at this moment I wish he was just a plain normal man.'

Still shaking slightly, Liv said, 'Everything will be well, I'm sure of it. But now we should all return to our homes.

We shall not see each other for a while, Mama. So please take good care of yourselves, all of you at Linden Allée!'

Sunniva was almost hysterical with fear. 'I want to stay with Tarald,' she screamed over and over again all the way out into the yard. 'He has promised to take care of me. I dare not live at Linden Allée – what if Grandfather brings plague to the house?'

'Let her stay here, Mama!' said Liv in an exhausted voice, as she came out onto the steps. 'With all her whining, she will do you more harm than good.'

Silje hesitated, not wanting to leave Sunniva in Tarald's home. Still, it all seemed very innocent. 'Oh, well, if you don't object, Liv …'

'Of course not!'

As her foster son helped her climb aboard the carriage, Silje turned and said quietly: 'Dag, please make sure Tarald and Sunniva don't spend too much time together.'

He nodded. 'I understand. I shall watch them, Mama Silje.'

On that note they parted company. There was no way they could have known, but for some, it would be their last farewell.

* * * *

Tengel rode silently on horseback between the two rows of linden trees lining the avenue. Tarjei and Yrja walked alongside him and Tarjei was chatting incessantly. Tengel tried hard not to look at Silje's tree as they passed it, for each time he did so, he suffered great pangs of anguish. He had at last come to understand her intense dislike of the lindens over which he had invoked incantations so long ago.

'First of all, Grandfather, we ought to wash ourselves thoroughly.' Tarjei was saying. 'You see, I have a theory about how all the pains in the stomach arise.'

Tengel nodded. 'I shall gladly wash myself, if that is what you wish.'

'You have to! And I mean every time you come close to a sick person – wash yourself.'

'There is not enough water for that,' laughed his grandfather.

'But you must! This is serious! I believe the malign enters through the mouth!'

'Evil spirits, do you mean? Yes, perhaps that is so …'

'Now, really Grandfather! You cannot believe in evil spirits! I do not know how the sickness gets into a person, but I think that water can kill it.'

'By drinking it do you mean?'

'No! No, in God's name, no! Never drink anything. Only wash yourself over and over again. I want the three of us – you, Yrja and me – to cover our nose and mouth to prevent the sickness from entering us. The people here need us now. What medicaments do you have, Grandfather?'

Speaking from memory, Tengel reeled off the names. 'Blueberry, camomile, St John's wort, saxifrage, coltsfoot, lady's-mantle, blood root, yarrow – they are all binding.'

'That's good – but I believe cleanliness to be the most important.'

'Agreed, but you are wrong on one thing, Tarjei. You do not know blood pestilence. It dries out the body – utterly and completely. Patients *have* to drink!'

Tarjei's confidence weakened. 'Well, yes, maybe. Perhaps you are right – we shall have to see.'

Tengel allowed himself a little smile. This boy was so eager, and a source of great pride for his grandfather. But Tengel was not about to be taught entirely by a thirteen-year-old! Although he had not been educated himself, he had nevertheless amassed a wealth of experience during his long life. Yet he did feel that Tarjei had made a good case when it came to cleanliness.

While these exchanges were taking place, Yrja plodded on heavily alongside them. She did not dare to speak, but carefully took in everything they said. Despite the danger, she felt very glad that she was being allowed to help in this vital task. As they entered the almost empty house at Linden Allée, Tengel halted, his face creased in a frown.

'I've just been thinking, Tarjei. What about drinking ale? Do you think it is cleaner than water?'

'Ale? I really don't know,' said the boy, uncertain. 'But *brännvin* ought to be pure.'

Tengel laughed loudly. 'We cannot make the whole countryside drink themselves senseless!'

'And why not – if that is what is needed?' replied Tarjei seriously. 'Then there's another thing. I've noticed something strange with water. I once boiled some very filthy water and afterwards it was almost clean.'

Tengel nodded. 'The same thought had occurred to me. But if we ask folk to choose between *brännvin* and boiled water, I think I know what the old boys will choose!'

Once inside the house, Tengel called the servants together and told them what had happened. They were asked to decide whether they would remain where they were or go home at once and stay there until the church bells rang out a 'good news peal'. The majority of them ran home in fear, but those loyal few whose only home was Linden Allée, decided to stay and attend to their beloved

Mistress Silje and the family. They were waiting together for her in a small group on the front steps when Silje arrived back from Gråstensholm a short while later.

As soon as he had helped Silje and the others from the carriage, Klaus bolted back to his smallholding, his eyes wide with fright. Using anything he could find, he barricaded the door on himself, Rosa and their growing children. Then he sat down on the marriage bed beside them all, biting his nails, while staring at the door as though expecting the plague to crawl in through the keyhole and pay him a personal visit. Rosa took his hand in her own and held it tightly. Without words, she appreciated that in his simple way, her young husband was demonstrating above all else that he was firmly shouldering his family responsibilities.

By this time Tengel, Yrja and Tarjei had long since left Linden Allée, having packed up all they needed and given orders to the servants on how to stay safe. Tengel had spotted Silje's carriage coming down the drive from Gråstensholm, but had decided not wait for it to arrive.

* * * *

Tengel, Tarjei and Yrja began their work at the pastor's rectory. They asked the churchman to send a rider to all the farms in the parish with instructions about staying isolated from others, cleanliness and boiling drinking water. However, they decided there would be no ringing of the 'plague bell'. Tengel knew from experience that this often inspired folk to hurry to other farms and villages in search of news.

They asked for a small outhouse to be made available to them, where they would live and store their herbs and potions. At first the pastor was not overly enthusiastic at the thought of his rectory becoming an informal meeting-place. But neither was he inclined to refuse them for, as Tengel pointed out, the plague had already affected his household. So the first patient they attended was the pastor's own servant, who told them he had visited the two stricken farms some days earlier.

Tengel mixed some herbs together in an infusion for the man to drink and gave him the same instructions that he had given to the pastor. His voice was slightly muffled by the strip of cloth wrapped around his face, because he and Yrja were following young Tarjei's advice to cover their noses and mouths, to wash themselves thoroughly after seeing to their patient and to burn his infected clothing. When they had finished treating him, they promised to return that same evening, but he was to be allowed no visitors and no food; also he was to drink only the boiled water that Yrja had brought with her.

'Am I to lie here alone to die?' the man asked.

Tengel's steady gaze calmed him. 'You are not about to die. You are not very poorly and you will get better, as long as you do as we tell you.'

'And do not put your fingers in your mouth either,' added Tarjei.

'What? Why not?'

'Because the pestilence finds favour on unwashed fingers,' Tarjei replied.

Even Tengel could not help pondering this. How much goes on inside this lad's head, he mused. Meantime the man was staring at his fingertips in abject horror.

'And I expect your master will come down and say a prayer for you,' Tengel told him wickedly as they left.

The situation was immeasurably worse at the two farms

on the outskirts of the parish and Yrja, Tarjei and Tengel were shocked by what they found there. At the first cottage, the farmer gazed at them as though they were angels of mercy. He and all the others in the cottage lay in bed, their faces drawn and eyes staring helplessly. The stench in that small space was indescribable.

'How long have you been like this?' demanded Tengel.

'We didn't know,' stammered the farmer. 'We didn't know what it was. First the stable hand got sick. Then everyone else fell ill, one after the other.'

Tengel turned to his two companions. 'Go home,' he told them calmly. 'This is too serious.'

Both youngsters shook their heads decisively and stood their ground. Yrja's heart was pounding anxiously, but it would never cross her mind to leave Master Tengel to manage alone. For his part, Tarjei was considering the science of what he saw – this was an opportunity to learn something new and test his theories.

Tengel sighed heavily. Suddenly he felt old and helpless. 'Where is the stable hand?' he asked in a resigned voice.

The farmer pointed to an alcove. It was just possible to see an elderly man in the shadows of the room. They had never seen anyone so wasted – he was nothing but skin and bones. His open mouth let out a groan, but he hardly had the strength to turn his head.

'Listen to me,' said Tengel. 'Where can you have caught the sickness?'

He tried to speak, but only unintelligible noises came from the old man.

'What strangers have you met these past days?' persisted Tengel. 'Anyone from nearby farms?'

With much difficulty the man managed to utter a single word: 'Nay.'

From the heap of rags that was her bed, one of the farmer's young daughters lifted a weak hand to attract their attention. Her hair was knotted and her skin was clammy from the sweat of fever. 'He was visiting Tönsberg but a week since,' she said in a feeble voice.

'Did they have the plague there?'

'We don't know. But when he returned he told of many sick.'

'Well!' exclaimed Tengel, 'at least we know now where the sickness has come from. But that is something for others to deal with. Yrja, you must run to the Helle house, out along the road to the next parish and tell them to place two strong men, preferably armed with muskets, to watch the road day and night. They must allow no person to enter or leave our parish.'

Yrja nodded obediently.

'Do not go into the house, but call them out to you. Ask them to send someone to Skogstorp at the other side of the parish to tell them to do likewise. Say that these are the words of Tengel, who wishes to free their countryside from plague.' He spoke his own name with great dignity, befitting the moment. 'Have you understood all that?'

Yrja nodded again and set off at a run. The Helle house was not far away.

Tengel would have preferred to send his grandson and get him away from this pit of filth and disease, but he realised that a lad of thirteen would lack authority and not be taken seriously. As he watched his beloved grandchild walking around, trying to find somewhere safe to step among all the disgusting rubbish on the earthen floor, a lump came to his throat. Tarjei was destined for far better things than this.

Looking up from the family bed, an aged grandmother

crossed herself reverently and said: 'No heathen shall come near me! Nought but the prayers of a priest will help us. They will free us from this scourge of Satan. Why does the priest not come?'

'A good question,' muttered Tengel, then continued in a louder voice: 'If you wish to lie here and wait for him, old mother, then I shall not stop you, but while you wait, I will see to the others.'

'I saw it!' said the old woman. 'I saw the sign in the heavens. A cloud in the shape of a cross, it was. That was the warning!'

'It weren't,' said the farmer's wife lying beside her. 'It were that harpy on the farm at Lower Tjärntorp. She be angry with us for our cows do milk better than hers. She done this terrible thing to us, you mark my words!'

'Nonsense!' Tengel's tone was harsh. 'This is a sickness that has been carried here from Tönsberg. The whole countryside is suffering. Don't start evil rumours about innocent folk!' Tengel always felt vulnerable where rumours were concerned.

Some time later, breathing hard, Yrja returned and told him that she had passed on his message. Everybody, she reported, had agreed to do as Tengel had instructed.

'Good, good. Thank you, Yrja!'

Ever since they had arrived, two young children in the cottage had been crying and the sounds were heart-rending. One of the children seemed a little stronger and healthier than the other, who was making much weaker and more plaintive cries. Overcome by the misery surrounding her, Yrja was suddenly seized by feelings of apprehension and panic. Whatever it was, she knew she had a strong desire to see Tarald at least once more before her life ended. Then she took hold of her courage and quickly banished such thoughts. Taking a deep breath, she made herself ready to help.

'What are we to do, Tarjei?' muttered Tengel. 'Where can we begin?'

'We have to make it clean and tidy. Nothing can be done while it is in such a mess.'

'Is there *anyone* here who is not sick?' shouted Tengel.

The farmer answered, 'Yes, my daughter and a housemaid. But they dared not stay in here. They are in the dowager cottage.'

They hurried out and found the two frightened women, who were both about twenty years old. They were pale and fear-stricken, but otherwise looked well.

Tengel looked at them for a moment then decided not to waste any words. 'If you have stayed well all this time then you have little to fear,' he told them kindly. 'You have apparently withstood the sickness. Now we need you to come and help us.'

Tengel's air of authority and strong personality won them over immediately. On his instructions they prepared the dowager cottage for the rest of the family and then buckled down to the task of cleaning everyone and everything who lived there. In the yard outside, they lit a fire beneath the tub that was normally used for brewing and, with Yrja's help, they took the sick, one by one, out of the house. There they were stripped naked and all their clothes were burned. Yrja and the two women scrubbed down adults and children alike from head to toe and this process itself helped each of them to feel less overwhelmed by disease. Last of all came the old crone. Tengel had taken her at her word and ignored her, but finally she screamed like a banshee at the thought of being forgotten.

Water fetched from the spring had been boiled in the dowager cottage and everyone was encouraged to drink

76

frequently. In addition, Tengel gave each of them a small tot of *brännvin* from the supply he had begged from the pastor's substantial reserves. Pails were also placed beside the door and very quickly they were made use of, when the water they drank began to course through their dehydrated bodies. On strict instructions from Tengel, there were to be no more soiled beds.

In time, everyone was moved into the dowager cottage. Everyone that is, except for the stable hand. He had died as they carried him from his ragged mattress and they buried him in a clearing in the woods, wrapped in his bed linen. Tengel marked the grave with a simple cross and asked Yrja to make sure the pastor came to bless it.

The two young women were given the task of caring for the sick, giving them boiled water to drink as often as they could and ensuring that they stayed warm and dry. Tengel would willingly have razed the main house to the ground, but that would have been a hard blow for an impoverished farmer's family. Lacking the time to clean it properly, he contented himself with barring the door and forbidding anyone to enter without getting permission from himself.

When they had finished their tasks, Yrja was standing in the yard, almost drowning herself in hot water and sniffing back tears as she worked on her own hands and arms with the scrubbing brush. Noticing her tears, Tengel walked over to her.

'Are you afraid?' he asked softly.

Yrja looked up, surprised. 'Afraid, Master Tengel? No, not at all – not any longer. I just feel so sad for all these people. How afraid *they* all must have been!'

'Yes,' he agreed as he also began to wash himself. They were joined a few minutes later by Tarjei.

'How many do you think will live?' asked Yrja.

Tengel shrugged. 'Who can say? I shall be thankful if we have saved just one. But no, I believe we have done good work here, my children, although some are fated to die. I think the infant will be among them.'

'Oh, no!' protested Yrja.

'Life can be very harsh, my dear young friend. But it was a weakling from birth,' Tengel added in a practical manner. 'Now, if you are ready, we can go to the next farm.'

* * * *

When they arrived at the second farm, they found there were fewer people afflicted. Also the disease had shown itself more recently, making their work easier. A fearless young farmhand helped them, and the sick were all moved into the main parlour while the other rooms and alcoves were thoroughly cleaned. But it all took time and when they had finished the day was gone. Exhausted, the three of them returned to the small cottage at the rectory, stopping on the way to see the solitary servant, as they had promised. They were all washing their clothing and hanging it to dry above the hearth when the pastor arrived.

'I – I expect I ought not come in … I mix with so many parishioners you see.'

'You must not "mix" with anyone for the time being,' Tengel said flatly. 'Will you come with us tomorrow and lend your help? Many have asked for you today.'

'Really? Well, yes, it is the sacred duty of a man of God, isn't it? How bad is it?'

'The folk at Svartmyren are very bad. The others will fare better perhaps.'

'And will this pestilence spread?'

'Most surely. Your servant was smitten, for example. But we have done all we can to thwart it.'

'The Lord castigates us! What have my wretched flock done to have Him visit this upon us?'

'Nothing,' replied Tengel coldly. 'It is simply one of the things we meet on the road of life.'

'But not without good reason,' said the priest sharply. 'Ungodliness, Master Tengel! Therein lies the reason! The Lord is passing his judgement on the ungodly!'

'Yes, and we shall bury an infant tomorrow,' replied Tengel.

Only Tarjei, who understood the man well, could hear the concealed rage in Tengel's voice – but nevertheless the pastor took a hurried farewell.

Unsurprisingly, he did not accompany them the following morning. None of them had expected him to. Instead he sent his curate, a young man who was studying for the priesthood. In return for performing simple clerical tasks alongside the incumbent clergy throughout the summer months, the curate was tutored by the church during the winter. The curate was a good-natured man with sincere beliefs and he went gladly among the sick, caring for their spiritual needs while Tengel and his helpers dealt with their physical suffering.

Yrja was more calm and detached than on the previous day. She had lain awake for a long time in the strange new surroundings, listening to the sound of Tengel and Tarjei's regular breathing. How different it had been from her home at Eikeby. And how wonderful it was to have a bed all to herself, even if it did feel a little deserted. She liked being with her two companions, the proud old man and the bright young lad with such clarity of mind.

She found that most of the time her friendship with them filled her thoughts, when normally she would only be thinking rapturously about Tarald. But this was not the case at night. Then there was only an aching despair again, as she tried to stop his image floating into her mind. In the deep darkness she yearned for him – simply yearned and yearned. Life, she reflected sadly, could be so cruel, so terribly cruel!

Fortunately, in the light of day, all such thoughts had left her and again the four of them worked well together. During the night there had been two deaths at Svartmyren, one of them being the infant, just as Tengel had predicted. Yet there now seemed to be hope for several of the others; one of the boys indeed was already up and about again. The day, according to their plan, would be spent cleaning the main house.

Then around midday came the news Tengel had been dreading: another farm had been infected. They were standing in the yard of the first farm scrubbing themselves clean after the loathsome work inside the house. Yrja felt nauseous and longed to be anywhere but where she was at that moment. However, she was determined not to give in. If the others could stand it, then so would she. She didn't realise that they were having identical thoughts.

'If only we had heard of this plague sooner,' mumbled Tengel pulling his shirt back on. 'Then we could have saved more of them and stopped this abomination from spreading. Come on, we must go!'

Yrja, who had just seen his incredible shoulders and hair-covered chest for the first time, had to make a conscious effort to stop herself from staring. There was something strangely fascinating about Tengel's 'wolf-man' physique and she thought it incredible that delicate

Mistress Silje would dare touch anyone like him – yet for some unknown reason she became disconsolate. Was it because she had realised how wonderful it was that two people, so different, could be so well suited to each other? That a living being as shockingly formed as Master Tengel could have found love and contentment with a beautiful warm-hearted woman like Silje? And would she in her turn, ever find a man to love her, despite her deformities? No, of course she could not expect that! It was far easier for the man to choose. And they always chose the best girls. Sadly, she was never in the running.

She had to set these negative thoughts aside as they hurried off to the next farm. Again they worked hard and Yrja believed that they probably succeeded in preventing a number of other deaths there, before they returned wearily to the cottage that had become their temporary home. That night the curate stayed with them and, to maintain decency, they partitioned off a corner for Yrja by hanging up a length of curtain. It had not mattered so much when only Tengel and Tarjei were in the room, but it was felt that with a young priest-to-be present, they needed to observe a greater degree of propriety. Yrja noticed however, that he was a very pleasant uncomplicated person, who took things as they came.

On the following day the situation worsened. One person died at Svartmyren and another at the neighbouring farm, while new cases of the disease were reported at two other properties. That evening they all collapsed into their beds from exhaustion – but not before they had again washed themselves and changed all their garments. Yrja was at a loss to understand what was holding her skin together after so many soakings. This amount of washing could never be healthy!

The days passed; they were invariably brutal and sapped every ounce of their strength. Despite that, each of them knew that without their help and guidance the outbreak would have spread more quickly and taken more lives in the surrounding countryside. As it was, many of the homesteads were unaffected – more by far than those that were stricken. Moreover they had succeeded in keeping the sickness in check in those places. But still the death knell sounded daily for the tragedies that no one could prevent.

Then out of the blue, fate played another cruel trick. They discovered this when a little stable boy ran all the way from Gråstensholm to find them. In a breathless voice he told them that the plague had spread to the estate! On hearing this, Tengel's whole body turned to ice. He could not even bring himself to ask who had been affected.

At the same time Yrja fell ill, worn out from her strenuous efforts. She simply had no energy left to resist. Then within the hour, it was the turn of the curate. Tengel was also tired beyond measure, as was Tarjei. As the two trudged back to Gråstensholm, Tengel tried to comfort himself by reflecting on the legendary stamina of the Ice People. But this did not bring any lasting relief for his anxiety and he remained deeply worried about what they would find when they arrived home.

They soon discovered that Charlotte had been first. Soon afterwards Jacob Skille had fallen victim; in addition Dag was already showing first symptoms of the malady. Tengel was mortified with dread – but he could not keep his mind from mulling over the situation. Seemingly, the kin of the Ice People, Liv, Tarald and Sunniva, had been spared!

Liv did everything she could to help her family, working slavishly at Tengel's side. He, on the other hand, was thinking of Yrja and the curate, left alone and forgotten at the tiny rectory cottage. They had helped so many, but now there was no one to help them.

But he could not go away from Gråstensholm; Charlotte was so poorly that he dared not leave her. He decided to send tough little Tarjei back to the rectory to look in on Yrja and the curate and also to see how the farms were faring. He hoped in his heart that the parish would forgive him for spending one day at Gråstensholm.

Down at the rectory cottage, in fact Yrja was feeling inconsolably miserable in her sickbed. So this will be my fate after all, she thought gloomily. But what a horribly shameful demise it will be – without any slightest trace of loveliness. A good thing that Tarald is not here to see it, she thought bitterly. Who then will mourn me? Will they not simply say, 'It was the best thing for her really, poor child. What did she have to look forward to in life anyway?'

Was this, she wondered the end she had always wished for herself? She tried to convince herself it was so. Haven't I wanted to be so sick, to have such pain that I should meet death as a release and without the slightest feeling of fear? Well if I did, she concluded, I don't think now it was such a good idea after all. Without any doubt she was deeply frightened. She wished so much she could have someone with her – preferably Master Tengel. But at the same time she still wanted to hide herself away with her misery.

The curate was suffering as much as she was – she could hear him with awful clarity only too well. She had thought to ask him to say a prayer for her, but she found she couldn't move her parched lips to speak. The water left beside her bed was finished, fever raged in her body and pounded in her brain; also the cramps in her stomach were telling her that she needed to get to the pail in the passage again – but in truth she had no strength left to rise from her bed!

'God!' she whispered to herself. 'Help me. Although I am worth nothing, I still want to live. I want to see the wildflowers in the horses' pasture at Gråstensholm – and the hedgerows at Eikeby – and the cat – and Mistress Silje and – no, now I must be going mad!'

Back at Gråstensholm Tengel was at that moment feeling deeply anxious about the lonely souls in the rectory cottage. Tarjei had still not returned – what had happened to him? What if he had also become sick on his long journey around the parish? But there was little opportunity to worry for long about what was happening elsewhere, because events quickly took a turn for the worse on the estate and the sick began to die.

Charlotte went quickly – she had no strength left in her and she passed away in Tengel's arms. Near the end she whispered one barely audible word: 'Dag?'

'He will be well. Do not worry. He is strong.'

'Good,' she whispered again. 'And Jacob?'

'I do not know, Charlotte. But it is not so good.'

She just nodded. 'Look after mine own, Tengel.'

'You know that I shall,' he replied, his voice full of emotion.

'Thank you for our long friendship,' she whispered very faintly.

'Thank *you*, Charlotte. Thank *you*!'

Then she smiled at him. 'Tengel the Good,' she breathed – and then she was gone.

Three hours later Jacob Skille followed her.

* * * *

In another part of the house, Liv was spending every minute with Dag and did not leave his side. It really did seem as though he would beat this blood pestilence. With his heart aching from sorrow, Tengel left Gråstensholm to travel to the rectory cottage and his thoughts were mainly of his Silje. She was not of the Ice People. Neither was young Meta. They would probably not have the strength to fight this disease, he thought. But fortunately the plague had not reached Linden Allée – yet.

And in the event, it never did reach the farm. Without reason, the pestilence just seemed to stop spreading and disappear. Furthermore, their parish had suffered far less than any other in the Akershus region. Eikeby, by some good fortune also stood unscathed. In an ungodly moment, Tengel reflected that a good clearout there might not have been a bad thing. But it was an unkind thought that he immediately regretted. To his amazement, Klaus found that the sickness had passed his house by and, with tears of joy streaming down his face, he hugged his family to him.

One of Tengel's last tasks during the epidemic was to try and save Yrja and the young curate. They had been left on their own for far too long. As he sat at Yrja's bedside, changing her clothes, he pondered how a beautiful personality could sometimes be found in the most unlikely body. A millstone could pass between Yrja's bowed legs; her spine was twisted in the shape of a letter 'S' and her hips and chest were joined as one, without the slightest sign of a waist between them. She smiled at him shyly, as though apologising for her disfigurement and the humiliating situation in which she found herself. Because there was an unspoken understanding between them, Tengel simply smiled back encouragingly.

But as the days went by, wonder of all wonders, both

Yrja and the curate survived. Somehow they both managed to pull through, perhaps aided by their decent forthright determination not to yield to the illness. Yet fate, capricious as ever, decided that the pastor, who had not shown himself other than to perform hasty funerals, should be shown no mercy. The malady seized him and he died speedily – and there was no more talk of God punishing the ungodly.

That was the last time the death knell sounded. Not long after the pastor's demise, the bell ringer was able at long last to ring out 'peals of joy'. The plague had been defeated.

Chapter 5

The pastor's untimely death left the parish without a priest. As a result, the church councillors asked the curate to take over, as he had almost completed his studies. They placed great value on the fact that he had selflessly carried out so many good works during the time of the plague and, to everybody's delight, the Bishop quickly came and ordained him. Very soon the whole parish realised they could not have wished for a better or more openhearted pastor.

Not long after the curate's ordination, people from the countryside all around gathered and made their way to Linden Allée. It turned out they were bearing a gift for Tengel. It was a printed Bible that the curate had helped them to buy with money they had all donated. Tengel was deeply moved and called Tarjei and Yrja to join him as he accepted the present.

A small part of him could not help wondering if there was a special meaning in the choice of gift. Was it suggesting that he should change his 'misguided' way of life and return to the conventional 'straight and narrow' religious path? Were they concerned for the state of his soul? Or was it quite simply that they just wanted to thank him with the best and most honourable gift they could find?

As he stood with a steady grip on Yrja's scrawny arm – her legs were still very weak – Tengel felt sure it was the latter. The village alderman gave an address extolling the virtues and courage of all three of them, recounting details of the 'miracle' they had performed. Nor in his speech did he forget to praise the curate, who at the time had not been ordained.

Tengel told the people of Tarjei's theories and how they had been proved to be of such help. Through it all Silje was constantly wiping tears from her eyes. She was so very proud of all of them and it was such a grand and worthy moment. The relentless and unceasing efforts they had all made, however, had taken their toll on Tengel and he decided to rest in bed for a few days. It was unlike him, but he needed to restore his strength and he thoroughly enjoyed being taken care of. Why, he wondered, had he never thought to do this before?

From his bed one morning, he heard the sound of a saw and axe being used in the avenue – Are was felling a tree that had suddenly withered and died and was threatening to fall across the path in the next storm. It turned out that it was Charlotte's tree – but Tengel decided he was not going to let his mind dwell on anything to do with the avenue.

In the weeks that followed, normality returned to the countryside. Tengel could now call the long-postponed meeting with his children and grandchildren. The meeting, with its empty chairs, reminded him just how much he missed Charlotte. And Jacob too, of course, although the former dragoon had always remained in the shadow of the dynamic Baroness Meiden. Everyone realised that an era

had come to its end with her death, and no one quite felt able to talk about her. The deep wounds of sorrow had not yet remotely begun to heal.

Naturally Yrja had been included in the meeting. Everybody agreed that she had become part of all their lives; besides, Silje no longer felt able to manage without her. Her help was invaluable and she always knew instinctively what Silje needed or wanted.

Liv had received a letter from Cecilie and now she read it to them all. It had taken a long time to arrive and Cecilie had no idea of the tragedy they had experienced when she wrote it.

'Dearest Mother and Father,' she began. 'Oh, I find myself so far from Gråstensholm now! I was so unsure and confused at first, but you know that it is your daughter's folly never to admit a weakness, so I kept up a bold appearance. In truth the journey went very well and my fellow travellers arranged everything and saw to my every need. Thank you, Grandfather, for the potion for seasickness; it worked perfectly. I shared it with all and sundry and became most popular, not least with the young Countess Strahlenhelm, who is very sweet to me. Please tell that to Grandmama Charlotte – she will be most proud!'

After those words, Liv stopped reading and there was a sombre pause. Liv discreetly blew her nose and wiped her eyes, but a minute or two more passed before she could continue.

'Yesterday Count Strahlenhelm presented me at Court. I saw nothing of His Majesty, but a great deal of his wife, Kirsten. I do not believe I like her. She looked right through me, as though I were invisible and asked: "Baroness Meiden? What petty nobility is she? Does she aspire to something in society?" Nor is she willing pay

anything for my services. It is as if this was to be a great honour, for which I should be made to pay! I am to be paid nonetheless, but without her knowledge. They do say that she is unbelievably covetous. And she is with child yet again. I have only made the acquaintance of two young girls – one is called Anna I think – and it is they I shall be caring for. Poor dear children!'

The letter concluded in a feast of descriptions of how impressive everything at the castle was. They all shared Cecilie's happiness and excitement as they discussed the letter with each other.

When they had finished, Tengel began to speak. 'You have all heard the legend of the Ice People, more or less in its entirety, so I need not tell it again here.'

'Good,' said Trond. 'We all know it inside and out already.'

Tengel turned to the boy and gave him a withering look. 'Yes, but something unexpected has happened Trond, and it is now necessary and important for us to talk about it again.'

The boy said nothing, but lowered his head in shamed silence.

'Once again it relates to Tengel the Evil, who swore allegiance to Satan 400 years ago. As you all know, I do not believe in Satan. He does not exist. Our sins, I am sure, are of our own making and we alone must answer for them without blaming him. But the first Tengel was an uncommonly evil man and his powers of wizardry were immense – *that* is beyond denial. You know that the evil legacy passes down through the generations, but to my great joy you have all been spared that fate. You know also that when he had his so-called meeting with the Devil, he is said to have buried a pot in which were placed all the

ingredients for an infusion to evoke Satan. His kin are destined to suffer the curse for as long as that pot remains hidden in the earth. This was done because Tengel the Evil wanted some of us to remain wicked enough to serve Satan. We will not be entirely free of this until the pot is found and dug up. We cannot be sure how much of this legend is to be believed, but one truth remains: monstrous examples of human kind do emerge among our kin from time to time.'

Tarjei interrupted him: 'Wasn't something once said about there being one person who would be born to our people who would have greater supernatural powers than anyone else has ever had in this world?'

'Yes Tarjei, that's true – but that individual has yet to be born. And we also know that the legacy is not all bad. It has brought with it great skills and knowledge of things unseen, as well as a vast store of ancient prescriptions and recipes. All of this I have passed on to Tarjei. He among you is best suited to oversee this treasure. And now the only descendants of the first Tengel of the Ice People are sitting here in this room. They are of course Liv, Are, Sunniva and myself.'

At the sound of her name, Sunniva awoke with a jerk from her reverie of admiration for Tarald. She stared hard at Tengel, her interest suddenly fully aroused.

From a chair beside Sunniva, Liv raised her hand tentatively to attract Tengel's attention. 'You have forgotten Cecilie, Father. She's not here.'

'Yes, you are right, of course,' he admitted with a rueful smile. 'My mind must be getting feeble.'

There was a little outbreak of noise around the table, as they all disagreed adamantly with him on that point and he had to hold up his hand for silence. When they were quiet again, Tengel repeated himself slowly.

'There is, of course, Liv, Are, Sunniva and myself – and as Liv rightly points out, Cecilie, but in addition to Tarald, there are Are's young tearaways Tarjei, Trond and Brand.'

The three young lads' faces lit up at the sound of their names. They were seated side by side on a bench under Meta's strict gaze and, from their delighted faces, it was clear that they worshipped their grandfather.

'That makes nine people,' said Tengel, 'nine people who could possibly be blighted by their awful heritage. You have been lucky not to be affected, and there are several of us here who hope that the potency of this inheritance is waning. Would that it were so!'

Every person in the room could tell from his tone that Tengel had reached the heart of what he was telling them and a breathless hush fell in the room.

'We shall of course do all we can to make sure that this evil inheritance does die out. This means that we must bring new blood into our kin all the time. In my youth I tried to hasten its demise by not taking a wife. I soon discovered that to be an inhuman way and not one that I would force upon you. But then I wed Silje, who was not of our kin. Liv married Dag, who despite growing up in our home, is not of our blood. Then Are took as his wife Meta, who came here as an outsider from Skåne. So to you, all my grandchildren, I make this fervent plea tonight: whatever you do, do not marry one of your kindred blood! If you do, catastrophe will result. The terrible curse will be passed on to your children – and your children's children!'

Tarald's noble face had turned as white as a sheet and beside him Sunniva burst into tears.

'Grandfather,' Tarald said with some effort, 'I have been waiting these last few days until you regained your strength, to ask for an exception to be allowed to this rule. I was going to come and speak to you, Mother, Father and Grandmama first. But you have forestalled my request. The simple truth is: I wish to wed Sunniva.'

'That cannot be allowed!'

Tengel's words came like the crack of whip and Tarald flinched, as though he had been physically struck. But the young man quickly gained his composure and reached out to take the hand of Sunniva, who was visibly trembling beside him.

'If you will not allow this, then I will have no one else.'

'Oh, Tarald,' thought Silje silently. 'Can you not see how much you are hurting Yrja? Are you so utterly blind, you self-centred and foolish oaf!'

Tarald remained completely oblivious to the focus of Silje's thoughts. He had never looked upon Yrja as anything but a friend. For her part, Yrja sat wringing her hands in her lap. Let me leave now, she was thinking. Do not put me through this agony any more!

Tengel gazed sadly at Tarald. 'You are so young my boy, and you will change your mind many times as you grow up. As the daughter of Sol and the grandchild of my sister, Sunniva carries too great a burden to be allowed to wed you, my grandchild. Can you not see this for yourself? Forget one another now before it is too late! That is my sound advice to you.'

Tarald, looking suddenly ashen-faced, stood up. 'It is already too late!' he said in an urgent whisper. 'Much too late.'

Every adult in the room gasped in horror at the same time. Then in the silence that followed, they heard Tengel draw a slow, menacing breath.

'No, Tengel!' warned Silje, reaching out to touch his sleeve in a restraining gesture. 'Don't do anything rash.'

Nobody but she and Sol had ever seen Tengel's anger rage. Now it broke loose with fearsome unbridled power and he stormed over to Tarald, brushing aside Silje, who rose awkwardly from her chair in an effort to put herself between them. As Tengel approached, Sunniva screamed with fright and hid behind Dag.

Tarald had become petrified in Tengel's still-powerful grasp and could not prevent himself from being shaken like a wet rag.

'What have you done, you imbecile?' yelled Tengel. 'What have you done?'

'No Grandfather!' screamed Tarald in desperation. 'No! You're hurting me. Help!'

'You *knew*!' Tengel hissed. The older man had become like a demon from hell, who had risen up from the earth to slaughter a mortal. He seemed to have grown in stature to an impossible size and his shadow fell across the entire room. As he peered fiercely into Tarald's face, his yellow eyes flashed mercilessly. 'You knew of the danger and still you did it!'

'I do not believe in superstition,' gasped Tarald, who by now was close to fainting.

'Children, go out and play,' said Are quickly to his sons. 'Go now, at once!'

Scared witless, the two youngest rushed out. But Tarjei, although pale and frightened, went no further than the door.

At last Dag came to his senses and tried to save his son. 'Father, think what you are doing!' he implored. 'Please think!'

Tengel had always felt a great respect for Dag and hearing his calm voice helped bring him to his senses. Almost instantly his rage ceased and his expression relaxed.

'Superstition?' he said exhaustedly. 'By all the saints – if only it were nothing but superstition …'

Everyone in the room breathed a sigh of relief. They were all very upset and dismayed by what had happened.

'If you had watched my mother die while giving life to a monster like me, Tarald, then you would not speak of superstition! Had you seen our beloved Sol in her darkest hours; then you would have chosen your words more wisely. Dag, you remember Hanna and Grimar, don't you? Why did you not warn the boy?'

'I have done so, Father. Both Liv and I have warned him – and Sunniva.'

'And still you did not heed them, Tarald?'

'I thought – they exaggerated,' stammered the handsome young boy, close to tears.

'And Sunniva,' said Silje, 'you promised me that it would go no further than kissing.'

'It wasn't my fault!' replied Sunniva at once. 'It really wasn't!'

Tengel pulled her brusquely from behind Dag's back.

'No, Sunniva, this time you will not put the blame on others,' he rasped, his fury growing inside him again. 'You will come with me and we shall be rid of your offspring this instant!'

The girl was sobbing with fright, but Tengel held her tightly by the wrist and began pulling her after him, heading for the door.

'No!' she shrieked. 'No, no, no! It is Tarald's child and mine! If you take it from me I shall kill myself!'

Tengel stopped. 'If you do not get rid of it, then the child will kill you. Have you understood nothing?'

'I don't believe you. I don't believe in all that!'

At this point Liv spoke up. 'Father, it has been many

years since anything happened – and all your grandchildren are without fault. Besides, Tarald and Sunniva love each other very much.'

'Liv, my dearest child, I cannot be responsible for what will happen.'

Silje came to his side. 'You must give up this child, Sunniva. I don't understand you at all – when you promised me you would not.'

'Oh, Grandmama,' the irritated Sunniva interrupted, 'you are so old-fashioned – you know nothing about true love – nothing of the ecstasy that overcomes you completely when ...'

'Enough, thank you, Sunniva,' said Tengel, his anger still burning. 'If there is *anyone* who knows the meaning of the word "love", then it is Silje, my wife. We have loved each other for forty years! And, whether you believe it or not, we can still lie together even now. So we understand very well. This situation, however, cannot be permitted. It is too serious, Tarald and Sunniva. You must be separated.'

'Then I shall kill myself!' cried Sunniva, rushing to the dresser where the knives were kept. She took out a sharp blade and with a histrionic gesture held it to her breast.

'Sunniva!' shouted Tarald.

'Hah! Pay her no heed. She is just testing us,' said Tengel. 'That girl would never thrust a blade into herself.'

Sunniva opened her hand and the knife clattered to the floor. 'None of you care about me,' she snivelled.

'Dear child,' Tengel retorted, 'if we did not care about you then we would not be so worried now.'

'But Tarald and I have sworn our love to each other for all eternity. You cannot make us break that oath.'

Tarald had plucked up his courage again. 'We will love the child, Grandfather, even though it might look like you.'

Tengel gritted his teeth in despair and, with an effort, said nothing.

'Tarald!' exclaimed Dag. 'Watch your words!'

'What? What have I said now?' asked Tarald; then suddenly he realised his mistake. 'Please forgive me, Grandfather, I did not mean it in the way you think.'

'Don't worry yourself about that,' answered Tengel wearily. 'Sunniva's life is more important.'

But the naïve girl did not want to understand. 'Tarald and I are normal, can't you see,' she pleaded. 'How can it not be a beautiful child? And we love each other – the Good Lord cannot wish us ill.'

Inside her mind, Silje was agonising for poor Yrja. How must she be suffering, listening to Tarald and Sunniva and their unending declarations of love? But whatever her feelings, she remained sitting, bolt upright, with a little sad smile on her face that seemed to reflect her pity for both of them. And so it did. The shocking news of a baby had sent shivers through her and made her see how foolish she had been. But now she felt great sympathy for Sunniva. Except for Master Tengel, Yrja knew nobody who was of the Ice People. And could there be a better person? His almost insane anxiety was beyond her understanding.

Cautiously Liv asked, 'I am too young to remember Hanna and Grimar, Father. But surely things are not as bad as that?'

'I have seen many more than them – too many.'

'But that was long ago.'

'I seem to remember a discussion like this,' muttered Silje.

Tengel cast a swift, melancholy smile in her direction. 'Yes, that is so. When Silje was carrying our first child, we said the same things. I would have killed the unborn, but I relented for Silje's sake – and Liv was born.'

97

'And Mother is normal and well,' said Tarald swiftly. 'There is no finer mother than Liv.'

Tengel nodded. 'We had the same argument over Are. That time it was Sol who stopped me from taking the life of the child.'

'Thank you, Sol,' whispered Meta softly to the room in general. 'Thank you.'

'In fact we have had the same anxiety and soul-searching with every child,' continued Tengel. 'For Tarald and Cecilie – and for Meta's three boys.' He paused for a moment. 'Liv and Meta, you remember, don't you, how I made you both swear not to have children?'

The women nodded silently in unison.

'Well, I have since changed my mind about that. It is too much to ask. For some reason the kin of the Ice People never have many offspring. With three boys, Are and Meta will hardly be bettered!'

Tengel fell silent, smiling faintly; he was obviously amused by the train of his own thoughts.

'Well then?' said Sunniva sulkily. 'You have been wrong every time. You gave in and the children were perfect. Why should I be different?'

'Have I not made myself clear enough? You are too closely related. And consider Silje's two deliveries! They were so fraught that her life was in danger both times. She might easily have died – that is how bad they were.'

'Yes, but that was Grandmama's fault. She was not strong enough. I am very strong.'

'Is that so?' Tengel's smile was gentle. 'You are such a fragile little thing. I don't exactly remember seeing you lift any heavy loads.'

Once again Sunniva's tiny doll-like face screwed up tightly, ready to start weeping again.

'Nobody understands me,' she sobbed. 'Nobody!'

Tarald was soon at her side, caressing her cheek. 'I do, Sunniva. You know I understand you very well.'

Tengel heaved a loud sigh. 'What say the rest of you? Silje? Dag? Liv, Are, Meta? I do not have it in me to fight alone any more.'

'I agree with you,' said Silje, loyally, 'with absolutely everything you have said.'

'That's not fair,' cried Sunniva. 'Grandmama nagged to be able to keep both her children, but I am not allowed to have even one!'

Tarjei, almost forgotten by everyone else, suddenly said in a low voice, 'Grandpapa Tengel is right, Sunniva. When there is frailty in a clan then family members should not marry each other – or the feebleness will attack.'

'You don't know anything!' Sunniva hissed at him. 'You are always so arrogant with all your learning. You think you're better than everyone else, you do!'

Ignoring the outburst, Tengel said, 'Dag?'

'I don't know. I'm still in two minds.'

'Things have gone so well until now,' said Liv hesitantly.

Are nodded. 'We all have wonderful children.'

Meta agreed with Are – she always did.

The two youngsters who were the centre of attention held their breath. After glancing round the room, Tengel sat down heavily on the bench beside Silje, suddenly feeling very, very weary. They are wrong, he thought. There is definitely another with the evil curse on them. Not long ago I noticed that yellow cat-like glint in a pair of eyes once more. I was right the other times as well. One of my grandchildren does carry the curse.

In reality, Tengel had already made up his mind to take the life of the unborn child. As he was getting nowhere with this discussion, he would have to administer the powder to Sunniva when she was not expecting it. This time there would be no Sol to stop him!

Then something came to him, as he thought of Sol. She had also tried to kill her own child – and that child was Sunniva. Yet she had failed. Sol, who knew as much as he did, possibly more, had failed. He no longer harboured any illusions about Sol. He felt certain she had taken several lovers and very likely killed several of her unborn children before, but this last one had shown a stronger will to live!

'Do what you will,' he said, his demeanour indicating that all his stamina had now been drained. 'But at the first sign that something is wrong with Sunniva, then I take the child – is that understood?'

There was a chorus of agreement from everybody and the young couple hugged each other in joy and relief. Yrja smiled – and kept smiling. But her eyes were dark pools of loneliness. She tried her best to be happy for the pair of them, yet the feelings of unhappiness deep inside her persisted.

Tengel rose and made his way towards the stairs to his bedchamber. 'It's best you see about getting wed then,' he said over his shoulder. 'And fast ... Damned foolish brats.'

Silje went with him, climbing the stairs slowly and deliberately. Halfway up he stopped and waited for her, offering a helping hand.

'Shall we move downstairs, Silje? Then you won't have to climb them.'

'No, I should say not! That would be admitting defeat. And besides we'll only have to move up here again once I'm better.'

'Yes, you're right,' he laughed, hoping that his laughter sounded sincere.

As she sank down onto the edge of the bed, she said: 'Has it crossed your mind, Tengel, that when we have our first great grandchild I will have known seven generations of our family?'

'How do you mean?'

'Well, I saw my great-grandmother briefly. That is three generations before me and I am the fourth. Now I have three generations after me – children, grandchildren and great grandchildren.'

'Yes, that's true. It is a harrowing thought.'

'Isn't it, though?'

'Then let me tell you a secret. I have known eight generations! I met my grandfather's grandmother! She was a proper old witch, and you know that the accursed ones of the Ice People can live for many, many years. Then again, I never knew my own mother. So maybe I shouldn't brag too much.'

When he had helped Silje into her bed and given her a herbal brew to help her sleep, he stood looking down at her. Inside his chest, his heart felt like a leaden lump weighing him down. I am able to help others, he thought. Hundreds, perhaps thousands even, have had my help. But for the one whom I love more than my own life I can do nothing. If she should go, then I would not have the strength to live on. Out there in the avenue, her very own linden tree is beginning to wither. She has not yet seen it, but Are knows. And Tarjei noticed it yesterday, although I have asked them to say nothing.

Tengel shuddered and took a deep, breath. I know this particular ailment and very soon I shall need to saw off her leg above the knee. I must do this before the harm can spread through her bone marrow to the rest of her body. I have no cure for this sickness. The warmth of my hands can at present ease the pain; but soon the relief will only last for a short while each time. It will not be long before I have no stronger potions to give her. Feeling sad, he climbed into bed beside his beloved wife. Life, he reflected, is sometimes so cruel and unfair.

* * * *

Silje realised that, despite being extremely considerate and kind to Sunniva, Liv and Dag had probably wished for a different future for their only son. Not that he should become an academic – Tarald was a landowner and would almost certainly devote himself to the estates. But Tarald was also a future baron – a noble rank that carried duties and responsibilities. They were not pretentious, far from it, but Liv and Dag probably had reservations about Sunniva's suitability as the lady of Gråstensholm.

In any event, that was how Silje saw it and for that reason she illogically sided with Sunniva from then on, despite sharing Liv and Dag's sentiments. It was in her nature to sympathise with the lass, hoping to make her feel wanted. Confidence and self-reliance were qualities of which Sunniva had too little.

As a result of these reflections, Silje showed Sunniva extra kindness during the difficult period following the storm of emotion directed at the two youngsters. Tarald, however, was left to manage largely on his own. He should have known better – and furthermore he had often taken his future for granted. Now he would find out for himself what happened when he acted selfishly, as though the world was his oyster.

The family had thought of having a small discreet wedding ceremony for the close relatives. Sunniva, however, wanted many guests to attend. Casting aside many moral scruples, they eventually agreed to it – for her sake. Yrja was invited of course, but she declined, saying that she was needed to help with the chores at Eikeby.

'I can understand how you feel,' said Silje one day, when Yrja was helping her at home.

'Yes, Mistress Silje, you know my feelings very well.'

'I do. But I have said nothing to anyone.'

'I thank you for that. There was a time when I thought it was behind me – when they told us they were expecting a child. But now it is even worse. Whenever he looks at me with his dark warm eyes – smiling as if I really meant something – I feel faint and have to hold on tight to something lest I should try to touch him.'

'Aah! How well I remember feeling just like that when I was young,' smiled Silje. 'That was how it was when I was drawn to Tengel.'

'So you see that I can think of nothing more pitiable than a rejected woman sitting in tears at the wedding of the one she holds dearest. Not that I ever thought he would look upon me that way! But the heart is a foolish thing, don't you agree?'

Silje took Yrja's hand in hers. 'You are so right,' she said quietly. 'It never listens to the voice of common sense, and that's a fact!'

'Baroness Meiden has asked me to be with Sunniva as often as possible in the months ahead,' Yrja said meekly. 'Of course I agreed, because Tarald and Sunniva have always been such fine friends. Yet I am so afraid that my stupid heart will ache so. What if I should start to cry?'

Silje had never grown used to the idea of her own

103

daughter Liv being called 'Baroness Meiden' and she felt so much sympathy for the Eikeby girl. 'If it is too hard for you, then blame me, Yrja! Say that I have asked you to help me and then you can come here and shed a tear!'

'Thank you, I will do that. I really want to help sweet gracious Sunniva – it seems that she too, is relying very much on my friendship.'

'I think she is,' muttered Silje. 'You are a good girl, Yrja. Tengel is very fond of you.'

Her eyes lit up. 'He is?'

'Very fond! I only wish … no I shouldn't say it.'

'What?'

'No, it would not be right, we are terribly fond of Sunniva as well.'

Yrja was not so foolish as to be unable to guess what had been left unsaid. She turned away, not wanting Silje to see the expression on her face.

'I shall try to overcome my feelings,' she said. 'It is such idiocy to be upset just by seeing a man who is utterly entranced by another woman – the one that he is to wed and who is the mother of his child. A man who – forgive me for saying – lies in her arms each night. I would never have thought that *I* could be so foolish, for I had always considered such thoughts to be unhealthy. Oh! Mistress Silje, I have been in such a rage with myself – I have beaten my head against the wall – I have *tried* to fall in love with other young men, whether or not they cared for me! Always there remains something in my heart that senselessly strives against me. It is then that I loathe myself.'

'My little Yrja,' said Silje, speaking gently to the big clumsy girl. 'I think the saddest thing is that you are too good for that young pup, that spoilt scoundrel, who is my own grandson! What shall we do with that heart of yours, you and I?'

Yrja gave a hopeless laugh. 'I don't know! But I do not believe that I am too good for Tarald. Nothing can be too good enough for *him*!'

'Now, now,' admonished Silje. 'You mustn't look at him through rose-tinted glass, Yrja! Truth to tell, I think that among all my grandchildren he is the one of least substance – him and Sunniva.'

'Yes, but they are so young!'

'You are the same age.'

Yrja chuckled. 'Does that make me sensible, do you think?'

Silje laughed with her. 'No, perhaps you're right!'

* * * *

Everything continued to go well for Sunniva. Whenever she was in pain at any time, she managed to shrug it off. Overall, she appeared to be surprisingly capable and lively, not wanting Grandfather Tengel to show concern over her health. However, what the others did not see, was how much of a burden she placed on Yrja, who had almost taken up residence at Gråstensholm through that winter and spring. Perhaps it was also true to say that anyone who did as little as Sunniva would have no difficulty in looking healthy and relaxed.

Furthermore, as Tengel had feared, the powder designed to induce a miscarriage did not work. Just as Sunniva, despite Sol's efforts to kill her, had fought tenaciously to survive before she was born, in the same way Sunniva's own unborn child stubbornly withstood all efforts to terminate its life.

So, in the end there was nothing more Tengel could do – except wait and hope.

Chapter 6

Cecilie was shocked and deeply dumbfounded. Sitting in her chamber at Fredriksborg, one of the King's many castles in Denmark, she stared in disbelief at the letter from her mother that she was holding in her hands. Grandmama and Grandpapa were both dead, it said – and she had not been with them!

Dearest Grandmama Charlotte, who was always so lively and enthusiastic, how could she be dead? How could life be imagined without her? Cecilie was not sure if she could bear to think about it. But it was true; it was not a dream. It was set down there, in black and white in her mother's handwriting, and eventually she would have to come to terms with it.

And Grandpapa Jacob as well! She knew, of course, that he was not her real grandfather – but he had always behaved as if he were with all the grandchildren. He had always been there and they had known no other. How often had Cecilie gone to him for help with this or that because of his practical skills? He was a big, reassuring and friendly man of whom people often took little notice because his dominating wife eclipsed him. Within the family, however, he had been their steadfast rock, and he had a wealth of knowledge where Gråstensholm was concerned. During his time, the estate had been brought into good order and he could usually be found making repairs or improvements here and there. He had always seemed so happy with his way of life. Now he too was suddenly gone.

Looking over the letter again, her heart skipped a beat when she realised that the news could have been even worse. Her own father had also fallen sick with the plague – and Yrja, too. But thankfully they had both survived. 'You were lucky to have left when you did,' her mother had written. 'Although you would not have been in any real danger – we of the Ice People will always endure.'

Not for the first time, Cecilie felt homesickness well up within her. The journey to Denmark and the circumstances in which she now found herself were not everything she would have wished them to be. The reality was not as much like a fairy tale as the prospect had seemed when she first heard of it at home. Here she sat now, alone in a rural castle in mid-winter, watching a pale sun go down across the freezing countryside of northern Zealand. Feeling sorry for herself, she shivered and pulled a blanket closer around her in the large chair she had placed in front of the fireplace.

She was alone in this part of the castle with only the two little daughters of the King in the adjoining apartment. The servants' hall was in another wing. Mistress Kirsten and her courtiers were attending a grand ball somewhere and King Christian was not in residence. The room in which she sat was furnished in the heavy rigid Renaissance style with dark polished wood everywhere – and the servants sometimes told her stories of ghosts that haunted this part of the castle. How very encouraging, thought Cecilie bitterly. It was a little irritating to have to admit it, but she did feel quite afraid. Now, on top of everything else, there was the deeply distressing news about the death of her grandmother and grandfather, which had just robbed her of all pleasure and enthusiasm for life.

Her duties were not particularly pleasant either. Arguments with the head housekeeper were an almost daily occurrence and Mistress Kirsten was difficult to deal with. Only three years older than Cecilie, she was an exceedingly arrogant young woman. The thing Cecilie found most distressing, however, was the housekeeper's harsh physical treatment of little three-year-old Anna Catherine. How many times had Cecilie found herself secretly comforting the poor child? Her sister, Sophie Elisabeth, was still too young to be beaten, but Cecilie felt horribly sure that in due course her turn would come, too. She had never known such brutal punishment in her own home, but here it was meted out for the slightest misdemeanour – mischief that any little child of three would get up to. Cecilie was very concerned for the child, but her appeals fell on deaf ears. She was ignored!

Outside she suddenly heard the sound of carriages driving into the forecourt and a noisy boisterous crowd of people began streaming into the castle. The ball had obviously ended, but from the sound of it, the festivities were continuing in the great hall below. Feeling no inclination to join them, Cecilie stayed where she was, sitting disconsolately in the chair. The news of the deaths at home had left her unable to sleep. There was also other disturbing news with which she was slowly coming to terms.

Tarald and Sunniva had married! The image kept nagging at her – it was not one she was happy with. Did they realise what they were doing – or was this merely youthful infatuation? After all, neither of them had met many other young people. But Cecilie, without realising it, did not have the full story. She knew nothing as yet of the child Tarald and Sunniva were expecting. Liv had not yet been able to bring herself to write about it.

Her gloomy thoughts were suddenly interrupted by the sound of hurried footsteps outside in the corridor. The footsteps stopped abruptly, as her door was suddenly thrown wide open and a man entered. At first he did not see Cecilie. He simply flung his cloak over a bureau and whistling abstractedly to himself, went over to stand before the hearth. Then he saw her.

'Oh! Please forgive my intrusion,' he said, taken aback. 'I did not know there was anyone here.'

Cecilie quickly tucked her bare toes under the hem of her skirt. She was so surprised that she could not think of anything suitable to say.

In an embarrassed silence, the man picked up his cloak again and made to leave. 'You see – I usually stay in this room,' he explained hesitantly. Then he paused and looked harder at her. 'But you seem unhappy. Is something amiss?'

His voice sounded so kind and friendly that Cecilie managed a weak smile in response. 'Everything seems to be amiss for me right now,' she said shortly. 'At this moment I can see not one single reason for living.'

He stepped closer, peering into her face. 'But what's so awful?' he wondered. 'Is there perhaps something I can do to help you?'

Cecilie had always been openhearted and trusting, and she found something reassuring in the man's manner. 'Yes, bless you, perhaps there is. Could you possibly sit with me a few short moments and remind me how many wondrous, joyous things there are in life?' Then she broke off, embarrassed by her own forwardness. 'No! You must forgive me! That was an unfair request!'

'No, it's not unfair at all.' His voice was soft and friendly and he asked if he might sit in the other chair. 'You see I too often feel as though I need someone to remind me of what is good in life.'

'You!' This surprised her. 'But you look so at ease with the world. You appear to be someone who has all he could want.'

Cecilie could see he was a distinguished man, whom she judged to be in his late twenties. His shoulder-length dark-blond hair was cut across his forehead in a straight fringe and she saw something noble and clean-cut in his manly features. But there was sadness too, in his brown eyes, and when she looked more closely, she sensed she could see bitterness etched into the corners of his mouth. The clothes he was wearing were certainly distinguished, but as he had just returned from a ball, he would probably have been wearing the best he had.

'All I want?' He laughed, but his laughter lacked joy. 'Yes, one can have everything – and yet have nothing! But I ask your pardon! My name is Alexander Paladin; I am one of His Majesty's cavalry, a captain in his Regiment of Lifeguards. My maternal grandfather was Duke of Schwarzburg. I am but a lowly marquis, an empty title without worth.'

'Paladin? Does that not mean "knight"?'

There was the flash of a smile. 'Oh, yes – and I feel like one too! Sadly I am the last of my line, so the name will die with me.'

Surely that won't happen, thought Cecilie, but she could not allow herself to make such an intimate comment.

'I am Cecilie, daughter of Baron Dag Christian Meiden,' she told him.

'Are you Norwegian?'

'Yes. I am here to care for the King's children.'

'Aha!' he said slowly, leaning back in his chair. 'Then you are the girl who dares to stand up to the housekeeper! You have true courage! I have heard both she and Mistress Kirsten are plotting to make mincemeat of you.'

'I do not like to see innocent children beaten.'

'No,' he said quietly, 'you are quite right. To do so can harm the soul – and it will not heal.'

Cecilie gave him a questioning glance, but decided not to pursue the thought at that moment.

'Thinking the way you do about the smacking of children,' he continued, 'I can well understand that you think life is hard. But you sit clutching a letter – does it have any bearing on your humour?'

'Most surely! I have just been informed that my paternal grandparents have died of plague. It may not sound that sorrowful – I know grandparents have a habit of dying, but in this case they meant so very much to me. They were wonderful, youthful, lively people despite their age.'

'I know what you mean. Relatives like that are to be highly valued.'

'They are, yes,' she carried on eagerly. 'And I have so many. My other grandparents are quite amazing! Should you ever meet them, I am sure you would like them. And my parents are so sweet!'

'But why then were you so disheartened?' he asked, amused by her zeal.

Cecilie waved her hand distractedly. 'Oh, it was simply that everything suddenly seemed to come upon me at once. The letter, my duties in this place, where I feel unwanted by everyone, except the children. And the weather – just look at that grey, cold picture of misery out there! And this drab, dismal room,' she hesitated, searching for words, 'but I suppose more than anything else it is loneliness. To be so far from the happy atmosphere of my home – which I did not value enough while I lived there.'

'It is natural to want to venture abroad at your age.'

'Yes, it probably is – and I suppose I could always return home. But that would be to give in. Besides I believe the young girls need me.'

'Most certainly they do!' he agreed. 'Stay true to yourself above all else – and I shall do my best to support you. While I have no influence over Mistress Kirsten or that other mare, I do have the ear of the King – and that is worth more than a little.'

'Thank you,' said Cecilie. She looked inquisitively at him. 'But you do not seem to be happy either. Is there something that I can do to help you?'

He drew himself to his full height and sighed. 'You are very observant – but as to whether you can help me, that's another matter. My very existence hangs by a thin thread, you see, my young Miss Cecilie.'

From what he said, she understood him to be seriously ill. How sad, she thought in such a fine man. She did not feel, however, that it was right for her to enquire directly as to his meaning.

'But what sort of company am I,' he laughed apologetically, 'to burden you with my woes?'

'Well, first of all, you have made no mention of your woes,' said Cecilie, laughing in her turn, 'and secondly I have forgotten all of mine – may I perhaps offer you a glass of wine as a mark of gratitude?'

'No, but thank you. I have already drunk sufficient this evening. It is dangerous for me.'

'Excuse my curiosity, but are you sick, Count Paladin?'

He bit his lip, saying nothing. Then he rose and ran his hand lightly across her cheek, holding her glance with his soft, sorrowful eyes. 'Goodnight, little Norwegian girl! And thank you for this moment!'

Cecilie jumped to her feet in alarm. 'I hope I have not offended you!'

'No, no, you have not offended me in the least,' he said, smiling suddenly at her. Forgetting decorum, she had cast the blanket aside without thinking and the sight of her bare feet obviously amused him. 'I felt such a strong desire to confide in you, and that is something I cannot do. You make sure you take good care of the two little royals! And do not forget that I will lend my support to you if you find life becoming too onerous.'

Saying that, he left abruptly and she heard his footsteps retreating down the corridor as quickly as they had come. As Cecilie prepared herself for bed, her mind filled with a hundred thoughts. She wondered how her other very loving grandparents, Silje and Tengel, were faring, and Are and Meta and their three sons. To her relief she found that her sorrows had diminished somewhat as a result of the chance meeting with Count Paladin and in its wake she was left with a more gentle melancholy. But it was a long time before she fell asleep.

* * * *

Some months later in glorious June sunshine, Are was walking through the fields around Linden Allée. But despite the fine weather, he kept looking up at the sky. It was a Sunday and he could instinctively feel from the atmosphere that thunderstorms were in the offing. What was more, they would be heavy ones, he could tell. Every little patch of field where he walked was showing green shoots. A downpour now would not cause as much damage as when the crops were ripened, but he would rather it didn't happen. The corn would be washed away if there was too much rain.

'It's going to pour down very soon,' he said to his two youngest sons, as they plodded along in his tracks. 'So let's hurry and get inside.'

Brand, the youngest, listened solemnly to every word of wisdom his father uttered about farming, while Trond, the middle son, who was more interested in playing, spent his time gadding about in the ditches among the tufted vetch, speedwell and buttercups. Tarjei had not gone with them on this occasion. He never involved himself in agriculture; he was always busy with other things. In the autumn he would be off to start school in Oslo – a clerical school, for there was no alternative. Furthermore the vocation of the priesthood was counted to be the most distinguished in any parish.

But Tarjei was not planning to become a priest. He had chosen the school as a path to university at Tübingen, the place where he would really be able to learn. It was there that his idol, Johann Kepler, had studied and Tarjei hoped he would perhaps one day be lucky enough to meet the great mathematician and astronomer.

This fierce thirst for knowledge learning typified by Tarjei and other members of the Gråstensholm and Linden Allée families had always been a thorn in the side of the old pastor of the parish who had died in the plague outbreak. In his time he was not so much old as narrow-minded, a man with ingrained fundamental beliefs. It had bothered him that there were others in the parish who were able to read and write as well as he could, because he felt it diminished his standing in the eyes of his congregation.

He could have accepted that a public notary like Baron Dag Meiden would be literate; it was only natural after all. But the women too – was that really necessary? Hadn't Baroness Charlotte, the notary's mother, tutored all the children from an early age? It was unheard of. She would have been burned as a witch if he had had anything to do with it. But Master Tengel always stood in his way. Those highborn gentlemen at Akershus had never allowed anyone to interfere with Master Tengel or his household. So all the children and grandchildren were able to read and write – and they had ideas and knowledge that did not become a layman. Ragamuffins, all of them who – he was forced to admit – knew more than he did. Before he died, this matter alone had troubled him greatly, taking him to the point where he was developing stomach ulcers.

In stark contrast, the two families formed an excellent relationship with the new pastor, who had been the curate at the time of the plague. Baptised Martin, he had taken the Latin form as his priestly name, Martinius. He had studied at Nidaros Cathedral in Trondheim before he came to Gråstensholm Church as curate and no one was more astounded than he at the speed with which he had risen to the priesthood. One reason, of course, was that the outbreak of plague had taken a heavy toll among the clergy. Many of them – unlike their honourable brother at Gråstensholm, also deceased – had bravely gone out and ministered to the sick and dying.

Martin was fully aware that it was Master Tengel and his grandson Tarjei to whom he owed his life and, despite the fact that Tengel never entered the church or showed any interest in Christianity, a deep measure of understanding had developed between the two men.

When Are and the two boys arrived back at Linden Allée, they found it almost deserted. Are immediately went upstairs to see his mother, because Silje never left her bed any more.

'Where is everyone?' he asked.

'If you mean your father, then he has hurried to Gråstensholm,' Silje told him cheerfully. 'If the baby gets a move on, then it will be a Sunday child.'

'Oh yes, of course the time has come,' muttered Are, sharing the anxiety that everybody felt about the birth of any child. 'But Tarjei was at home today when I went out. Where has he gone?'

'Where do you think? He follows his grandfather everywhere – especially to exciting medical cases!'

'And why are you sounding so happy, Mother?'

'I am glad that Sunniva has been in perfect health throughout her time. When I think of how terrible *I* was before I had Liv, then Are, I truly believe that this bodes well. Just think! My first great-grandchild!'

'Of course everything will go well.'

'Yes, I *know* it will,' she replied confidently. 'Because Hanna told me that I should have one great sadness in my life. There can be no greater sorrow than I felt at Sol's death. So everything will be right with Sunniva.'

'Of course. But is it really proper for Tarjei to attend a birth, Mother. He is but fourteen years. Is it not going too far?'

'You know that Tarjei is an unusual boy – and he already looks at the world as a man of science. This will be an experience for him.'

Are gazed through the window. 'A man of seventy-three

and a young lad of fourteen – there is no doubt Sunniva needs help!'

'She could find no better help anywhere! Liv will be there, and Yrja, as well as the midwife Tengel has sent for. Rest assured, Sunniva will be in good hands.'

'And has the new pastor been sent for?'

Silje's smile faded. 'Why should we do that?'

'To bless the child I mean,' Are answered quickly.

'Well, that won't be necessary. He only gets called to baptise a newborn who will not survive. Ahh – the air is so heavy today, isn't it? It is scarcely breathable.'

'That's not surprising! There is an awful thunderstorm building.'

'Ooh, I don't like thunder and lightning! There is nowhere to hide from it. Lightning finds you, wherever you may be.'

'Has it ever found you, Mother?' asked Are with a grin.

'No – but you can never tell!'

'Linden Allée is quite safe, but Gråstensholm stands on higher ground.'

'If that thought was supposed to comfort me, Are, then it was unsuccessful.'

'Yes, I suppose it was,' replied Are, turning away to hide his smile from her. His mother's age-old fear of the powers of nature had always enchanted him. In spite of all she had been through in her life and all the wisdom she had gleaned, she had never lost touch with those primitive beliefs. It was one of the things that made her so lovable.

But Are was also pondering something else: it was quite strange to think that his own sister was already becoming a grandmother. The years had passed so quickly and almost unnoticed. Are himself had not changed very much. Now thirty-five years old, he had remained soft-spoken, reliable and realistic about life. His relationship with his sons and Meta was comfortable, even though his wife's timidity in tight situations sometimes tested his patience. Occasionally, because of her position as the wife on a large farm she could be meddlesome. But she was devoted to him and it was always a joy to come home to her after a hard day's toil.

Are and Meta often regarded their eldest, Tarjei, with wonder and disbelief. Sometimes they were unable to grasp that they had given birth to such a sharp-witted and intelligent boy. Sometimes Are could not escape the thought that Tarjei was in more ways Tengel's grandson than he was their son.

'Can you pass me that shawl, Are?' said Silje, breaking in on her son's deep thoughts. 'My shoulders ache badly today. It's probably the weather.'

'Yes, gout can be uncomfortable.'

Are tucked the garment she had requested tenderly around her. He was one of the few people who realised that his mother's illness was worse than gout. After a lot of thought and discussion with Are, Tengel had not been able to bring himself to amputate her leg. They knew that it was highly likely that such an operation might be fatal. Powerless to do anything, they had watched her disease spread – all the while hoping in vain for a miracle.

Silje smiled her thanks, as Are adjusted the shawl around her. She could not conceal the fact that she was delighted and excited by what was about to happen at Gråstensholm. The previous day she had spoken to Yrja for a little while to find out how she was feeling about the impending birth.

'I hear that Liv and Sunniva want you to be there at the birth,' Silje had said. 'How do feel about that?'

Yrja had hesitated before she answered. 'May I tell you a secret, Mistress Silje? Yesterday I met one of the lads from the farm at Hellegården and he – well, he asked if he could be my "night-suitor"! Everything would be very respectable of course, you do know that?'

'Of course,' smiled Silje. 'Why I too had a "night-suitor" once, in my first flush of youth. So what did you say to him?'

'It was all so sudden. I told him I would think about it – but he is quite nice.'

In fact, all of this was a lie. Yrja had simply made up the story on the spur of the moment, because she knew that Silje was worried about her. She felt it was not right that Mistress Silje should have anything else to worry about in her weak condition.

'So you've put everything else behind you, then?' Silje asked eagerly.

'With Tarald? Oh, yes, thank the Lord. At last I have. So I told Sunniva that I would be happy to be there.'

'Oh, that's wonderful! You know how much Sunniva relies on you, don't you?'

Oh, yes, Yrja certainly knew that. Sometimes she even imagined that Sunniva was aware of her weakness for Tarald and that she deliberately tormented her with displays of affection for him or by giving Yrja orders when Tarald was in earshot. But deep in her heart, Yrja didn't really believe that Sunniva could be so evil-minded – it was more likely that she was just thoughtless.

But Yrja's love for Tarald? Despite what she had told Silje, that would never ever die – and how she despised this strange condition. Yet somehow she was totally incapable of freeing herself from it.

* * * *

That night, dusk fell early over Gråstensholm. The evening was much darker than usual because of the blue-black thunderclouds that seemed to be pressing down towards the rooftops. Then, with sudden and unmitigated violence, the storm broke.

In Sunniva's room, Liv looked up anxiously at the window and thought about the tower, reaching up high into the sky above the house. She was wondering anxiously whether the lightning was about to strike it. In the next room, where they were waiting, the same thoughts were making Dag and Tarald feel very uneasy.

They were all weary, exhausted from the stress of a day at Sunniva's bedside. It was worst for Sunniva of course and her eyelids were swollen from the pain and the constant tears. Dag and Tarald had been ordered out of the room – it would not be long now, they were told. The contractions had started a long time ago, but they seemed so far not to have had real effect.

Desperately Sunniva squeezed Liv's hand, while Yrja wiped her brow. To say that she was a brave and determined woman in labour would have been an overstatement. But nobody could ask her to endure much more after such a day of misery.

As he watched and waited, Tengel was resolute, determined to do anything he could to help. He was keeping his thoughts focussed purely on the present and not allowing them to stray to what might be. Similar concern was also etched in the midwife's face. But she could not understand it. Why had the child had not yet been born?

At Tengel's side, Tarjei remained alert, his eyes taking

in every detail. He had been with his father many times in the barn when different animals gave birth. But this would be the first time he had been present at the birth of a human child. From outside, they could hear the dull rumble of thunder growing ever closer. Inside the room, the air was becoming so heavy it was almost impossible to breathe.

'Will it be over soon?' whimpered Sunniva, her voice deeply agitated. 'You don't know how much it hurts!'

No one answered her any more – she had been asking the same question for hours. Then without warning, she gasped and screamed piercingly, as if long knives had suddenly been thrust into her. Tengel was nearest to her and he drew a long deep breath. 'Get out, Tarjei!' he snapped. 'Get out at once!'

The boy began to protest. 'But I ...'

'Go! Now!'

Feeling hurt and finding it hard to comprehend, Tarjei went out to the room where the other two were waiting. He turned briefly in the doorway to see the consternation on the faces of the others as they huddled round Sunniva. By now she was screaming incessantly and insanely – and louder still were the screams coming from Yrja and Liv.

In the anteroom, Tarjei stood beside Dag and Tarald, unable to move. Through the door came the sounds of Sunniva's crazed shrieking, Tengel's tense voice of authority and running footsteps; then more panic-stricken voices added themselves to the cacophony.

A moment later Yrja's face appeared at the door, as white as a sheet. She looked as if she was about to faint and her clothes were splashed with blood. 'Fetch the priest someone – hurry!'

'I'll ride over,' said Dag.

With anxiety churning in his belly, he rushed out.

'Oh, Dear God,' whispered Tarald. 'I must go in to her.'

Tarjei barred his way. 'No! Stay here! Grandfather would not send me away without good cause.'

Tarald's face was contorted with dread. 'Sunniva! Oh, Sunniva!' he moaned.

To his horror, he realised that one noise was suddenly missing from among all the others: the heart-rending screams of Sunniva herself. Gradually the sounds of the other voices subsided too; then they ceased altogether. After that there was only deathly silence from inside the room.

* * * *

At the bedside Tengel suddenly noticed that he could no longer see clearly. He took a very long and deep breath in an attempt to stop any more tears flowing. Then he carefully wiped his eyes.

Looking around, he saw only expressions of horror on the faces of the others. Liv was ashen-faced and shaking violently from head to toe; Yrja, weeping bitterly, was crouched on the floor with her back to the wall. The midwife was slumped in a chair shaken, inadequate and unable to move. And on the bed, Sunniva lay dead, her body broken and bloodied.

In the beautiful crib that had stood ready …

Behind them the door had been opened without them noticing and Tarald, looking scared, came cautiously into the room.

'Is it over?' he asked, attempting a hopeful smile.

Liv quickly drew a sheet up over Sunniva's body. But she could not hide all the terrible pools of red still spreading everywhere.

'Is she sleeping?' asked Tarald uncertainly.

The question was pointless. It only served to show how desperately he wanted to keep alive the pretence of hope and success. What person would sleep with such a frozen expression of terror and pain on their face? Nobody had the energy left to answer. Neither did anybody have the energy to prevent him from walking over to the crib.

Tengel himself was afraid. He watched how the young man leant forward over the crib; then stopped abruptly. Like the biblical pillar of salt, he seemed frozen, unable to move. His stare was fixed and unwavering. Also unnoticed, Tarjei crept into the room behind him.

Only slowly did Tarald become conscious of his surroundings once more. He stared wide-eyed with horror all round the room before his gaze finally settled on Sunniva. Then he understood fully that this time she would not wake up from her slumber.

At long last he made a sound, a choking howl of fear, as he rushed out of the room. He ran on without stopping, out of the building, out into the rain that was now falling torrentially in the darkness. He ran blindly on and on into the depths of the forest until finally, when his strength ran out, he stopped. There he retched and sobbed for a long time, feeling sick to the core of his very being.

Tengel found he could not leave the room or sit down. He stood beside the crib like a statue, his face contorted into deep furrows of sorrow. Very gently his right hand closed around one of Tarjei's hands – the boy was standing motionless at Tengel's side, looking down into the crib. What he could see disturbed even his logical realistic soul.

'The poor child,' was all he said.

But somehow those few simple words helped to ease the sense of horror and loathing that everyone else had been feeling.

'Yes,' Tengel said softly. 'The poor child.'

In the crib, the child's eyes were closed. It made no sound and the only signs of life were occasional short jerky movements of its hands and feet. The shoulders of the infant were oversized and pointed, and in time would undoubtedly come to resemble Tengel's own shoulders. But the child's head sat directly on a barrel-like torso, with no neck, and its long arms were ape-like. Coal black hair covered most of the body – and the most disturbing aspect of all was its face.

Tarjei and the rest of those who had never seen Hanna or Grimar could scarcely believe their eyes. They could never have imagined anything so repugnant. Liv, although she had a vague memory of the old couple, thought that the monster in the crib was infinitely worse than them; and yet she could not help feeling an agonising affection for the unfortunate little boy.

When the pastor arrived, Tengel led him and Dag outside, where he explained what had happened.

'Do you want to baptise him at once, Father Martinius?' asked a grey-faced Dag. 'And perhaps say a prayer for his mother's soul?'

'Of course.'

All three of them returned to the room where Sunniva lay. Despite being forewarned, it was an effort for Dag and the pastor to hide their shock. Dag was the only person, apart from Tengel, who clearly remembered Hanna and Grimar, and at that moment, as far as he could see, the future resembled a dark tunnel with no light at the end of it. But it was likely to be worse by far for the infant in the crib.

Looking round the group, the priest's friendly young face was full of sympathy for each one of them. 'Who will name this child?' he asked.

'His father is not here,' said Dag clearing his throat. 'But if I may be permitted to suggest a name, it will be Kolgrim. Tarald can add another later should he wish.'

The priest nodded.

They all thought it a suitable name. 'Grim' the child most certainly was and 'kol' or 'kohl' was the word for black, like his hair.

'May I add a name too?' asked Liv.

'What is it?'

'The Cherished One.'

On hearing this, Yrja burst into tears again. Liv had obviously understood how much the child would suffer in life.

'So be it,' said Father Martinius and the monstrous newborn infant was duly baptised 'Kolgrim the Cherished One'.

During the brief ceremony, however, something very distressing happened. Liv chose to hold the child for the baptism. She had to steel herself before lifting him, but told herself it would get easier as they grew accustomed to the child's monstrous appearance.

Just before the moment of baptism, however, the child's eyes opened unexpectedly and they all gasped. For a long moment, two green cat-like slits stared unblinkingly at Liv. In that instant a terrifying thought crossed her mind, one that she never would reveal to another living soul: how can a newborn, innocent child look so *evil*? It hardly seemed possible!

Tengel had also noticed the brief opening of the baby's eyes. This had terrified him as well and made him feel so weary. He recalled his own childhood – was this child going to suffer again just as he had done?

* * * *

As soon as they had attended to Sunniva's pitiable dead body and done all that could decently be done for her, Tengel took Tarjei to one side. 'You know, don't you, that you are to have the Ice People's whole supply of medicaments? I have spoken to Liv and Dag as well as your father about it.'

The boy nodded. 'Yes of course I know, Grandfather.'

'Then Tarjei, please heed me well now! This is important beyond measure! Never, ever permit that child to touch any of them! He must never have even the smallest herb! And teach him *nothing*. Not one *word* – do you hear?'

'Yes, Grandfather. I too saw the look in those eyes. If all this had not been so tragic, I would have found it most interesting.'

'Tarjei, my dear young friend,' said Tengel putting his hands wearily on the boy's shoulders, 'never forget that you are a *man* first and a man of *science* second!'

'I won't forget, Grandfather.'

After Tarjei had left him, Tengel went out to Dag and Liv.

'Tell me – do you want me to ... give the child something? Before it knows it has a life?'

'No, Father, please don't,' replied Dag, without any hesitation. 'I know what you mean, but he is our grandson.

127

Although we dread the sight of him and fear for his future – well, it is strange, but I feel a fondness for the poor mite.'

'I do too,' added Liv. 'We have just spoken of this – we will try to help and guide him in life. You have told us of your wretched upbringing, Father, and we promise that he will be better cared for.'

Tengel nodded his acceptance of their decision. 'There will be changes in him of course. The hair will soon fall from his body and his features will mellow perhaps. No newborn is a pretty sight!'

'Very true,' agreed Liv.

Tengel rubbed a hand distractedly across his face. 'Will you forgive me if I leave all this for you to deal with now? I have become too weary to do any more.'

'Of course, Father. Thank you for everything you have done.'

They both thought he was referring simply to the hardships they had endured together through the long day, but in his own mind there was a deeper meaning to his words. He felt a strong yearning to embrace them both at that moment, but he knew that would have seemed out of character to them and might have alarmed them.

'I should thank you, my children! Tell Tarald not to forget that the child is a small living creature that needs him.'

'I will go and search for him presently,' said Dag.

'No. He will return in his own time when the terrible wrenching sorrow for Sunniva has begun to wane.'

'We will care for the boy, Father,' Liv assured him. She looked tired and very sad. 'Yrja has promised to help me – if Mother can manage without her.'

Tengel turned to Yrja and placed a hand gently on her cheek. Looking into his face, she could scarcely believe how this mighty man had aged!

128

'You are needed here now, child,' he said very quietly. 'So stay – and bless you!'

And with that he left Gråstensholm.

* * * *

The rain had stopped, but as usual the thunderclouds had continued to circle the heavens and were approaching the estate once again. Tengel walked slowly along the path between the two farms, his massive shoulders slouched forward. Above all else he felt tired, so desperately tired. For Silje's sake, he had tried to keep himself youthful and strong, but at that moment he felt all of his seventy-three years. It was a good age. Few people ever lived so long.

Stopping on a sheltered part of the path, he lifted his eyes to the leaden late-evening sky. Silje, he knew, lay at home, waiting expectantly for news of her first great-grandchild. How brave she was, seldom complaining about her discomfort and pain. He felt a sudden pang of guilt that he had not told her she was suffering from a sickness worse than gout, although he knew in his heart it was for the best. But now on top of everything else, he was about to go home and dash her hopes with news of this deeply tragic day: the death of Sunniva and the monster in the crib.

Surely it would crush her spirit! It would take all joy from her life, every ounce of happiness she had left. No one had felt as much compassion for the orphaned Sunniva as Silje. Oppressed by these thoughts, Tengel could not resist the weight of the anguish he felt pressing on his chest.

Tears welled up inside and he whispered fiercely aloud to the gathering thunderclouds, 'Are you satisfied now with what you have done, Tengel the Evil One? I know that you are not to be found up there, but these dark clouds will serve as my witness. Do you know how you have poisoned the lives of those I hold dearest – and my own? Yes, you know right enough – and now you laugh in triumph. Once again you are the victor!'

When he walked on, it was with a heavy heart and a heavy tread and it took him a long time to reach home. After much reflection, he felt absolutely certain of one thing above all else: evil had been born again that night. The scourge of the Ice People would seemingly always ensure that a few of their kin would come into the world who were evil incarnate. This new child was surely proof of that. The fact that the baby's grandfather had been Heming the Bailiff-killer probably did not help. There had been very little good in that man.

Tengel desperately wanted to sleep; he felt indeed that he wished to sleep now without ever reawakening. He lacked the will to go through it all again, having to relive his own bitter childhood through the life of this newly born infant. He no longer had the strength to fight human ignorance and injustice. He wandered on through the darkness, but finally the weather forced him inside, when the dark clouds opened once more.

But he did not go straight to his rooms. He went along instead to the new and grander part of the house that Are had built. The doors, he knew, had been left unlocked for Tarjei, but he had decided to stay overnight at Gråstensholm. Very quietly he crept into the boys' room and stood in the darkness for a long time, looking down at them.

Eventually Trond woke up and, on catching sight of Tengel, he immediately sat up in his bed. 'What is it Grandpapa?'

Tengel sat down on the edge of the bed and Brand then woke up too.

'I just wanted to see you,' he whispered, 'and tell you how much I care for you both.'

The boys were both delighted. 'We love you too, Grandpapa,' they said and threw their arms round him. They stayed in that embrace for a long time and neither of the boys noticed how their grandfather wept. At last he stood up and wished them goodnight.

'Tell your mother and father that I hold them both very dear,' he whispered to them as he left.

When he entered their room in the older part of the house, Silje also sat up eagerly in the bed. She had obviously been anticipating his return for a long time and her lined face was alight with expectation.

'So Tengel, you're back. Did everything go well?'

Tengel bent to pick up her shawl, which had fallen to the floor, and cleared his throat in an effort to disguise the hoarseness of his voice.

'Yes. Everything went well!'

'Then *tell* me! Are we great-grandparents?'

He straightened up said cheerfully, 'Yes we are! To a big healthy boy!'

'Oh! How wonderful,' she said excitedly. 'Nothing is wrong with him?'

'Nothing at all!'

'And Sunniva?'

'Sunniva is doing well. They are all very pleased.'

'Oh, Tengel! Dear Tengel! And how we worried ourselves – needlessly! I knew that it would be all right. Do you think I could get up tomorrow – to go up and see them at Gråstensholm? To get a glimpse of the little one?'

Tengel took a deep breath before he answered, 'Yes, we'll

do that. We shall take the carriage and drive round the road.'

'I'm so happy – but are you all right? You sound as if you have a cold.'

'Yes, I must be coming down with something, Silje,' he replied. 'Anyway, we must celebrate the birth! I shall fetch a bottle of wine. It is our last one and only half-full. But it will be enough for us. Besides I need something for the cold.'

'Now! Drinking in the middle of the night?' she laughed gleefully. 'Yes, let's!'

He paused. 'Oh – and I almost forgot to say – Tarjei and I have made a herbal potion that we think will help your gout – not only the pain, but the gout itself.'

'No! Really? That would be wonderful! Because, if I am honest, I am now sometimes in great pain – and look how thin I am! It is as though the gout has robbed me of my appetite.'

Tengel gave her a quick hug. 'Then we shall try it at once! We'll take it with the wine so that it doesn't taste so bad. Don't fall asleep while I fetch everything, will you?'

She laughed again and Tengel hurried down to the workroom that he shared with Tarjei. They had not discovered a new medicine, although they had tried and tried, investigating everything they knew from every point of view. Inside the workroom, he went directly to where he kept the most secret and dangerous potions. He would need two of them. The first was an opiate. It made a person light-headed and induced pleasant dreams. He poured a measure into a small glass, drank it down and poured out the same amount for Silje.

Then he reached for the second. He hesitated a moment before he grasped the small leather pouch and tipped a large portion of the powder into the bottle of wine. He sniffed, dried his eyes and went back upstairs.

'Here, take the small glass first. It is a special concoction and tastes quite nasty, so you can wash it down with the wine afterwards.'

'As you command!' she laughed, pulling a face as she swallowed the brew.

'Silje! You are almost naked,' he said sternly, 'and you with your gout!'

He found her finest nightgown and helped her to change into it before he put on his own nightshirt, which he seldom wore.

'I need to keep warm to fight this cold,' he told her quickly.

She cuddled up close to him. 'I have been so frightened, lying here alone with all that thunder and lightning outside – but I knew you were needed up at the big house. I can't tell you how happy I was to hear your footsteps at the door.'

He was able to laugh again now; the drug had started to work. 'Allow me to propose a toast to our great-grandchild, Silje!'

'And to us, Tengel! Oh, how blissful I feel now!'

They drank the wine together and then lay calmly side by side, listening to the distant thunder. It seemed to be coming closer again.

'What a lovely sensation,' Silje said thoughtfully. 'Can it be the potion is already making the gout better?'

'It's not impossible.'

Tengel was starting to feel the euphoria – the light-headedness – brought on by the opiate.

'Tengel, have you ever longed to return to the valley of the Ice People?'

'No, strangely enough, I never have. Have you?'

'No. We have had such a wonderful life here at Linden Allée. But Tengel, do you remember the time we made love against the wall of the house in the valley?'

He laughed easily; he was no longer conscious of the present and all the terrors it held. He was back in his youth once more with the young Silje resting on his arm and no words would ever describe the happiness he felt then. Silje snuggled closer to him in the bed and gave a tiny contented sigh before she slept. A few moments later Tengel also fell asleep.

Although the storm was now venting its rage far away along the horizon, it had already taken its toll on the badly withered tree in the avenue at Linden Allée, and suddenly the linden could withstand no more. It fell with a roar, its roots torn bodily from the earth. As it came crashing to the ground, it tangled its branches with the tree on the opposite side of the avenue and brought that down too.

Chapter 7

Liv, her arms full of flowers, picked her way through the little churchyard towards the gleaming new headstone that caught the eye among the older stones because of its freshness. She stood before it for a minute with her head bowed, silently reading the inscriptions. The first two names were given in bold script along with their birth and death dates. Below these, a simple epitaph had been appended. The first part of the inscription read:

TENGEL THE GOOD of THE ICE PEOPLE
Born 1548   Died 1621

His Wife SILJE ARNGRIMSDOTTER
Born 1564   Died 1621

Their Love Inspired All Who Knew Them

'You can never be replaced,' whispered Liv reverently. 'Not in our hearts, nor in our minds, nor in our memories.'

Letting her gaze move further down the gravestone, Liv read the third inscription. It said more simply:

SOL ANGELICA of THE ICE PEOPLE
Born 1579   Died 1602

In Memoriam

Sol had no known grave. In their disappointment at finding her dead on the very morning they were due to subject her to their special display of torture, the authorities had kept her body. It had most likely been burnt and thrown into an unmarked burial pit. All Dag's efforts to have the body returned had been rejected out of hand. For that reason, Liv, Dag and Are had asked for the inscription to be added to the gravestone of Tengel and Silje. Sol would probably have been furious had she known that her name was written in a Christian churchyard, but they had wanted to do it nonetheless. This way they felt she would be at peace and no longer alone.

Still holding the flowers, Liv gazed again at the names of her beloved parents. I know what you did, Father, she thought, and I do not blame you. You did what was right both for Mother and yourself. You knew she would die and you would never be able to go on without her. You freed her from knowing an unbearable truth and from terrible pain and suffering – of that I am sure. But we are so alone now both of you are gone. So awfully alone!

Father Martinius had also realised the truth behind the deaths of Silje and Tengel on that fateful night – but he chose to pretend otherwise. Without a word he had prepared a plot for the grave of Tengel, mercy-killer, suicide victim and atheist. It was not in his heart to separate Silje and Tengel in death, and there were heathens far worse than Tengel buried in the churchyard – even if they had paid lip service to the Church.

He had also readily agreed to Sol's name being added to the headstone. It had all happened so long ago that most people had forgotten her. In any event, Martinius could think of no finer, more striking people than the members of the Meiden family and the Ice People.

Standing before the grave, with tears dampening her eyes, Liv continued her reverie. She wondered what age Tengel might have lived to, had he not taken his life. In some ways he had always seemed somehow immortal. At that moment, for some reason, Hanna forced her way into her thoughts. Because she had been so young when they lived in the Valley of the Ice People, Liv could barely remember Hanna. But she recalled that she had been really ancient, and might have lived many more years if she hadn't been murdered.

Then Liv shuddered, as she thought about her newly born grandchild. How long would *he* live? With an effort, she tried to push all thoughts of him out of her mind. 'I love him,' she told herself defiantly. 'Of course I do!'

She bent down to place her flowers in a pot that stood by the grave and gave them some water. Then she walked the few steps to the Meiden's family crypt. It was the resting-place of the old Dowager Baroness and Charlotte, together with Jacob Skille. Now there was also a new coffin in there – for Tarald's wife, Sunniva. After another moment of quiet reflection, she arranged the rest of her flowers around the vault.

As usual, her son was sitting outside the crypt. As she

approached, he buried his face in his hands. Without speaking, Liv placed a loving hand gently on his shoulder.

'At least she was much loved,' she said comfortingly.

Tarald uncovered his face and stood up. 'Ahh, Mother, you don't understand!' he said in a haunted voice. 'You can know nothing of the anguish that burns and consumes me inside!'

Without another word, he hurried off, leaving his mother nursing a sense of guilt, thinking she had chased him away. That was not what she had intended. A few seconds later Pastor Martinius emerged from the church and, on catching sight of Liv, came straight over to greet her. They talked for some time about the weather and other everyday things, before he said: 'You seem troubled today, Baroness.'

She gave a little start. 'Do I? Yes, perhaps I am. It is not only the deep sorrow my son is suffering that concerns me. I am also worried about the circumstances of my daughter, Cecilie. She is with the Court in Copenhagen.'

Martinius had heard of her, but he said nothing.

'She is unhappy, Pastor. All goes well with the royal children she is caring for. She now has two more in her charge – a girl, Leonora Christine, and a boy too, much to the King's delight. But it is their mother, Mistress Kirsten, who is so unkind to Cecilie. Nor is she permitted to travel home to visit us – and – no, how awful of me! I shall stop my tales of woe! Now tell me, Pastor Martinius, I hear that you are to be wed. I am very happy for you.'

'Thank you. Yes, one might say she is my childhood love. Her name is Julie, the daughter of a dean and we grew up as neighbours. Such an enchanting girl; so pure and so beautiful. As a boy I could do nothing but dream about her. But since becoming priest in this parish I have dared to court her, and she has said, "Yes"!'

'I should hope so too!' laughed Liv. 'I should have done so, if I were she. Don't misunderstand me now. I am true to my Dag – but he was also my childhood sweetheart. So we have something in common, you and I.'

He smiled. 'It would appear so.'

'She has a friend,' said Liv thoughtfully. 'Did you know?'

Martinius was momentarily dumbfounded. 'Who? My Julie?'

'No, No! Forgive me – I was thinking aloud – I meant Cecilie. She has a friend at Court who is helping her counteract the wiles of Mistress Kirsten and the unpleasant head housekeeper. He is a marquis, by the name of Alexander Paladin.'

'What a noble name! It carries responsibilities, I'll be bound!'

'Yes. But I cannot quite grasp the nature of this friendship. Cecilie's letters sound so lacking in substance when she writes about him. Almost as though *she* is slightly enamoured, but not *him*, if you see what I mean. But no matter – she has received plaudits from King Christian for her kindness to the children. He visits them often and they have spoken warmly to him about Cecilie. She writes that he is most satisfied. I understand that this marquis has also put in a good word for her. The head housekeeper would have her gone, but cannot because she is admired by the King. Oh – it worries me so! If I could but travel to see how she is! But we also have a "little conundrum" at Gråstensholm that prevents me from leaving.'

They stood in silence. The Kolgrim 'conundrum', they both knew was not by any means a little one.

* * * *

A distinct change had come over Are after the death of his father, Tengel. Always the most unassuming of all the children, he seemed very quickly to grow out from the shadow under which he had always lived. Almost overnight he found authority and significance and became a proper 'pater familias'. His deference to Tengel had been so overwhelming that, without being aware of it, he had suppressed his own wishes and opinions. Tengel for his part had not realised the influence he had on his youngest son.

None of the children had been as devoted to their father as Are – except he had not understood it until then. But now he was the real Master of Linden Allée – a responsibility he would take very seriously. Meta watched admiringly as her husband grew fully into the role of country farmer, although ironically theirs was a relatively small estate.

Hitherto they had imagined that much of the hard work Are had done on their lands had gone unnoticed. But now he and Meta realised how many of the other farmers in the surrounding countryside had copied much of what he had discovered and developed. They imitated the way he broke new ground in areas of rough forest; they also copied his forestry skills to make better and more efficient use of woodland; they learned from him too, how to chose the best seed for the following year's planting.

Meta was very proud of Are – more than she could say – especially as she was now regarded as one of the leading farmers' wives in the district. How shocked the other wives would have been had they known of her early life; that she had been the wayward, scared, illegitimate child of a harlot in a village in Skåne – a young girl begging in order to survive. It was a wonder that her spirit had not been broken a hundred times in those formative years, but she had been strong enough to leave her past behind and prove herself worthy of Are's love.

Without doubt, the three boys were their pride and joy. It was true that Tarjei's distinct qualities were a little beyond their understanding; Are in fact often felt awkward talking to his eldest son, sometimes almost wanting to apologise for his ignorance. Trond was more relaxed and more fun to talk to. Just like his cousin, Cecilie, he could be cheeky at times, but for Are and Meta, Trond's intellect showed in more down-to-earth ways – with his simple humour and an unpretentious turn of phrase. But would he be the right person to inherit Linden Allée? They were not sure that he was. It was true that nobody harvested as effectively as Trond, that no other was so skilful with their hands or so easy to approach when help was needed – but did he have sufficient tenacity and fortitude for the inheritance?

As the eldest son, Tarjei was the natural heir, but nobody had even once considered making a farmer out of him! His path was clearly taking him in other directions. Instead one immediately thought of Brand, the youngest, who loved the earth, just like his father, and whose life centred on the farm. Would they be able to bypass Trond? Well, the answer to that question lay in the future. Children could change unexpectedly as they grew up.

Although they would never show any preference, Brand was Are's favourite, just as Trond was Meta's. And Tarjei? No, he had been Tengel's special grandson, his great delight. Now there was no one of sufficient stature left to take him under their wing – intellectually he had grown too far apart from the rest of them. Only his cousin Cecilie would be his equal.

* * * *

In Denmark Cecilie had been made a governess of sorts to little Anna Catherine. There wasn't much one could teach such a small child, but she got on well with the girl and Cecilie thought that to be important. The child primarily needed someone with whom she felt safe and secure. More compliments and fine words were heaped on the little princesses than was good for them, but within the great chambers and halls of the castle, they had nobody who showed them real affection.

When it arrived, the message telling Cecilie of the new series of tragic events back home involving Tengel, Silje and Sunniva had almost broken her. She decided to speak to Alexander Paladin, whom she had seen only briefly on a few occasions during the previous months. But she knew he must be watching events discreetly, making sure the housekeeper did not bully her too much. Not that it was a simple task to bully anyone so defiant as Cecilie, but her position was fragile and she had to be careful.

When she had reached the marquis's lodgings, not far from the castle, she heaved on the large bell-pull and stood waiting. A manservant opened the door, and with a look of surprise, bade her come inside and wait in the entrance hall. After some mumbled conversation behind a closed door, Alexander Paladin came out to greet her. His face showed his surprise and, she thought, a trace of alarm and she was starting to wonder whether she had made a terrible mistake in coming.

Feeling a little uneasy, she falteringly told him the reasons for her visit: how she had lost three more of her loved ones and needed someone to talk to in this foreign land – someone whom she felt would understand.

He showed her into a comfortable salon, where they then spent the whole afternoon and evening talking. Cecilie told him all about her extraordinary family. She found that talking about the three precious relatives who had died while she was so far away somehow helped to lessen her sorrow. Alexander himself spoke of being brought up by a loving but over-protective domineering mother, although he said very little about his adult life. The conversation later moved on to art and literature, society in general and some of the historical events that had shaped their time. Cecilie, who was well read, blushed with pride when he complimented her on her understanding of so many subjects. Then suddenly noticing how late it was, she panicked.

'Oh, dear,' she gasped. 'I fear I have compromised you completely.'

That made him laugh. 'Me? Compromised? On the contrary, Mistress Cecilie!'

Somewhat confused by this remark, which he did not explain, she had thanked him for his kindness and hurried away.

Later she remembered what Kirsten Munk had once said to her. 'Well you might take care of my children, Mistress Meiden, but believe me it will earn you no favours! I dislike your impertinent manner towards my housekeeper and in other circumstances would have dismissed you instantly. But this advice I give you: have more taste when choosing your patrons!' And at that, with a rustling of skirts, she had left an amazed Cecilie staring after her.

* * * *

Yrja was sitting in Gråstensholm with Kolgrim on her lap, trying to feed him. He was a big wild-eyed boy, now almost a year old and was hard to deal with. He had determination far greater than anyone else Yrja had ever encountered and never showed the slightest sign of good humour.

Lank wisps of hair fell in tangles over his yellow eyes – although the black hair that had covered most of his body had gone – and no one could help but shudder at the sight of the child's unbelievable face. He was no longer as ugly as he had been at birth, but there was now something else that was horribly repulsive in his features. It was malevolent yet otherwise indefinable – but it was undoubtedly there. While Tengel had possessed the appearance of a demon, it had been an appealing one. Nothing at all about Kolgrim was appealing.

Perhaps that was why Yrja felt so sorry for him. She and Liv took turns to look after him, but they would invariably be worn out after a few hours. Dag was too busy with his duties to do a lot, and even though he tried admirably to show an interest and demonstrate affection for his only grandchild, the two women could hardly fail to notice his relief when the time came for him to leave the house.

Tarald was seldom, if ever, seen anywhere near the boy. He bolted like a startled mare at the very sight of his son, as if he was unable to believe that something so terrifying could result from such unbounded love and beauty as he had shared with Sunniva. When he was not working like a man possessed looking after the estates, Tarald spent every spare minute at the churchyard beside Sunniva's grave. Liv was worried about him and thought he would exhaust himself, but Gråstensholm was unquestionably better managed as a result. Jacob Skille had been both clever and industrious, but had not fully understood the complicated workings of a large estate; and Dag had never really been interested in running it.

The boy Kolgrim himself was hard to fathom. He had never been seen to smile by anybody – and after a year he still wasn't speaking. Every waking hour his eyes watched the adults harshly, even hatefully. For the most part he allowed them to change his soiled clothing without complaint and he tolerated their friendly chatter. But if ever he was denied anything he chose to do – like climbing up the stairs – he would fly into a rage and his hoarse roar would reverberate throughout the house and farmyard. He never cried and he never screamed. Invariably he just bellowed like an angry bull.

At times like that Liv found it hard to calm him down. The many bite marks on her arms and hands bore testimony to her efforts. But fortunately Yrja was always on hand to assist.

For Yrja it had been a difficult day, almost a whole year ago, when she had broken the news about her potential new role to her parents in Eikeby. She had been surrounded then by innumerable younger siblings, the offspring of her older brothers and sisters, and hordes of cousins. When she revealed she had been invited to move into the big house, her overworked mother just stared across the table at her.

'Move up to Gråstensholm?' she echoed. 'In heaven's name, why?'

'The Baroness has asked me to help her care for Tarald's new son.'

'So now you're a nursemaid as well? Stay up there always, you say? And what will become of us without your wage?'

'Mother! You well know that it was Mistress Silje who paid me out of kindness. Now she is dead – God bless her memory!'

Her father, his unshaven face brown with ingrained grime, grunted, 'More room for us here if she goes, Tilda. Will you be paid, girl?'

'We have not spoken about wages. I haven't thought about it.'

'P'raps they want you to work for nothing – and you give not a thought for us,' he grumbled. 'Living in finery up there in the big house. Are we to have no reward for bringing you into this world? Look at us! I marries them off one after t'other, but they all come back wi' their womenfolk an' their menfolk an' all their brats. Ain't one o' you as can stand on the' own two feet. You be gone! It'll be one mouth less t' feed here then!'

Her mother glared at her: 'I warn you! You see you gets paid, and you come home wi' every shilling! D'you hear? We'll have something for all we done for you.'

Yrja knew, without being told, that she had been the most commendable of all the children, despite her sickly start in life. Later on she had not been allowed to work at home – they had wanted her to go out and earn. She also knew that only very seldom did children who left home receive a wage. Poor food and a squalid bed – often shared with other servants – was the most they could hope for. It kept body and soul together and for that they were grateful. They might have been reluctant to admit it, but Yrja's parents knew that she was worth a lot to them. Yrja, on the other hand, had no burning desire to ask the Baroness for money. She wanted to help her, not profit from her.

Yrja did, however, have some sympathy for her mother. Life had been hard on her and nobody would have believed that she was not many years older than the elegant, refined Baroness Liv Meiden. She was gaunt with a tired disillusioned stare, her veins and sinews protruding, hardly a tooth left, and thinning hair. She was pregnant again and Yrja felt certain that this would be her last child. She hoped desperately that it was, for her mother's sake.

Touching Yrja's arm suddenly, her mother lowered her voice and cupped a hand to her cheek to speak in a stage whisper. 'Is it true what they say? Is it a strange child – a changeling?'

'A changeling?' repeated Yrja aghast. 'No, I can swear to you that no troll came into that room to replace the infant with his own.'

'Oh, pity …' said her mother, sounding disappointed. 'But be sure you get pay!'

Yrja sighed and said nothing, wondering how she would get out of this awkward situation – but in the end it was resolved more easily than she dared hope. The first week after the conversation with her parents had passed without event at the big house and she had not managed to find the courage to raise the subject of payment for her work. Then her salvation came in the form of Baron Dag Meiden.

'Yrja,' he began hesitantly. 'I am aware that Mama Silje set great store by you. I also believe that she used to give you some coin now and again, didn't she?'

'Yes, Baron, every Saturday. But I don't want …'

He held up one hand to give her pause. 'I understand, young Yrja! But you know how grateful we are for your warm-hearted help with the boy. Yes, I will even say how *desperately* we depend on it. We know that you would never ask for anything in return, so please take this as a token of our gratitude. Please.'

She swallowed hard, nodded and said nothing.

Dag's hair was thinning as the years passed and his waist was now much larger from attending too many official dinners with worthy gentlemen. But in one respect he had not changed at all – his heart was as warm as ever towards those he loved and he smiled gratefully at her.

'Mama Silje also mentioned that you left your little coin at home and kept nothing for yourself. That was a fine thing to do, but you no longer live at home. I think we should do this: you shall have a large coin that you give to your parents, and a small coin that you keep for yourself and tell no one about. I would like it to be the other way round, but I don't think you would agree, would you?'

'No, Sir – Mother has too many mouths to feed. Thank you,' she said and curtseyed low.

The Baron looked at her so compassionately that she was quite moved. Dag these days sported a pointed beard, perhaps to compensate for his balding pate. He was fashionably dressed in an elk-skin jacket, similar to a frock coat, which hid his expanding girth. A shirt with a lace collar and puffed sleeves and generously cut breeches, tucked into knee-high boots, completed his attire. Smiling warmly at her, he put his hand gently on her head in a gesture of deep gratitude and affection, and Yrja, in her turn, beamed back at him in delight. Liv and Dag had long since forgotten her disability and ungainliness. They saw only the warm-hearted girl, Yrja – a human being whom they greatly cherished.

* * * *

Yrja often went to the churchyard with a small bunch of wild flowers. She liked to sit close to Mistress Silje's resting-place – close to the only person who had known the bitter secret in her heart. On one particular day, she found Tarald there, standing near to Sunniva's grave in conversation with Pastor Martinius. Unsure if she should go on, Yrja stopped, but they waved her over to them and she walked across, hoping that she would not blush too much.

'Come, young Yrja.' The pastor's voice was friendly. 'We were just talking about the plague – and how you did so much to help stop it.'

'Oh, that,' she said speaking dismissively to hide her shyness. 'Yes, it was a terrible time! Do you remember, Father Martinius, when we each had a corner of that tiny cottage? We lay there helpless, taking it in turns to run for the pail, so that we didn't bump into each other – or shouldn't I have mentioned that?'

The pastor laughed, 'In such circumstances one must leave convention behind. We did so once, Master Tarald, collide I mean. It was awfully embarrassing, but I gave way, gentleman that I am.'

'And waited?' asked Tarald.

'Wait? Master Tarald, when one has the blood pestilence in the body, one does not wait! But I had a change of garments with me!'

Yrja smothered a smile. 'It is easy to laugh about this long afterwards. But while I was suffering … Oh, Dear God, I was so afraid then!'

'I, too. It was Master Tengel and young Tarjei who saved us. But you know that, of course?'

'Yes – but it was so embarrassing those last days, when we had no strength to leave our beds and Master Tengel had to change our clothing. I was so ashamed, I could have died.'

'I thought you would say that you were saved by the Lord Our God, Father Martinius,' retorted Tarald aggressively.

'Why should He save Yrja and me, yet strike down so

many others in the parish? Are we so much better than they?'

'A sensible point of view,' said Tarald. 'And an unusual one for a man of God.'

'But I will confess that I prayed to God to save my life – as I prayed for the lives and the souls of everyone.'

Tarald nodded. 'That is only natural. Now, tell me, Pastor, if you will, how it feels to be wed?'

The pastor turned away. 'Mmm, yes,' he muttered, as though uncertain what to say.

'That is good news about your marriage,' said Yrja politely. 'A good pastor's wife is an asset for the parish, as well as its priest.'

'Yes!' said the priest, with such acrimony that they both looked at him with amazement. He seemed to be unaware that he had even replied and simply stood before them, deep in thought. So much despair and anger showed on his handsome young face that the other two were momentarily at a loss for words. They had met his young wife, a very pretty girl, and she appeared to perform her duties as pastor's wife with great diligence. She visited the sick, arranged help for those who needed it and, in desperate cases, provided a little charity. She did all she could and her beautiful smile had already become a legend.

Gathering himself, the priest gave a start. 'I ... forgive me – my mind was elsewhere. What was it you were saying, Yrja?'

'I was only saying that a good pastor's wife is a great asset.'

'Yes, That's right! And there is nobody better than my Julie. I am truly lucky to have her!'

His eyes smiled warmly again, but Yrja gave a little shake of her head, trying to clear her thoughts. What had the priest been thinking about inadvertently in those few moments? What might be amiss in his life?

It was a cloudy day, damp underfoot with rain hanging in the air and, in the uncomfortable silence, Tarald turned his attention to the crypt once more and began pulling out some weeds from around the opening.

Softly the pastor said, 'How good it is to see such devotion, Master Tarald.'

The young man gave him a strange look, but didn't answer. Instead he turned to Yrja and said, 'And I see you have picked flowers for Grandmama Silje's grave again.'

'Yes ... Oh, I forgot. I must find a place for them.' Dismally she looked down at the sad bunch of harebells and daisies she was clutching.

'If you put them in water, they'll soon recover,' said the priest.

Yrja did so and placed the pot among the carpet of flowers that lay around Tengel and Silje's grave. She noticed that someone had recently lit candles there as well, presumably to honour their memory at the recent Olsok festival, which commemorated St Olav each autumn.

'They were indeed two greatly loved people,' said the priest, as the three of them made their way towards the churchyard gate.

'That's hardly surprising!' retorted Tarald, holding the gate open as the other two went through. 'They both gave very generously of themselves to others.'

'Indeed, they did,' agreed the pastor.

Yrja's heart was thumping. To think that she, ugly, hopeless Yrja was walking along having a quiet conversation with the pastor and Tarald! If only her mother could have been there to see it!

'It's true that Grandfather once scolded me so badly that

I felt I was worth less than horse droppings,' Tarald said. 'But he was perfectly right to do so! I had acted very irresponsibly.'

'You must not blame yourself for the birth of little Kolgrim,' Martinius told him. 'A passion such as yours will not be ignored.'

'It's not the child I was thinking of,' answered Tarald impatiently.

'It's natural also to feel that the death of your wife weighs heavy on you.'

Tarald lost his self-control. 'Yes, of course it does! Oh, my God, how my conscience condemns me! I *have* to come here – I *must* sit by her grave every day – for my soul is as black as the darkest night!'

'But you could not help what happened,' Yrja said softly. 'Still, I understand why you grieve.'

'Grieve!' Tarald exploded. 'You understand nothing – neither of you!'

They had stopped at the very place where, many, many years before, a verger had died after being poisoned by Sunniva's mother, Sol. Yrja and the priest looked at the young widower in astonishment. Tarald seemed to want to free himself of the burden of guilt that he had carried for a long time.

'I come here as penance,' he almost screamed at them. 'For she went to her death for my sake – and unloved by me!' He held his hands to his face, obviously feeling he could bear the shame no longer.

A grey mist lay close to the ground all around, cutting the three of them off from the rest of the world. The church, the churchyard and a little avenue leading to it were all they could see. Gråstensholm had disappeared, Linden Allée as well and there was no sign of the distant hills.

'Unloved?' repeated Yrja, hardly moving her lips. She didn't understand. 'How can that be?'

Tarald looked at them again, but now his face was ravaged and tormented.

'It was euphoric for a short while – madly, crazily euphoric. Oh, I loved her – I suppose I worshipped her completely, my creature of grace and beauty. She was everything – my first journey to the realms of love. No, I cannot find the words to describe what I felt.'

'We understand,' the pastor's tone was relaxed. 'I believe we understand.'

'I was bewitched. But once we were wed, then ...'

For a long time they waited in trepidation for him to continue. After staring into the mist for a long time, he lowered his head and when he spoke, his voice sounded tired and defeated. 'But at the end, in all honesty, I found her insufferable.'

'Why?' enquired the pastor, very gently.

'Because she thought of none but herself. That's true isn't it, Yrja?' he pleaded, suddenly turning towards the girl from Eikeby. 'Tell the pastor that's the truth. She spoke only about herself – always. How unhappy she was and how she had no one in her life. It was her greatest lie, for she had a large family that took good care of her. Everyone did all they could to make things right for her.'

'Yes, that is true,' confirmed Yrja, her voice almost inaudible. 'I can't deny it.'

Tarald nodded distractedly. Then he ran a hand over his forehead and turned his gaze towards Gråstensholm, which lay hidden by the mist.

'It was as though she had no love for *me,* but wanted only to see the love I felt for her shining in my eyes. No, forgive me! It's no good – I cannot talk properly today!'

'I do understand what you're saying,' said the priest. 'You mean that she adored being the object of your love and admiration – yet she gave nothing in return.'

'Yes, that's almost right. She always wanted to be waited on. In the beginning it was charming, but later ... I once heard my mother tell my father: "There is nothing of Sol's inner strength in Sunniva." "No," my father answered. "I think she has much of Heming the Bailiff-killer's ability to hide away from trouble. She always blames others and abuses folk's goodwill. Sol was much more honest, even though she fell on the wrong side of the law – and that's something Sunniva will never do." Although I never met the fabled Sol, I agreed with them then, and I always will.'

He lowered his head again; then continued, 'Oh, I was so tired, so tired of Sunniva! I almost hated her! Then when she died – it was as if I had wished it to be! I blamed myself for everything and believed that child to be a grotesque consequence of my resentment. The boy was a punishment!'

The priest had stayed silent while he listened to Tarald, but now he took charge of the situation. 'I think all three of us should now go into the church to pray. I can well understand your doubting soul, Master Tarald, and only the blessing of the Lord can grant you release. Follow me please!'

Making no effort to resist, Tarald went with him. Yrja hesitated, but Father Martinius motioned to her to join them. Once inside the quiet little church, they knelt together in silent prayer. But Yrja found it hard to join in. Profane and unforgiving, an inner voice was crying out over and over again: 'He didn't love her ... He didn't love her ... He really didn't love her!'

Then, somewhat perversely, with her next breath, that

same inner voice was saying: 'Poor little Sunniva! Poor little Sunniva.' And the truth is, she meant that with all her heart.

Chapter 8

Following his churchyard confession to the pastor, Tarald's relationship with his hideous-looking son started to become more relaxed. There seemed to be a new hint of compassion in his expression whenever he looked at the boy and his gestures too were less dismissive and uneasy. Only a few days later, Yrja was sitting with Kolgrim on her lap, singing a nursery rhyme. Her spirits were low and it was impossible to say whether Kolgrim found the rhyme entertaining or not. But his eyes remained steadfastly fixed on Yrja's mouth and they were following every movement of her lips.

Then, without warning, Tarald came into the room. Yrja stopped singing, thinking that the rhyme might sound silly and that her singing might make it sound even worse. But Tarald took no notice of her; he was staring at his son as if seeing him for the very first time.

'He looks like Tengel,' he said shortly. 'I swear it.'

'Yes, indeed he does,' replied Yrja reassuringly, realising that this was Tarald's one hope. 'And Mistress Silje once told me that Master Tengel would have been an impossible child.'

A tiny glimmer of optimism showed on Tarald's face. 'Was *he* ugly as well?'

'Almost certainly.'

'And Grandpapa was the finest person I have ever known.'

'I could not agree more! But look, the boy's features are becoming more normal. You can almost see them change with each day that passes.'

'Yes, that is true, isn't it?'

Tarald crouched down and gazed at the boy.

'Hello,' he began in a careful whisper.

Kolgrim's cat-like eyes glowered at him through his tangle of coarse ragged hair and the wide unpleasant mouth opened to let out a low warning growl.

'Good God!' cried Tarald as he jumped to his feet in panic. 'Why does he do that?'

'He's not dangerous,' Yrja told him. 'It's just his way of talking.'

'Then Heaven help us!' He looked at her hands. 'And he has bitten you too, I see.'

'Yes, he can be stubborn. But he accepts me.'

As if to prove her point, Kolgrim grabbed Yrja's chin and pinched hard. There was no sign of fun in the actions of the boy and she endured the pain without a sound.

'Does he walk?' asked Tarald, who had now retreated to safety, leaning against the wall nearby.

'Of course you do, don't you Kolgrim?' said Yrja.

The boy slid off her knee and took faltering steps towards his father.

'Reach out to him,' said Yrja in a soft voice.

'He understands what we say!' said Tarald in amazement and he tentatively stretched out his arms to his little son.

157

'Yes and why shouldn't he? Did you think he was ...? Well he's normal for his age in every way, in body and in soul.'

Kolgrim stood wavering and Tarald was wise enough to move himself closer to the boy almost unnoticed; a moment later he allowed him to fall against his arms without losing face. Tarald had a lump in his throat as he drew the child awkwardly towards him. At last he embraced him gingerly, still looking anxious, and Kolgrim rewarded his efforts by biting his ear so badly that it began to bleed.

* * * *

As the boy grew older, it soon became clear to everyone that he would never be another Tengel. Yet the changes that had been predicted by some members of the family at his birth began to occur. The grotesque face became less ugly and the features began to show signs of a developing personality and identity. His body had grown and was now in better proportion to his arms. He also now had a discernible neck.

However, despite his improving appearance, his worst traits remained unchanged. What did it matter that he was more pleasant to look at, when there was still no sign of any positive emotion in those amber-coloured eyes – and he still displayed no sense of fun or jollity? The physical hideousness they had all witnessed at his birth was now little more than a memory, but Yrja would have much preferred him to have remained disfigured, rather than having to deal every day with the sinister glare in his eyes.

A person with a disfigured body could still find love and be loved, she reflected, but a depraved soul would never know affection.

In desperation she would tell herself he was only a child and truly deserved all the love they lavished upon him. Sadly though, their affection was not returned. The women, Yrja and Liv, he tolerated to some degree because he had a need for them and could exploit them, but he had a total disregard for everyone else. Nonetheless Tarald made strenuous efforts to get to know and understand his son, but often came close to tears with frustration. Kolgrim did not lack intelligence. Indeed he soon learnt the power of words – especially 'no', a little word that he used cunningly and vigorously.

Yrja had untold patience with him. Very often Liv would be unable to cope. She would become exhausted by the infant's tantrums and call wearily for Yrja, who would calmly let him rage. Eventually, when he saw that his behaviour did not provoke anger and despair in his nursemaid, as he had hoped, he stopped and became sullen instead. Never would either of them have believed that such a small child could be so thoroughly infuriating.

One day Liv received a letter from Cecilie that she read to Yrja. 'I long to come home again, Mama!' she had written. 'Now, when Yuletide is almost upon us and I think of all that needs to be done at Gråstensholm, I yearn for home even more. Yet I cannot come home this year as everyone is going away. I am not privy to where or for what reason, and I shall remain almost alone with charge of the children. You must not think I am unhappy in Denmark for I have many friends – it is purely that I have not come back home for so many years. Tarald's little boy will soon be two and a half years old; Grandmama Charlotte and

Jacob are gone, as are Sunniva, Grandmama Silje and Grandpapa. So much has happened and I have not been there with you! Not for a wedding, nor a funeral, nor a birth. I am so afraid that something else will happen, and yes, I have thought the most dreaded thing: that I must travel home again before somebody else dies! If only I could come home for just one Yuletide! I miss you all so much!'

Liv put the letter down. 'My poor little girl,' she said shaking her head. 'I must speak to Dag and see that she comes home to visit soon. I have missed her so terribly, of course. But she always seemed to be enjoying her life there.'

'Yes, it would be lovely to see Cecilie again,' said Yrja, as she fought to dress Kolgrim in his outdoor clothes, something that he hated.

Some months previously, Tarald had gleefully announced that he had found himself a new young lady. Yrja had spoken of it to no one. She had tried to make light of the heartbreak she felt, while everybody else was saying how happy they were for him.

The girl, young, pretty and titled, had come to visit and been received with warmth and hospitality. Then she saw Kolgrim – Tarald's child – the angular shoulders that had caused the death of Sunniva; the face, still with traces of its most ghastly features; and the instinctive piercing glare of jealousy from eyes filled with an inhuman hatred.

She had politely stayed on for the few short days of her visit, but she never returned. Tarald had received nothing more than a coldly worded letter of regret, following which he shut himself away and could not bring himself to see his son for a long time.

There was a lot said about Kolgrim in the village and the surrounding countryside. The rumours of a changeling

160

in their midst continued, despite unending denials from both Yrja and the midwife. Did folk not understand that they had all been there during the birth and seen the creature emerge from its mother's belly with their own eyes? No troll or demon had been anywhere near them and besides the priest had baptised the infant almost as soon as he was born.

Others maintained that Sunniva must have conspired with Satan – something that caused Liv great distress. The pastor tried to silence such babble by declaring that the child had been baptised in the Lord's name, but curiosity remained rife. Everybody was anxious to see this monster that the servants from Gråstensholm had been whispering about for so long.

Until now they had deliberately kept the boy at home, but Yrja had finally grown tired of all the wagging tongues. Despite all the difficulties, she felt great empathy for this child, having herself suffered similar callous treatment meted out by people to someone with a flawed body. So, five Sundays before Yuletide, she dressed Kolgrim carefully in his best clothes, combed back his hair until it was hidden under his hood and put him on the sled, before setting off for church. Except for Liv, the rest of the family had left earlier in the large sleigh. Liv herself had decided to stay at home with a sore throat and remained unaware of Yrja's plans.

The stares and murmurs started on the lane leading up to the church, but Yrja calmly lifted the boy out of the sled and led him by the hand up to the church entrance. She may have looked calm on the outside, but her heart was racing so much inside her chest that it hurt. The first signs of difficulty came as she entered the porch. Kolgrim tugged and twisted her hand in protest, reluctant to enter this strange cold house.

If he screams now, thought Yrja nervously, then it will all be ruined. Everyone will be convinced that he is a demon-child, with the Evil One for a father. In anticipation, she had brought with her some sweet Yuletide treats pilfered from the larder and she quickly put one in his mouth.

'There will be more,' she whispered to him, 'if you stay quiet and come in with me.'

The bribe had the desired effect and Kolgrim remained silent. Then, to her relief, Pastor Martinius came out to the porch. Ever since they had suffered together during the outbreak of plague, she had felt able to trust him in a special way. Almost immediately he walked over and greeted them. As he did so, Yrja lifted the child in her arms, although he was now getting too heavy for her to hold for very long.

'Father Martinius, may I ask a favour of you?' she asked quietly.

'Certainly, Yrja.'

Yrja leaned closer to him to whisper in his ear and they continued the conversation in hushed tones, as the parishioners filed past, casting sidelong inquisitive glances at them. When they had finished speaking, Martinius led Yrja to the Gråstensholm family pew and helped them settle. Tarald froze with alarm upon seeing his son there, in public view. In his turn, Dag welcomed them with a fixed smile.

Luckily Kolgrim's attention had been drawn to the flickering candles, and he remained engrossed, staring at them for some time. Yrja then pointed out the ship hanging high in the rafters. When he had tired of looking at it, he stood up on the pew, looking backwards over the congregation and everybody present greedily feasted their eyes on him. Yrja sensed that they were all horrified up to a point; but she fancied they could not hide a certain degree of disappointment, because the boy was not as awful as people had been saying. But from close by, she half heard a muffled whisper.

'Look at them eyes!' said an old female voice. 'If them aren't the eyes of Satan, what be they?'

Yrja was aware that several members of her family from Eikeby were in the congregation. She was certain that if her mother were among them, she would be wishing for the church floor to open and devour her at the shame of seeing her daughter, sitting relaxed in the Gråstensholm pews with a demon-child in her arms. Luckily Kolgrim was an unusually quiet child when he was in a good temper, and to keep him happy Yrja continued feeding him a sweet whenever he began to talk or become restless.

Then came the moment when the pastor turned, unexpectedly, and addressed the congregation directly. Yrja sat up straight; this was the moment! Would they take his words to heart?

'We have with us in our church today a new young member of our congregation, a small boy – one whom I myself baptised shortly after his poor mother had died while giving birth to him. Now, much foolish and spiteful gossip has been spoken about this child, but I want to tell you all a little of his background. Can you see whose appearance he has? Look at the shoulders and the black hair ...'

In the Gråstensholm pew, Yrja pulled back the hood, so that everybody could see clearly what the pastor was referring to. Kolgrim did not move or speak.

'And see those remarkable eyes! He has the looks of another man who suffered an equally unfortunate start in this world – taking the life of his mother that he might live – and tormented by his fate as he grew to a man. A man who we learned to know as the finest, most noble and self-sacrificing person anywhere – a man we all loved. That man, Master Tengel, was the father of this boy's grandmother and he too was said to have been a difficult child. Are we then to make young Kolgrim's childhood as tragic and lonely as that of Master Tengel? Or shall we welcome him among us with love as Our Lord Jesus Christ has already done?'

Pastor Martinius paused. Not a sound could be heard in the church. Then he began his parish announcements, births and deaths and other parochial matters. In her seat Yrja closed her eyes and said a silent prayer of thanks. The ice had been broken. Everybody from Gråstensholm and all of Are's family from Linden Allée also breathed quiet sighs of relief.

Unfortunately Kolgrim's good behaviour ended at that point and Yrja was forced to stand up and to carry him outside in a hurry. He had taken a sudden interest in the pulpit – apparently intent on climbing the steps to join Pastor Martinius. As she carried him away, he continued to voice his reluctance to leave with all the power of his young lungs. Yet despite the overall success of the church visit, Yrja felt faintly depressed by what had happened. It wasn't really possible to compare Kolgrim with Tengel, because she knew instinctively that something very fundamental was missing in the boy. Tengel had felt a deep compassion for his fellow man; Kolgrim, for his part, felt only contempt.

Later that evening as she was putting the boy to bed, Tarald entered the room. He stood watching them both for a long while, saying nothing. His presence was making her nervous and awkward, and she dropped one of the boy's shoes on the floor. Tarald immediately bent to pick it up and handed it to her.

'Thank you,' she murmured without daring to look at him. It was then that she felt his hand on her shoulder.

'It is I who should be thanking you,' he replied, with an unmistakeable note of affection in his voice. Then without another word, he turned and left.

After that he made a habit of coming and sitting with them to chat at Kolgrim's bedtime. Although Yrja looked forward to these moments, they also frightened her. On the one hand she enjoyed talking to Tarald very much, but on the other she was afraid he would discover just *how* much she enjoyed it!

* * * *

The New Year, 1624, began in the midst of a cold, bleak winter. For Yrja, the freezing days were also a struggle in other ways, because her tangled emotions were being challenged constantly on two fronts. Her efforts to keep Kolgrim in a good frame of mind were an unending strain, but she was also finding it increasingly difficult to conceal her undying love for Tarald.

One morning a letter arrived from Cecilie, saying that she would be coming home the following Yuletide and there was some rejoicing at this news. But on the very same day, very different news came from nearby Eikeby: Yrja's mother had died, quite needlessly, in childbirth. She had been too old, too worn out and abused by everyone – most of all by her husband. But Yrja's father, finding himself alone with his large brood, ordered Yrja back home.

Liv was tight-lipped on hearing this. She could understand the reasons of the crofter at Eikeby, but how would she cope with Kolgrim without Yrja? He could never be left alone for a second, she thought, as she trudged wearily up to the boy's room following Yrja's departure. Tarald was coming home from the fields as Yrja emerged from Gråstensholm's front courtyard, heading for Eikeby with her few belongings wrapped in a bundle. He stopped in front of her and looked directly into her face.

'They will be the death of you, as they were of your mother!' he said in a despairing voice. 'And we *cannot* be without you here. Only you can cope with Kolgrim when he is in a stubborn mood.'

'Father has no one else,' said Yrja, lowering her bundle to the ground. 'All my other sisters have husbands. I am the only one unwed.'

'Then marry me!' he blurted. 'Marry *me*, Yrja!'

They stood in the courtyard gateway in a stunned silence, gazing blankly at each other. Then, without answering, Yrja bent and picked up her bundle of possessions again.

'It's best I go now.'

'I mean it, Yrja!'

'No, you cannot. Not when I am as I am! And what about Gråstensholm?'

An unkind thought had crept into her mind as they spoke. Was Tarald doing this so that folk would believe Kolgrim's looks were her fault? No, she decided, regretting the idea, such considerations were truly beneath him. Besides, he was not so calculating.

Without speaking, he had taken her bundle from her hands and now drew her after him across the courtyard towards Dag's empty study. 'We had best talk this through calmly and thoroughly,' he said over his shoulder. 'It's too important to rush.'

166

She went with him without protest, but inside her mind she was at a loss to understand why she felt so sad. After ushering her into his father's chair, he sat down opposite her, close enough for their knees to touch. Yrja discreetly moved hers to one side and continued to look unflinchingly at the floor.

She did not need to see his face – every inch of it was etched deep into her memory already: she only had to close her eyes any time, anywhere, to see his beautiful arched eyebrows and the curve of his eyelids over deep-set dark eyes. He had a perfectly straight nose and his jaw had begun to lose much of its juvenile weakness. It had become so well defined and strong that she had often wanted to follow its contours with her fingertips. Despite inheriting the high cheekbones of the Ice People, there was a lot of Meiden in him, although he did not have their long narrow face. His throat and neck were as straight as a Hellenic god's, his torso was that of an athlete and, as ever, she found him beautiful to the point of distraction.

'Yrja, this is not a sudden impulse,' he told her seriously. 'I have pondered this idea a good deal in recent times – but I did not feel I had the right to ask you.'

'Did not have the right?' she repeated. 'What do you mean?'

'Please wait until you have heard what I have been thinking.'

She said nothing further, but sat waiting, as he had asked, feeling she was unable to quite grasp any of this.

'I need you, Yrja,' he said in an urgent tone. 'I need you so desperately because of my unfortunate son. I can offer you a title, a secure future – and my unfailing friendship. You know how highly I regard you and the affection I have for you, because you are so faithful and loyal.'

167

As she listened to his words, her sadness was becoming even harder to bear.

'You understand that I shall never be able to re-marry thanks to that child. You saw what happened when I tried. But you know him and he ... he can *tolerate* you, which is the closest that child can come to liking anyone. On the other hand, he treats me with perpetual scorn.'

'That isn't so,' said Yrja swiftly.

Tarald smiled ruefully. 'When I enter the room, does he smile or make any positive sign? If ever I try to show him fondness, he just turns away – or bites me.'

'It is not in his nature,' she muttered.

'No, and that is why I can never take another woman for my wife. Whoever would choose to risk giving birth to another child like him – and maybe die because of it?'

Yrja remained seated and unmoving, but something told her she was about to be humiliated.

Tarald studied his hands for a moment: 'I cannot offer you my love, Yrja. All of that gift I gave to Sunniva. You shall of course have your own chamber and I should never disturb you there.'

'Oh, what blessed innocence!' thought Yrja.

'And what will My Lord do on that day he finds another woman to love? One who will take both you and the child?'

'That won't happen!' he snapped. 'And please, Yrja, don't say "My Lord" like that. We have been friends since childhood – and now I am proposing marriage to you. Don't you understand that?'

'Yes, I understand only too well,' she sighed, 'and I am grateful. But Tarald, you do not know whether you will find a new woman in your life. Let us say that you do before too long – what then becomes of me?'

If Tarald's senses had been keener, he would have paid

more attention to her choice of words and the nuance in her reply.

'Well, then naturally you would be released from your vows.'

Thank you, thought Yrja silently, her heart heavy with tears. She did not move or speak again for a long time.

'Well?' prompted Tarald eventually. 'What do you say?'

'I think you are wrong when you say "another child such as him". It was only the union of Sunniva and you that proved so fateful.'

He thought for a moment. 'Yes,' he agreed, 'you are possibly right.'

'Then, I think you should not act in haste, Tarald.' She hoped he would not notice how her voice was trembling. 'You can still find a new love and have more children.'

'Nothing would please me more than to have one more child. I'm sure you can understand that. It would help me put aside the feeling that I have failed. However I am certain that no woman would ever want me, when I wear the millstone that is Kolgrim around my neck. But even if I were to meet another, yet more beautiful than Sunniva, I could not love her. No, my heart has been left barren by all that happened before. I couldn't love again!'

Yrja could find no words to say to him. It felt as though a deep, dark pit of emptiness had opened up inside her. Her emotions seemed to have been fatally dulled and a cloak of disappointment and exhaustion weighed heavily on her. Father needs me, she told herself, and I must not let him down. But in her heart, she knew that if her brothers and their families all worked together, sharing the burdens that they had always placed on her mother, then her father would be able to manage – whereas here at Gråstensholm, she was truly indispensable.

'As long as you can see it that way,' Tarald was saying, 'wouldn't that be acceptable?'

Lost in her own thoughts, Yrja had not been listening properly and had missed much of what he had just been saying. 'What was that?' she asked apologetically, shooting him a questioning glance. 'I don't think I quite understood?'

'No, of course, I can't ask that of you!'

'Tell me what it is!'

He hesitated for a moment. 'Well, I was just saying, "Unless *you* would want to have my child …"'

For some moments Yrja could scarcely breathe. Then she leapt out of the chair with a muffled scream and picked up her bundle of belongings. Without looking back, she ran out of the room, out of the house and down the road leading towards Eikeby, as fast as her heavy strides could take her.

Although it was late winter, there was no snow on the ground. The pastures and fields through which she hurried were frozen under a glistening frost, and mist rose up over the ponds and lakes. When she reached the path that led off towards her father's farm, she found herself walking more and more slowly, because her thoughts were increasingly in turmoil.

What was her future at Eikeby? Father, with his stifling austere piety, his blatant exploitation of others … How would that life compare with the freedom and independence of Gråstensholm and Linden Allée, which was unmatched anywhere in the parish. At Eikeby there would be her small brothers and sisters, young cousins and many other family offspring, all demanding her constant attention – they would use her as they had always used her mother – until finally she too, was fit only for a grave.

So had she the right to seek another life – to be a wife? Who would marry Yrja, the clumsy, ugly, twisted, bow-

170

legged Yrja? The Thistle! Well, Tarald of Gråstensholm, the love of her life, wanted to – but under the most humiliating of conditions. Yet could she afford to refuse? How foolish would it be to turn down his offer? Was she not, in truth, the least worthy of all?

But it was his last request that had been too much for her – he proposed to use her as a brood mare, a convenient means for him to have a child! 'Oh, Yrja, stupid girl!' she castigated herself suddenly. How else will you have the child that you so long for? And with Tarald! Yet, whichever way she looked at things, it still it felt as though it was a stark choice between which humiliation was the better of the two – a life of slavery at Eikeby or unending emotional torment at Gråstensholm!

Yrja suddenly realised that she had been standing on the same spot for a very long time and was becoming very cold. It was time to decide – and so she made up her mind at last and set off at a brisk pace towards Eikeby. When she arrived she found the atmosphere inside the farm cottage was doleful and stifling. Her mother's corpse had been placed in the barn prior to burial and her father sat in the main room, surrounded by his many offspring. The moment she stepped through the door, holding her bundle of belongings, the relief was plain to see on all their faces.

'Well, 'bout time too,' said her father ungraciously. 'Get some gruel in the pot for us – we ain't had any food since last evenin'!'

Yrja stood looking at them expressionlessly for a long moment. Suddenly she knew that her father's words were the last straw that had finally broken the camel's back. Nothing in the world, nothing at all, could make her return to the scene before her.

'You can get your own food and that's a fact,' she

snapped. 'You are all grown-up people – and there so many of you, as well! I have come merely to take farewell of my dear mother. After that I shall return to Gråstensholm.'

'What! Has pride made you witless, girl? Yo'r wanting to leave us? Yo'r duty is here!'

'My duty is to my master and husband. I'll not be worked to the bone for the sake of you idle pack, or be hounded to death, as mother was! I will not be staying,' she said loudly. 'I am soon to be wed!'

She walked out again, slamming the door loudly behind her. She managed to say a hasty and sad goodbye to her dead mother in the barn, before she spied the swarm of irate relatives coming after her. Without waiting to hear what they wished to say, she took to her heels and fled as fast as she could back to Gråstensholm.

* * * *

During Yrja's absence, something extraordinary had taken place in the great house. Liv was, of course, completely unaware of the conversation that had taken place between Tarald and Yrja. She was simply terribly upset and concerned that the girl from Eikeby was leaving them. She was sad for purely practical reasons, now that she would have to manage on her own, but it was not only that. Yrja had been more than just a nursemaid at Gråstensholm. What would life be like now in the great house, Liv was wondering, without Yrja's dependable, warm friendship?

Kolgrim, now almost three years old, was standing at the window as Liv mulled over these thoughts. 'Ware Yrra go?' he asked in his harsh voice.

Liv put down the embroidery she was working on. Her sorrowful mood made her voice sound sad and despondent.

'Yrja must leave us, Kolgrim,' she told the boy gently. 'She is to live at home with her father and be of help to him. They are so many in the family, you see.'

The boy gasped and panted as he stared down at the road to Eikeby. He could just see Yrja's ungainly figure growing smaller in the distance as she headed away from Gråstensholm. He watched in silence for a long time; then began to emit a slow wailing howl that grew louder as he beat at the window with the palms of his small hands.

'Yrra!' he screamed. 'Yrra!'

Liv jumped up and lifted him away from the window.

'Yrja *has* to go,' she said, as she tried to calm him.

But Kolgrim was not to be consoled and he started to kick and scream like someone deranged. She tried several times to hush and placate him with promises and treats, but nothing had any effect.

'Dag! Tarald! Help!' she yelled. 'Please come and help me.'

Dag, awakened from his midday nap, came rushing in, meeting Tarald in the doorway. It took all three of them to hold the boy down on Yrja's bed – his own bed being too high for them to lift the struggling child onto.

'Look!' exclaimed Dag in amazement. 'He is sobbing! He is shedding real tears!'

Tears were also streaming down Liv's face – tears of both emotion and exhaustion.

'Oh, my dear child,' she whispered. 'My dear child!'

'We must have Yrja back again,' insisted Dag, as they strove to quieten the boy. 'We can't let her go under any circumstances.'

Tarald, in his efforts to quieten his son, made the stupid mistake of putting his hand over Kolgrim's mouth – and instantly let out a roar of pain.

'I did my best to get Yrja to stay,' he panted, pressing his bleeding hand against his midriff. 'I even offered her marriage.'

'You did? Well, at last you did something sensible!' said his father scathingly. 'And what did she say?'

'She just ran off.'

'Kolgrim, dearest,' said Liv, trying in a gentle voice to calm the boy down. 'Please do not carry on so. We will do our best to get Yrja to come back.'

But the frenzied toddler went on howling at the top of his lungs, his unpleasant-looking head wagging wildly from side to side. Nothing they could do would placate him.

Above the noise, Liv shouted to Tarald, 'How on earth did Yrja come to say "No" to you?'

'I really can't understand it myself either,' he yelled back. 'I offered her a title and a secure future, where her wishes would prevail over Gråstensholm. And I said, even if I could not offer her my love, I promised her I would give her my everlasting friendship …'

'Why did you put it like that?' asked Liv, frowning.

'Well, I explained to her that I would not be able to marry again because of … you know what I mean. And she could have her own chamber and live without any unwelcome approaches from my side. But yes, I did also go so far as to offer to have a child with her – as you know, I would like to have another – and it seemed to be that which frightened her. You know, another changeling perhaps.'

Liv straightened up to ease her back and moved away, leaving the two men struggling to quieten the boy. Then after a moment or two, without any warning, the usually gentle, docile Liv exploded, hissing at her son like a savage cat.

'You have always been the weakest of our children, Tarald! Cecilie is far stronger than you!'

'Have I not done all that has been expected of me, and much more besides?' he replied hotly. 'Can you not see how Gråstensholm has grown and developed under my hand?'

'That is not what I am talking about now! Yes, you are a clever farmer, but you know nothing, absolutely nothing at all about people's feelings. When it comes to emotional matters, you are as clumsy as an elephant!'

Tarald stood before his mother as indignant as any Roman emperor – noble to look upon, but his mind in turmoil. For long moments they continued glaring angrily at each other and almost forgot the yelling child they were trying to soothe.

'Quick, someone help me please,' gasped Dag. 'The boy is getting loose!'

Liv shrugged and began to walk away from them. 'What does it all matter anyway? Yrja has been frightened off forever by the moron we have for a son. And our life from now on will be nothing but unending toil with a child who never ...'

She had been glancing idly out of the window as she spoke and her voice tailed off suddenly. After a pause, she let out a joyous shriek.

'Yrja is coming back!' she cried. 'Look, she's carrying her bundle and everything! Is that not Yrja – there, far off towards Eikeby?'

Tarald rushed over to join her at the window. 'Yes, of course it's Yrja. No one waddles along with such a funny step as she does. I'll run down and meet her!'

He ran out and plunged helter-skelter down the staircase, with his mother shouting warnings after him that he couldn't hear or understand. He seemed to fly across the courtyard and down the carriageway and he met Yrja a long way down the road.

'You came back!' he said, trying to catch his breath. His eyes were shining with a genuine delight. 'You came back!'

'Yes, Kolgrim needs me more than those spoilt oafs in my family.'

Tarald took her bundle from her. 'He went wild when he saw you leaving, Yrja. He cried real tears for the first time!'

Yrja was bewildered. 'Kolgrim? I didn't think he would care.'

'Neither did we. Mama was so upset. Yrja ...' he began hesitantly, 'have you thought ... any more about my suggestion?'

'Yes, I have,' she answered solemnly.

'Well?'

'I accept, thank you. I have so little self-respect you see.'

'I am at a loss to understand you. As if it could be a step down for you to become the Mistress of Gråstensholm?'

'I never said that.'

'Oh, I see, you mean that you are not worthy? You have no reason to be ashamed of accepting my proposal, not at all! You know how much we need you. Papa said that proposing marriage to you was the most sensible thing I have done – then Mama told me off for scaring you away. She called me a clumsy elephant and I became quite angry, for I did not deserve *that*.'

Yrja smiled to herself. The Baroness had always been a sensible woman.

'There is one thing, though,' she said and stopped as they approached the house.

'Yes?'

'Can we wait a little while before that second child? I don't think I'm quite ready for that at the moment.'

Tarald squeezed her hand, 'Of course, I understand. Take all the time you need!'

In fact Tarald understood nothing. He thought she meant having the child – carrying it for so long. He couldn't see that it was the act of conceiving itself that she feared most. Also it was almost more than she could bear to think of lying together at last with the man she had adored for so many years, knowing that he cared no more for her than for any other available fertile brood mare.

They carried on walking in silence for a while, before Yrja said: 'Who says that I shall be able to have children anyway? When I was very young I suffered from rickets, as anyone can see. I may not even be able to carry a child. You ought to choose someone else.'

'But it is *you* Kolgrim wants,' insisted Tarald. 'For him, nobody else will do.'

That answer, Yrja told herself as they walked on, was all she had to soothe the pain and heartache.

Dag and Liv had hurried down to the entrance hall with their odious grandson struggling between them, his small legs straining to reach the outer door. He had stopped screaming, but his puffing and sobbing still echoed around the walls. Dag opened the door and they were pulled out onto the steps, just as Tarald and Yrja arrived. Kolgrim tore himself loose and ran to her with outstretched arms, greeting her with another long howl. Yrja lifted him up and he threw his arms around her neck.

'My sweet little child,' she murmured comfortingly, as she stroked his repulsive bulky shoulders. 'Don't be afraid. I will always be with you from now on.'

They were all touched by what they saw. Against all their expectations, Kolgrim had for the first time shown feelings for another human being. Liv was the only one who could see the expression on his face above Yrja's shoulder and she looked expectantly for some sign of pleasure. But when she caught sight of his expression, her blood ran suddenly cold: a hideous, cunning sneer of triumph distorted Kolgrim's young features and it remained unchanging as he gazed steadily back at her. Liv tried to tell herself she was mistaken in her interpretation of what she saw. She could possibly be wrong. Perhaps that was the only way the three-year-old boy could express his happiness?

* * * *

If any of them had thought Kolgrim would be easier to handle after Yrja's dramatic return, they were soon disappointed. He became more of an ogre than before, fully aware now of the power he held and how he could use it. In the same way that Silje had once found with the young Sol, they soon realised that punishments were bound to fail. Filled seemingly with fierce hatred and a lust for revenge, the boy became a threat. In time they managed to tread a fine line between affection and discipline – but the effort put a strain on all of them that was almost unbearable.

No, he was not, by any measure or means, another Tengel the Good. Liv indeed, had often toyed with the profane idea that he might be another incarnation of Tengel the Evil. But be that as it may, he nonetheless belonged to them, a little child who had not asked to come into this world. He needed them and he was their responsibility. Also, deep in their hearts, they all felt compassion for him, as well as a barely concealed anguish for what fate might have in store.

Chapter 9

Because Yrja and Tarald had found a way forward together that everybody welcomed for differing reasons, Gråstensholm became the setting for yet another family wedding. This time, however, realism rather than romance was the main spur. As they talked over the arrangements together, Liv and Yrja acknowledged this without any reservations.

'May I suggest that we make it a very simple celebration, this time?' said Liv with a wry smile. 'We once had a very splendid wedding here – my first one to Laurents Berenius – and never has there been a more unhappy marriage! My second wedding to Dag was far quieter and smaller – and you know how happy we are together. Tarald and Sunniva's was quite grand – and that ended very badly too – so shall we agree on a quiet ceremony this time?'

Yrja smiled too. 'Yes, that sounds safer. But I should like to have asked my father and perhaps ...'

'My dear child, it goes without saying that all your relatives will be welcome to come, as will all of ours from Linden Allée. But no outsiders this time.'

Nevertheless, Liv could not hide faint feelings of alarm when she and Yrja drew up the list of people from Eikeby and other relatives living in the countryside nearby. With all Yrja's siblings, uncles and aunts, children, cousins and the folk from Linden Allée, there would be eighty-five guests, which was no small number for a 'quiet' wedding. But in the event, all proceeded smoothly without incident and afterwards, when they had finally managed to usher the last of the unpretentious guests from Eikeby out of the mansion, the exhausted family and the servants were all able to heave a sigh of relief and relax. Admittedly they did find one of Yrja's cousins lying drunkenly asleep under one of the tables when they started clearing everything away – but otherwise everything passed off in an orderly fashion. Yrja and Tarald had duly become man and wife.

The pastor performed the ceremony well and gave a short endearing speech, saying how pleased he was that his two friends had found each other. Throughout the reception afterwards, his young wife Julie, pretty as a porcelain doll as usual, sat with a tight-lipped acerbic smile on her face, occasionally fingering the wall hangings, tapestries and cushions to test their quality. As a result, Tarald and Yrja suddenly saw her in a new light and began to understand the reason why Martinius had seemed so bitter that day in the churchyard. It became even more apparent later in the evening, when Julie had the audacity to start talking to Liv in a most patronising way. It was clear from her manner that, as she saw it, nobody was to think themselves above the wife of the priest in the parish!

As she listened, Liv felt a sudden sense of devilment rising in herself and her eyes sparkled mischievously. Without any preamble, she raised her glass high in Yrja's direction.

'Welcome then into the family, my little Baroness!' she called out gaily. 'We all wish you good health and a long and happy life!'

In the silence that followed, everybody heard the subdued snigger from the pastor's wife – and at the same time noticed the faintly embarrassed expression of the pastor himself. But nothing was said and so the wedding ended. After the guests had left, the family retired to their respective chambers. Outside the door to Yrja's room, Tarald and his bride stopped and faced each other.

'Thank you so much for this day, my dear friend,' said Tarald softly. 'You have done all that was expected of you in the best possible way. Now it is my turn to fulfil my duties.'

Yrja was startled briefly, wondering what was coming. But Tarald in fact did no more than to reach out to take her right hand and hold it in both his own. 'Goodnight, Yrja!' he said smiling gently. 'Kolgrim could not wish for a better mother!'

Having said that he turned and walked quietly away to his own quarters.

After watching him go, Yrja entered her own lonely room, where the door leading into Kolgrim's nursery stood open. To her relief he was lying quietly asleep and did not stir. For a very long time she lay on her bed, staring blankly into the darkness and she did not finally fall asleep until the early hours of morning.

* * * *

In spite of its unpretentious beginnings, the marriage was a happy one. Tarald showed more consideration to Yrja than he had ever done before, and Liv and Dag found their affection for her deepening too. After Kolgrim had been

181

put to bed, the four of them would often sit up late during the dark winter evenings and talk or amuse themselves with a parlour game. They were all happy in each other's company and Yrja was never regarded differently because she was illiterate and of lowly birth. They recognised that she was their equal in the most important ways – a wise and warm-hearted woman.

One day in the middle of March, Tarald and Yrja were together in Kolgrim's room. He was standing with his back to her, staring reflectively out of the window.

'Yrja, have you ever thought any more about having a second child?' he asked unexpectedly.

His words startled her so much that she almost let Kolgrim fall from her arms. She had not expected the matter to be raised so soon, but she successfully concealed her surprise.

'Yes,' she replied quietly, 'I have thought about it sometimes.'

'Do you think you are able?'

Yrja hesitated for a moment. 'Do you mean carrying it for so long? And the birth?'

He nodded, still looking absently out of the window.

'Yes – whenever you wish.'

Still without turning from the window, he said: 'Would this evening be agreeable?'

'Oh, my poor heart,' thought Yrja. 'Do not beat so hard or you will burst!' Then aloud in a calm voice she murmured. 'Yes, that is agreeable.' She almost added, 'Thank you', but managed to stop herself at the last second.

* * * *

Without losing any time, Yrja went to bathe and wash her hair. Her hands were shaking so badly that she was unable to pour the water into the tub. In frustration she sat on the bench in the laundry room, covered her face with her hands and burst into uncontrollable tears. Liv, who was bringing some clothes down to be washed, heard her sobbing and came anxiously into the room, closing the door behind her.

'My dear Yrja, whatever's the matter?' she said in a concerned voice. 'What is it?'

Yrja, dressed only in her linen shift, could not answer. Liv put her arms around her daughter-in-law and sat with her until she had regained her composure.

'I am so afraid,' sobbed the girl.

'Tell me why.'

'No. This is something I cannot talk about.'

'Whatever it may be, you cannot face it alone.'

'But this concerns only Tarald and me.'

Liv didn't move. 'Has he mistreated you?'

'No. No, not in the least!'

'Because he is my son, then maybe I can help?'

'I am so afraid – that he will think badly of me ... of my body. And that I shall not be able to ... keep him from knowing ... how fond I am of him!'

Liv closed her eyes. 'Oh, God,' she thought. 'What has my hopeless son done now? How much has he hurt this girl?' Then looking at Yrja again, she asked: 'Do you mean that you have never – lain together?'

Yrja choked back her tears. 'No, never. But this evening he wants me to be with child. I wanted to bathe and look nice and put my hair up, just as Mistress Silje showed me. But I can do nothing about my legs!' Her voice rose to a thin squeak as she finished speaking and she started sobbing again.

'Oh Tarald! How can you be so cruel?' Liv wondered

despondently. Are you not our son, and the grandson of Charlotte and Tengel and Silje? Where did your heartlessness, and your foolishness, come from? Was it from your grandfather, Jeppe Marsvin – or Charlotte's unpleasant father?

Thinking these thoughts, Liv's anger suddenly boiled over without warning.

'Listen to me, Yrja! You are worth a thousand of him, insincere blockhead that he is. Never forget that! It is he who should be grateful that he may come to you, and he who should feel humbled by your devoted affection. You have loved him for some time, is that not so?'

'Yes, for many years. Mistress Silje knew of my love for Tarald.'

Oh, even *before* Sunniva, thought Liv sadly. How bitter those long years must have been.

'Yrja, I cannot get too involved in this. If I should go to Tarald and speak about you, and tell him how he ought to feel towards you, then I would only make things worse. But if I should find that you are sad or in pain tomorrow – well! Then I shall thrash him – as big as he is! Believe me when I tell you that I know what it is to suffer in a marriage. I have gone through nearly the same as you – with Laurents Berenius – and I was even younger than you are. Now you finish what you were doing here and then you come along to me and we shall see what we can do together. I have a little perfume and some cochineal rouge for your cheeks and lips. You will be so pretty that that my dim-witted son will forget about anything as trifling as your legs.'

Yrja sniffed and gave her a cautious smile. 'Thank you, Baroness. You are very kind.'

'Now then, you're falling back into your old ways! There are no titles any more – not between us Baronesses!'

Yrja fretted about in her room, randomly picking up ornaments and other trinkets from one place and putting them down in another. She was dressed in Charlotte Meiden's splendid regal old nightgown that was fit for a bride of far higher birth. Her brown hair had been brushed straight, to fall over her shoulders and down her back. It nearly reached to her waist and was pinned up at the front, so that her face was framed in graceful curls.

Liv had applied a hint of rouge and make-up before spraying her with rose-scented perfume. Yrja could not help thinking that she looked quite pretty; in fact she had never looked so pretty before. Also for the first time ever, she had closed the door to Kolgrim's room.

Suddenly there was a knock on the other door, the one opening onto the corridor. Yrja jumped up and tried to say, 'Come in', but only managed a tiny squeak. She took a deep breath, tried again and managed to get the words out more clearly.

When Tarald entered, she was standing motionless at the side of the bed, looking for all the world as if she had been carved from stone. In her anxiety she barely nodded to him and he also stood quite still, looking at her in the glow of the tallow candles set into the walls on iron brackets.

'Don't look so frightened,' he smiled reassuringly. 'Everything will be all right.'

That's easy for him to say, she thought. But I must make myself forget that he has held Sunniva in his arms in mindless, joyful ecstasy. I must! He despised her at the end, didn't he? But I must not think like that either – it is unfair to Sunniva. Then almost losing patience with herself, she thought impatiently: 'Oh – to hell with Sunniva!' and in some strange way, such a blasphemous sentiment made her feel much better.

'You look grand, Yrja! You are really very pretty.'

Tarald was wearing only a thin shirt and dark coloured breeches. Cautiously he walked over to her and placed his hands on her shoulders. She was so nervous that she almost collapsed as he touched her.

'We ought to be unemotional and rational about this,' he told her amicably. 'Then it will be easier – you'll see.'

A voice inside her wanted to scream out loud. Is that what you think? Unemotional and rational! You, who are to me the most beautiful and dearest on this earth – it's no good, I can stand no more – I want to run away! But he had already begun to lift her nightgown and obediently, like a child, she raised her arms.

'Perhaps we should snuff out some of the candles?' she whispered bashfully.

'Soon. Lie down my friend, you have nothing to fear.'

Dear God, how bow-legged she is, thought Tarald, shocked at what he saw. It's hardly surprising that she walks so badly! And her body is completely without form or shape. Little wonder that she understands Kolgrim so well, when she too has been born with deformity. But of course she wasn't born that way – it was the rickets that had made her so. 'Thistle' they had nicknamed her and yes, that was the right word.

As he looked upon her, a wave of anxiety rushed over him. What if she could not bear a child after all? What if this was to be all in vain? She was already lying on the bed, curled up as if to hide her disfigurement, so Tarald pulled off his shirt, loosened his belt and then lay down beside her.

'I shall not be able to do this,' he thought desperately. 'Her body is so unattractive that I am not aroused at all.'

However he found when he touched her that she was soft and warm, but she was shaking like a leaf on a windblown tree, although the room was not cold. He had no real desire to caress her, even less to kiss her – after all they were only friends, so that would have been silly.

Yrja was trying to stop herself shivering, but without success. Then she felt the touch of Tarald's skin against her breast. He was there at last! The one she had loved in her dreams for so long. Now he was there and lying with her. How could she hide her desire? How would she stay in control of her hands – her whole body – her very being?

Tarald lifted himself up on one elbow, looking down into her face.

'Dare I rest my hands on his shoulders,' she wondered, 'or is that the wrong thing to do? Oh, I am so ignorant and so frightened. I am so frightened that he will find out. Aah, no I cannot go on. I can feel a throbbing and burning deep down in my body – I am ready for him, but he must not know. Oh God, I shall die of shame! He must not find out! I shall be unemotional and rational, I shall … but my arms are touching his back – I did not mean that to happen!'

She realised her determination was weakening and a tear ran quickly down her cheek. Unable to resist the surge of her feelings, she pressed herself hard against him.

Poor Yrja! She was unsure how she should ready herself to receive him and she tried to make sure he would not be unwelcome. Tarald was flustered – and the heavy pounding of his heart took him by surprise. He had told himself that the deed had to be done and the sooner the better. Then suddenly he felt aroused and ready. And so soon – he had not expected that!

Pulling Yrja under him, he started to remove the rest of his clothing. Her lips were caressing his neck, moving slowly from side to side, and her eyes were shut tight. When she felt him undressing himself, she let out a gentle moan.

I love you! I love you! I love you, she repeated over and over inside her head. But I must not say that aloud, she cautioned herself. Neither must I show it, because he would be offended by the thought and certainly turn from me.

Any woman who feels there is something unattractive about her, will normally find it difficult to become aroused. But by now Yrja had passed that point and her body was no longer heeding her wishes. She could not recall lifting her knees – it was not of her doing. Her body seemed to be moving itself instinctively and independently of her conscious will.

She gasped and began to breathe more rapidly, as she felt him push against her. Her whole being seemed to be engulfed by a raging inferno – she trembled with a burning desire that seemed to equal the worst torments of hell. She screamed aloud, then bit her lips fiercely to muffle the sound. Oh, no … oh, no … why did it hurt so much?

'Be gentle, Tarald,' she begged, her voice hardly more than a whisper. 'Please be gentle with me.'

But although Tarald had started this conquest in a cool and businesslike fashion, he had by now lost all self-control. He was bewildered by the ferocity of his response and found he could not help himself, despite seeing the pain she was obviously enduring. It was proving difficult for Yrja, because her pelvis had not developed normally and although he tried with all his might to restrain himself for her sake, he found he could not.

He had never known desire of such depth and intensity, and it drove him on with its own force. He heard Yrja try to stifle an ecstatic cry, as their bodies joined fully at last; but she too was unable to control herself. Yrja's arms were tightening convulsively around his neck and her open mouth was pressing desperately against his cheek. In his own frenzy he turned his head and pressed his lips fervently against hers. The kiss deepened and seemed to engulf them both in emotions neither had ever felt before – and it did not end until their two bodies had been ravaged by the final, violent throes of their shared passion.

Tarald slumped to her side, exhausted. He realised then that Yrja was weeping softly. Feeling alarmed, he touched her cheek tenderly with his hand; but a moment later she lifted her head to look at him and, without any warning, her sobbing turned suddenly into a burst of joyous laugher.

'Well,' she said, struggling to regain her breath, 'if that doesn't make a baby, then I don't know what will!'

With great relief, he joined in her laughter. 'Yes, but just to be absolutely sure, perhaps we ought to try again in a few days. When the pain has gone I mean. And maybe the next evening too, and the one after that – and the one after that! Because it was so wonderful – I so enjoyed it, Yrja!'

She breathed a deep long sigh of satisfaction, but found she could not speak.

'Only if you want to, of course,' he added anxiously, fearing that he was presuming too much, too soon.

'Always, Tarald,' she whispered, replying without any hesitation this time. 'Whenever you want me, I will be ready.'

* * * *

When Liv saw Yrja in Kolgrim's room the following morning, she could tell immediately from her glowing expression that her son had treated her with dignity and respect.

'So … everything went well I see,' she said tentatively.

'Oh, yes! Tarald was so gentle and kind and wonderful, Mistress Liv. And he remained with me until morning – although that was because he quickly fell asleep and I didn't dare move my arm. It still has no feeling. But I am so happy, Mama!'

Liv was touched that Yrja, without thinking, had called her Mama. But almost without pausing for breath, Yrja continued: 'Naturally I didn't tell him how much I loved him and there was no question of that on his part. He was simply fond of me and wanted to be with me, Mistress Liv – and he *desired* me! Just imagine that. Tarald desired *me*! And wants to be with me again!'

Liv smiled. She had been about to give Yrja a warning – the words were on the tip of her tongue – not to be grateful for such little crumbs of comfort. But she thought better of it and instead decided to encourage her in a different way.

'Do you want to know what I think?' she asked in a cheery voice. 'I think it sounds like Tarald is making a very promising start to falling in love.'

'Oh, God,' whispered her daughter-in-law. 'If only that were true.'

* * * *

As it happened, Yrja conceived very quickly. Even so, Tarald continued to lie with her and they shared the same

190

chambers every night, always leaving the door to Kolgrim's room open. Then one summer's day, when Yrja was out in the garden with Kolgrim, trying to teach him not to pull up every one of his grandmother's flowers, she looked up to see Tarald standing there before her in his very muddied working clothes. She smiled warmly at him in welcome, but his expression remained serious.

'I love you, Yrja,' he said calmly. 'I love you more strongly, more deeply and more passionately than I ever loved Sunniva. You give me so much more, both by day and by night.'

An overwhelming feeling of joy immediately rose up within her. Unable to stop herself, she fled up the steps into the house, covering her face with her hands to hide her tears.

'What in the world is going on?' cried Liv who was tending to her plants a short distance away. 'What have you said now, Tarald?'

He shook his head in bewilderment. 'I only told her that I loved her. I don't understand …'

'No! But I do!' said Liv, advancing on him with a serious look on her face. 'It's time for you to hear the truth! Yrja has been in love with you, unselfishly and adoringly, since long before you had your mindless episode with Sunniva. Yrja has suffered at your hands for many years. You brought a new girl home, but thankfully she did not want you. Then you tortured Yrja with your cynical proposal of marriage. When at last the day came that you deigned to visit her chamber in the evening, I found her sitting in the laundry room sobbing for fear that you would dislike her legs – and she was also afraid that you would discover just how much she had always loved you. But I am grateful for what you have been to her *since* that night my boy! And thank you for what you said to her just now!'

191

Tarald stared at his mother dumbstruck for a long time. 'But why has she never said anything before?' he asked at last.

'I despair,' Liv sighed. 'I sometimes think you've got your grandfather, Jeppe Marsvin, to thank for the empty peacock's brain between your ears! Women can feel both shame and pride at the same time – even those like Yrja who are untaught. She couldn't tell you because … Oh, help, look – the boy!'

They both raced to the foundation walls of the house, where Kolgrim was attempting to commit early suicide by climbing the tall sheer blocks of grey stone. Tarald quickly lifted him down, amid angry howls of protest, and left him in the care of his Grandmama. Then he ran swiftly up the steps after Yrja. He found her eventually in their bedchamber, trying to wipe away the signs of her tears.

'My beloved, dearest Yrja, why have you never said anything?' he asked as he took her in his arms. 'Mama told me of your long enduring love for me. We have lost so much time!'

Yrja, despite her tears, was ecstatically happy. 'No, we have lost no time at all. The last apples of winter need a long time to ripen.'

'Are you comparing me to a winter apple?' he laughed. 'Yes, I suppose I am slow on the uptake. I would have to agree with you. But please forgive me, my dearest for all the pain my thoughtlessness has caused you!'

She shook her head dismissively. 'You know how happy I have been of late and now at last I will be able to show you how much I truly adore you.'

He looked steadily into her eyes for a long time. With each passing moment, his gaze became more intense. Then without warning he reached out for her with both arms.

'No! Tarald!' she squealed and giggled. 'Let me go! We can't do this now – you have brought half the field indoors with you on those clothes of yours!'

* * * *

Down in the garden, Liv was still struggling with Kolgrim, who had grown bigger and stronger with each year. Sometimes his strength seemed almost equal to that of the two women caring for him and he seemed to be increasingly aware of this.

'Will you stay on the ground, you little ...' she began and then thought it best not to say exactly what she was thinking.

At that moment Dag came into view, riding back from a session at court. On catching sight of him, Kolgrim stopped fighting his grandmother. He knew that he might be lifted up to join his grandfather on the horse if he behaved well. His calculated action quickly had the desired effect and he was soon sitting astride the horse in front of its rider.

'So,' Dag inquired of his wife, 'is all well here?'

'We have a letter from Cecilie,' she replied, trying to tidy her hair after the fray. 'She really is to be allowed to come home for the Yuletide season – and she will stay for two months.'

'Well now, that is good news! And how is Yrja today?'

'She is grand – and happier than usual, because Tarald has finally come to realise that she is *the* woman in his life.'

'Mmm, yes – that lad has always been a bit slow to see the obvious.'

Liv glanced up at Kolgrim. His eyes were gleaming amber as he tried to urge the horse to set off at a gallop down the road. To his disappointment, however, Grandpapa and Grandmama kept a firm hold on the animal.

'Dag, I am quite worried, though.'

'Why? Everything is going splendidly, isn't it?'

'I am not so sure about that,' she murmured cryptically. 'How do you imagine a certain "young nobleman" will greet a new sibling?'

Glancing speculatively down at Kolgrim, Dag sighed. 'I suppose it is anybody's guess. Particularly as the young nobleman in question is so attached to the expectant mother. Perhaps we can only hope for the best.'

'It will be a new balancing act, and that frightens me,' said Liv anxiously. 'You don't know how often I have wondered whether we might have given the wrong answer that time …'

'When Tengel asked if he should end it quickly, you mean?' enquired Dag. 'When the tiny life was barely one hour old? Yes, I have to admit I too have often asked myself that very question. But I believe we chose correctly … from a Christian point of view.'

'The Christian point of view often forces people to choose between the lesser of two evils. To save *one* life, only then to spend every day preventing it from taking another.'

'Oh, now I think you're being too hard,' said Dag who was more of a believer than his wife. 'And of course we love him, don't we?'

'You're talking too openly – small heads have big ears. But yes we do, although it's a desperate kind of love tinged with sadness – no, Kolgrim, don't poke the horse in the eye! Come down, now. It'll soon be time to eat!'

References to food and eating were terms that Kolgrim always readily understood and he slid down from the horse at once. In truth, he already understood a great deal; indeed he had an underlying intelligence that never ceased to surprise them. But what his deepest thoughts and feelings were nobody could fathom, and speculation on the subject was endless when the boy was asleep.

That summer many of the local children caught mumps – including Kolgrim and, shortly afterwards, Tarald contracted the illness too. He quickly became seriously ill as the sickness spread through his glands. On a home visit from his studies in Tübingen, Tarjei came to treat him.

'Tarald, I think you have been lucky,' said Tarjei curtly, 'that Yrja is already with child, I mean.'

'What has that to do with my mumps?' asked Tarald.

'This will be the last child you will father.'

The colour drained from Tarald's face. 'How can you know that?'

'It is better to catch mumps when you are still a lad. It can badly affect a grown man's ability to procreate.'

When his cousin had left, Tarald lay thinking over what he had told him. If this was to be his last child, then everything must go perfectly. But he was already horribly afraid. Yrja was having a difficult time, with pains in her back and swollen feet – and that young maniac Kolgrim needed to be held constantly in check.

Tarald was surprised by his new sense of devotion to Yrja. His love for Sunniva had always been something of a game; they had been like two butterflies flitting after each other across a pasture. He had adored watching her, holding hands with her and living with her in a make-believe world of beauty. They never held a conversation with one another, but skipped about, acting the fool and speaking baby talk to each other. Sunniva, because she knew how sweet and beautiful she was, spent all her time striking poses. She adored her young, divine beauty to the exclusion of almost everything and it was for this reason above all else that Tarald had grown tired of her.

In contrast, Yrja was a person with whom he could talk about anything. She always listened and understood, never mocking him or laughing at his ineptitude when he had to confess that something was beyond his intellect. He was increasingly aware that he felt a deep tenderness for Yrja. Sometimes when he was out in the fields, a warm pleasant feeling would well up inside him, making it hard for him to catch his breath or swallow or even see clearly. What did he care about how she looked? She was Yrja, his beloved, and to her belonged a pair of deformed legs, a shapeless body and a heavy, touchingly friendly face – but he loved every part of her.

He told her so over and over again. It pleased him to think that his words made her happy. Then there was all the wonderful love she gave *him*! Somewhere in the back of his mind Tarald was beginning to sense that his wife was playing a large part in turning him into a mature man with a resolute and tenacious personality.

* * * *

Cecilie arrived home just as everything was being prepared for the Yuletide festivities. Her arrival lifted everybody's spirits, because her wit and happiness were immediately infectious. She was so obviously overjoyed to be home again at last and, in no time at all, Gråstensholm bustled with new life and vitality, as if she had painted colourful flowers on every wall.

Life at Linden Allée was also very cheerful, because Tarjei was back again from Tübingen. It was easier for him to travel home more often than Cecilie, because Grandpapa Tengel had secretly given him a large part of the income from his medical practice. He had in no way neglected his other heirs, but Silje and he were agreed that Tarjei had something about him worth nurturing, and that required money. Besides, Tarald and Cecilie would share in the wealth of the Meiden family and for this reason alone, it was not too surprising that Tengel had decided to be more generous to Are's sons.

So as Yuletide drew near, the family's two most gifted members had come home after long absences. As a result, everybody was in an unusually joyous mood. There was an almost tangible feeling of anticipation in the air – but nobody realised just how eventful the festive season would turn out to be.

Chapter 10

Cecilie had barely closed the ornate, beautifully carved doors of Gråstensholm's main entrance behind her before everyone started asking questions at once. They crowded round her excitedly, unable to restrain their feelings of pleasure at seeing her again after such a long time.

'Am I allowed to remove my cape before I answer?' she chirped happily. 'It will only take a moment.'

It was in fact a very fine cape, stylishly black and made from fur-trimmed high-quality woollen broadcloth. Until the moment that her daughter made her sudden appearance, Liv had been single-handedly lime-washing the great brick-fronted fireplace. She climbed down from the stool on which she had been standing to help take her daughter's outer garment. But unsurprisingly, Cecilie refused her offer: she did not wish to have any white marks on that magnificent cape, thank you!

'Oh, how marvellous it feels to be home again!' she cried. 'And how fine everything is looking too! But dear Mama, please go and wash that off your hands. I want to hug all of you – oh, now look, I'm beginning to weep and I really must not. I had promised myself I should not

… Oh, Papa, I do miss them all so terribly much.'

With that she threw herself into Dag's arms, overcome with sadness for all those beloved relatives who were no longer with them: Charlotte, Jacob, Sunniva – they had all been such a large part of her home and her earlier life. And of course the very heart of the family at Linden Allée had also disappeared – Tengel and Silje. It took quite a while before Cecilie regained her composure, but then mother and daughter retired together to the 'petit salon', Cecilie's new name for the room beyond the great hall, to talk in private.

'So tell me, what happened with the young nobleman, whatever he was called?' asked Liv eagerly, pretending to have forgotten the man's name. In truth she had spent many quiet moments contemplating the prospect of Cecilie as a Marchioness, after gathering from her daughter's letters that he seemed to be a pleasant person.

'Alexander Paladin, you mean, I think,' she answered nonchalantly. 'Hmm, yes, I see him from time to time. But then I have so many suitors.'

'You do?' Liv was intrigued.

'Oh, yes. I have but to choose … Heavens, there's that old jar, I didn't know you still had it. Oh dear, now I'm getting very sentimental …'

Cecilie chattered on very animatedly without pause, to hide pain she did not wish to reveal at that moment, and it was not long before she excused herself, saying that she wanted to go to her chamber to recuperate from her journey. As soon as she was alone, she began to unpack her travel chest, and as she did so, she found herself repeating aloud to herself the name of the man about whom Liv had so recently enquired: Alexander Paladin.

Although she could not reveal this to her mother, she could not forget that she had often dreamt about

199

Alexander Paladin. She spent most of her time at Fredriksborg's Castle, north of Copenhagen, because the royal children lived there. The marquis spent time there too, but only occasionally, and sometimes they would meet in Copenhagen on one of her infrequent trips to the capital. However, they more often met by chance, walking along a castle corridor or at a social gathering. In whatever way it came about, they always found time to talk, although it was never Cecilie who initiated their conversations.

He had always told her he would 'keep a watchful eye on the little Norwegian maiden who was so innocent of the intrigues of the Court', but he remained otherwise extraordinarily remote. Once or twice he had contacted her to ask her to accompany him to some concert at the castle or to the performance of a play – or any other spectacle the King had commanded. She accepted gladly and always enjoyed his company. But she couldn't help but notice the restless, almost hounded look in his eyes or the enigmatic glances they both received from others.

Not once had he ever said anything that implied he might be a little fond of her – and he never touched her unless they were in company. Then he would place a confiding hand on her arm or shoulder and whisper something banal in her ear – smiling as though they were a very intimate couple. But afterwards he would leave her at her door, kissing her hand and politely thanking her for such pleasant company.

Yes, they seemed to find it easy to talk to each other, but Cecilie remained confused and could not understand his conduct – until a terrible sequence of events began to unfold one by one. Recalling them again, she found, was already making her cheeks burn. At the same time, she also realised she had stopped unpacking her clothes and was sitting on her bed, as if her legs had given way beneath her. Tired from her travels and her mind in turmoil, she lay back on the bed with her arm resting over her face.

The first event had occurred when Cecilie was waiting to accompany the children to Dalum Abbey, where they were to be educated by their maternal grandmother, Ellen Marsvin, a distant relative of Cecilie's own ne'er-do-well grandfather, Jeppe Marsvin. The relationship was so distant, in fact, that it could almost be ignored. It would be far more pleasant for the children at Dalum Abbey, thought Cecilie, because Mistress Kirsten was not a good mother to them. Because she had a violent temper and was so impatient, she often beat them black and blue. She treated Anna, the oldest, worst of all because she took after her father, King Christian; something that Kirsten Munk found impossible to tolerate. It was always left to Cecilie to comfort the girl after these episodes and as time went on, the bond between the two of them became stronger.

It was also heartening for the girl to know that the King himself delighted in her, and in that way young Anna had helped to ensure that Cecilie remained as the children's governess. The King wanted her there, Alexander wanted her there and so did the children. Faced with this, Mistress Kirsten and her housekeeper could do little to oppose her. But slyly they found ways to torment her beyond all measure with taunts, threats and evil gossip. The fact that the children fared little better at the hands of Grandmother, Ellen Marsvin was another story.

One morning, shortly before they were due to leave Fredriksborg, Cecilie entered the children's chambers to begin her duties for the day. She saw the chambermaids standing in a huddle, whispering among themselves, obviously sharing some sensational gossip. They stopped when they saw her come in and, still sniggering, went about their work.

Very soon, however, the head housekeeper appeared. 'Ah, there you are, Mistress Cecilie. What will become of your *special friend* now then, eh? The Marquis, I mean.' She had pronounced the words 'special friend' with exquisite sarcasm and Cecilie's heart beat faster, as she wondered what she meant. She knew that Alexander was staying at Fredriksborg, but before she was able to frame her reply the older woman continued in the same unpleasant tone. 'Has he proposed marriage to you yet?'

All the chambermaids within earshot started to snigger uncontrollably.

'I'm afraid I do not understand you,' said Cecilie, flustered. 'Please explain further.'

The housekeeper's eyes were glittering with triumph. 'Somebody might very well whisper in His Majesty's ear that a young boy was seen leaving the Marquis's chambers at four o'clock in the morning.'

All eyes were looking expectantly at Cecilie, yet she remained nonplussed. 'Yes, and what of it?' she had wanted to say. 'I have seen a youth go in there previously – a couple of times. What is so strange about that?' But she said nothing, because she could see from their faces that Alexander was in serious trouble. Had he been involved in spying – or conspiring against the King, or in some other form of treachery?

She did not have to wait long, however, to discover the truth, because a moment later the housekeeper clarified the gravity of the situation.

'The King will not be pleased to learn of this! Should His Majesty happen to be in a good mood, then perhaps the Marquis will be dismissed dishonourably from his service and cast into oblivion. Should His Majesty happen to be less well disposed, then …' She stopped speaking and silently drew her forefinger across her throat.

Cecilie's mind had been racing, but she had at last managed gather her thoughts. Because the Marquis had always been kind to her, she decided it was the time for her to stand by him. The housekeeper's uninterrupted tirade had meant that her contemplative silence had gone unnoticed and she took her chance to speak out now in a forthright tone.

'You are quite right, Alexander Paladin did have a visit from a young man last night,' she said in a firm clear voice. 'I don't know if you are aware of the fact that the Marquis has suffered from undulant fever for many years. Late last night, as he was escorting me to my door, he felt the onset of an attack of fever. I bade a young man we met to help me take the Marquis to his chamber and then come to my rooms, where I have medicaments to help cure the sickness. The man did so and then, following my orders, he returned to the Marquis with a potion. Nothing very remarkable, I'm sure you'll agree.'

She turned to see that the King had entered the chambers and had obviously overhead what she had said. Cecilie curtseyed at once, as did every other person there and they waited expectantly for His Majesty to speak.

'What a damnable amount of running along the corridors there must have been,' he observed dryly at last. And with that, the subject was closed.

The following day, however, a large bouquet of autumn flowers arrived at Cecilie's rooms and with them a card. The message on it read: 'Thank you! Will you dine with me tonight? Your devoted friend, Alexander.'

That evening they had enjoyed an excellent dinner in his

chambers with servants in attendance, cut-glass goblets and porcelain plates. His manner had been delicate, almost ethereal, yet she began to sense that underneath his surface good manners and good humour, he was unsettled and nervous. She tried her best to respond to him in a similarly moderate, intellectual tone and after the meal they relaxed together with a board game on the table between them. But the quantity of wine they had drunk made concentration difficult.

Then out of the blue, Alexander said confidingly: 'Cecilie ... about that night-time visit ... and the undulant fever you found I was suffering from ... We are greatly indebted to you, my friend and I.'

'It was the very least I could do,' she replied with a smile. 'Considering all the kindness you have shown me.'

A silence fell between them and Cecilie's expression became serious again. She scrutinised his face carefully for a long time before speaking again.

'I have no wish to be impertinent and enquire as to what reason the King would have to cast you into oblivion,' she said at last. 'But I feel obliged to ask anyway. You need not of course feel compelled to answer. But I hazarded a guess that you may be plotting against the King in some way – and that is awfully dangerous isn't it?'

Alexander's strong beautiful hand had opened and dropped the token it had been grasping. He stared back at her for what seemed like another age.

'Plotting against the King? Have you taken leave of your senses?'

Filled with confusion, she looked at him blankly. 'But you are not serving His Majesty abroad, are you? So are you here to spy? And you are yourself a foreigner, isn't that so?'

'No, I am no foreigner!' he exclaimed. 'My family was Danish long before I was born ...'

Cecilie sat waiting, but he did nothing to explain or elaborate further. Instead he sighed and leaned his elbows heavily on the gaming table, burying his face in his hands.

'Good God!' he whispered between his fingers, 'do you mean that you have not understood? That you have not *known*?'

'Known *what*?'

Alexander raised his head again and looked at her. His eyes had a haunted look and his fascinating face was suddenly care-worn and confused.

'Cecilie! My, oh my! Young innocent Cecilie, my country lass from Norway! My dear friend, how could I have treated you so abominably? I thought you *knew*! You have met my young friend Hans a couple of times and when you said nothing, I assumed you understood. Oh, my dear child!'

Tears had begun to well up in her eyes. 'What is it Alexander? I get so upset when you look so unhappy. Is ... he ... is he your son, perhaps?'

Alexander glanced at her indignantly. 'My son? No, now that's enough! That could be regarded as offensive! How old do you think I am?'

'Please, no! I don't know. But I could think of nothing else so terrible and so secret that would cause the King to see you harmed! But you must forgive me, I shall ask no more questions.'

In the new silence that followed, his eyes studied her, but his mind was elsewhere.

'Tell me, Cecilie, what are your feelings towards me? No! Don't tell me, I do not want to know! Oh God, how much misery have I caused you, my dear young girl?'

'You? You haven't caused me any misery. You have always been very kind to me.'

'No! I have used you – betrayed your friendship and trifled with hallowed emotions. In God's name I hope I have not harmed you and destroyed something precious within you! But in this atmosphere of decadence I had not imagined that you did not know. I could not see how pure and unsullied you are. No, ask me no more, Cecilie, for your virtue puts me to shame. All I can tell you is that I have a vice that must remain secret – and as a result I have many enemies here at Court. While they may suspect me, they can present no proof. I have the King's favour, but should evidence be presented to him, then I am finished. In an instant! From now on Cecilie we must go our separate ways – forever! For your sake it gladdens me that you are to leave Fredriksborg and be free of me. Your friendship has been my strength, but God forbid that it should be more than friendship! I would not wish such pain on you.'

Cecilie had already got to her feet and stood looking at him, shaken and unhappy. It was all beyond her understanding and she didn't want to be parted from her best friend – and yet there was no hint of compromise in the way he spoke.

So she had left Fredriksborg, but her new mistress, Ellen Marsvin, displayed as little compassion as her last. The fact that the head housekeeper would be going with them did nothing to improve the situation. She did not meet Alexander Paladin again before she was allowed to return home to Norway for her first visit in several years – but she still missed him terribly.

On the journey from Oslo to Gråstensholm, she finally found out the truth. She had arranged to meet up with Tarjei in Oslo and he had waited a day for her just so that they could travel home together. Her ship had made good time and they took a carriage together. As it rattled along on the homeward journey they had told each other eagerly of all their adventures and experiences.

Naturally Tarjei had enquired about her suitors and whether or not she had found someone special. Despite being five years older than he was, she had always been able to confide in Tarjei. So she naturally had told him everything about Alexander Paladin and as he listened to her story, his happy expression had gradually changed. He became silent and serious, biting distractedly on his bottom lip while wondering how to explain to her what she had apparently not understood.

'What is the matter, Tarjei?' she asked worriedly when she noticed the change in him. 'There's something wrong, isn't there?'

'Do you really not understand?'

'That is precisely the same question Alexander asked. So do you know something?'

'Yes, it's not hard to guess. Are you in love with him?'

'I don't know that I am in love – but I am terribly fond of him.'

'I would not want to destroy any of your fine sensibilities – I think perhaps it might be best for you to remain ignorant.'

'No!' she exclaimed, grabbing his coat collar. 'This time I want to know! It seems as though I am wandering along a dark tunnel, feeling around for something nice to hold onto. But there are so many horrible things everywhere that I dare not touch anything.'

'Yes, that's probably a very good description of the way it is.'

'What? Tell me now or I shall not talk to you any more.'

'And is that a promise – or a threat?' he teased. 'All right, now I am going to be very serious. Have you never heard people talk of men like Alexander?'

'How? What sort of men?'

Tarjei pulled a worried face. He felt uncomfortable at the thought of bringing the walls of Cecilie's little citadel of innocence tumbling down about her ears.

'One thing is certain, Cecilie. You must not expect any love from him in return.'

She was taken aback by his words and huddled back into the corner of the carriage. 'Why not?'

'Because there are men who … Oh, Good Lord, girl! Don't you realise what that young man, Hans was doing in Alexander's room at night?'

'No.'

'They … Cecilie, use your imagination! There are men who care nothing for women and never will. They cannot love them – they love other men instead!'

The shocking words took a long time to sink into her brain. What he was saying was unfathomable; he seemed to be talking utter rubbish. She herself was at a loss for words of any kind.

'I can quite understand that your friend's position at Court is in the balance!' Tarjei said bluntly. 'Such things are punished very severely – sometimes even by death.'

'Do you mean that they …' Her brain felt as though it was made of wool. She could not think properly.

'Yes, I do mean that,' said Tarjei. 'They don't just sit and hold hands!'

'But Tarjei …' Cecilie began slowly, 'that's not possible!'

'What is possible is their affair,' he said gently. 'I only know that their love can be as great and pure as yours or mine – but sometimes it can also be a thousand times more confused.'

208

Hans? Hans – what did he look like? Yes, she did vaguely remember him. Cultivated, beautiful – and awfully young. And he was her rival? At last pictures began to form in her mind.

'Stop the carriage!' she mumbled almost incoherently. 'I have to get out, I must have some air!'

Before they reached Gråstensholm, Cecilie had managed to collect her thoughts and the two of them had discussed the problem thoroughly. Tarjei told her there were also women who had similar feelings for other women. The veil of naivety had been lifted from her eyes and she saw for the first time an entirely new world that had previously been beyond her comprehension. Of one thing she was certain: she never wanted to see Alexander Paladin ever again. 'The Paladin' was how he was known at Court, after the twelve knights of Charles the Great – 'Christian IV's Paladin'.

'To hell with you, Alexander!' screamed Cecilie very loudly without any warning, as the coach rattled along the last mile approaching Gråstensholm. 'To hell with you!'

It was a hopeless cry of desperation, but at least it told Tarjei that she had got over the worst. As the great house came in sight through the carriage windows, they had both begun to laugh uproariously.

* * * *

To everyone's great surprise at Gråstensholm, Cecilie quickly won Kolgrim's affection. Although he had shown little or no sign of that emotion to anybody else, his manner in Cecilie's presence was quite markedly different.

When she came down to the breakfast table in the mornings, she would call out: 'Where is the little beast?' and Kolgrim, who was by now almost four, would rush forward and crash into her knees, trying his best to make her keel over.

'Heavens above, are there no brakes on this wagon?' she would sigh and lift the boy into her arms. He in turn would snigger with delight and ruffle her hair.

'Will you stop doing that, you full-blooded little devil!' she would yell and a wild chase through the corridors and rooms inevitably ensued. Kolgrim would tear along in front, braying with uncontrolled laughter, while Cecilie followed rapidly behind, shouting after him every curse she knew.

Eventually he let himself be caught and she pretended to beat him soundly before he cuddled up close to her while she ate her meal. The others told her not to wear herself out keeping him amused, but she assured them that she had received plenty of excellent experience with the King's children.

Furthermore she would not admit that he was ugly. 'I think you've all had your eyes closed,' she said lightly. 'In a few years time he will enthral any woman, can't you see it? He will be one of those completely fascinating and handsome men who are irresistible.'

Cecilie was right. It needed a certain perception to see such a thing, to decipher the emerging attraction in Kolgrim's unusual features. Had Sol lived to see her grandchild, she would have recognised him instantly. In time Kolgrim would grow to look exactly like the man she had met during her séance at Ansgar's Klyfta, the ravine where witches had traditionally gathered over many centuries. He would come to resemble his incredibly handsome ancestor, who had eyes as cold and bright as ice and whose seductive appearance had made Sol tremble with desire – until she saw the severed head of a woman that he clutched in his hands. But without any shadow of doubt that same man's features were now beginning to show themselves in the face of Kolgrim, that very face which had been so grotesque at birth.

'Have you done anything nasty today?' Cecilie might ask him. 'You know what I mean by "nasty", don't you? Not harm anyone – man or animal – because that is just stupid and not something a clever young man like you would do. But something like tying knots in the window drapes or hiding Grandpapa's shoes – things like that.'

Kolgrim usually shook his head artfully, but the following morning Yrja would discover that he had had tied enormous knots in his bed linen – and this made her furious.

'Don't be upset,' smiled Cecilie. 'The boy needs a way to get rid of his mischievous impulses. Better he does this, than to run wild with all and sundry. But you shouldn't be untying those knotted sheets, my dear – here, let me do it. You sit and rest.'

Yrja was happy to do as she was told and Cecilie went over to her and fondly stroked her cheek. 'I am very glad that you are my sister-in-law,' she whispered warmly. 'Very glad indeed.'

Yrja was so moved by these words that she could do no more than nod, hoping Cecilie would know that she felt the same.

During supper that same evening, Kolgrim threw his bowl of gruel in Cecilie's face to see if she would become angry. When she simply threw her food at him instead, he was taken completely by surprise – but lacking any sense of humour, he immediately went into a rage. Eventually she calmed him down and wiped the mess from his face and hers. Then she sat him on her knee.

'You and I, Kolgrim, we are two sides of the same coin,' she announced to him. 'We are both of the Ice People.'

'Cecilie,' cautioned Liv, 'you ought not to speak to him of the Ice People.'

'Why not? Why deny that which is a fine and noble part of us? And we must accept the less dignified strain in the Ice People along with the rest. Kolgrim, did you know your grandmother could do magic?'

'Cecilie, really!' said her father, Dag.

But she would not be stopped. 'Yes, she could – she was a proper witch!' The boy listened eagerly. 'Many of the Ice People were witches and wizards. My Grandpapa was a wizard, but he didn't do magic.'

'Silly!' muttered Kolgrim.

'No, that wasn't silly. But you mustn't forget that you are also a Meiden. A little baron.' Then she mumbled to herself, 'And what a baron, God help us.'

'Meiden is poo,' announced Kolgrim. 'I am wizard!'

'Hardly,' rejoined Cecilie. 'Your grandmother – they say she was very beautiful – she could move things just by looking at them very hard. Grandpapa Dag and Grandmama Liv have said so.'

Kolgrim's eyes widened. 'Move things? How?'

'Well, you see this little bowl – she could look at it and by thinking and thinking, very, very hard, she could make it come over to me. Do you understand?'

The boy glared at the bowl so intently that he went boss-eyed.

'Move, silly bowl! ... It's not moving!' he protested.

'No, what did you expect? Your grandmother Sol practised for many years before she learnt how to do it.'

Cecilie turned to the others and said with a sigh, 'You know, sometimes I feel very strongly as though I have lived before. It is a feeling that is both bewitching and frightening at the same time.'

Dag and Liv glanced uneasily at one another. They both remembered that Are had reported back to the family Sol's very last words: 'I feel that I shall return in a different, more gentle incarnation.' Of course, Cecilie knew very well that she sometimes reminded them of Sol. But she had never in fact, heard those words spoken herself – and nothing had ever been said in her presence, because they had been unsure how she would react. By consensus, they had all felt certain that Cecilie would want to be her own person, not someone else who had 'returned'.

'They moved!' screamed Kolgrim suddenly. 'Look Aunt Cecilie, the bowl moved!'

'Ha! You cheated, you spawn of a viper!'

'Did not, so!'

'Oh, yes you did! Did you think I couldn't see your arm out of the corner of my eye? Come on, Kolgrim, shall we go and find something exciting to do … and be a little bit naughty together as well?'

'Yeees!' the boy yelled. 'Mama, clothes!'

Yrja helped him to dress, grateful that Cecilie was looking after the lad. Liv was busy preparing for Yule and everyone else had work to do. Yrja was due to give birth any day and she was finding the unending attention demanded by Kolgrim extremely tiring.

Then the day before Yuletide Eve, traditionally known as 'Little Yule', they sent for the midwife.

Cecilie admonished her brother. 'Couldn't you have planned the event more sensibly, Tarald? Who can find the time to give birth when everyone is dipping candles and making sausages?'

'All those things were done weeks ago, Cecilie,' said Liv.

'Don't start making Tarald more nervous than he already is! He has painful memories of childbearing in this house, don't forget!'

'Hmmm, he wasn't the one suffering the pain, though!'

'A soul can also be in agony, Cecilie. You must not be so cynical.'

'Don't you think I realise how serious this is?' she asked solemnly. Then with a gleeful yell she called, 'Where is my little monster?'

As if from nowhere, Kolgrim rushed up and head-butted his favourite aunt quite hard.

'Come, Troll, you and I shall leave,' said Cecilie. 'I don't think we can be of help here. Mama Yrja is going to give you a new brother or sister – what do you think of that?'

Kolgrim reached up to the table and grabbed a knife. He stabbed wildly at an imaginary sibling again and again, his eyes gleaming with delight.

'No Kolgrim! How could you?' Cecilie's tone was icy. 'If you do such a thing to the new baby, then I shall never be able to take you with me to the Trolls' Great Feast. Only trolls who have not harmed their little brothers and sisters are allowed. Because the Terrible Great Troll, who is a thousand times bigger than all of Gråstensholm, comes and asks: "Have you all been up to lots of mischief?" And all the little trolls answer, "Yes", but *then* he asks, "Have you been really nice to everyone who is smaller than you?" That's very important to a troll, you see.'

Kolgrim nodded, wide-eyed and open-mouthed. He was so engrossed that he swallowed air instead of breathing properly, which caused him a moment's panic.

'And all the little trolls again answer, "Yes",' Cecilie continued. 'But the Terrible Great Troll looks all about and then he says, "But Kolgrim has not been nice to his little brother"– or little sister, whatever it may be – and he will point straight at you and say, "Be gone from here! We never want to see you again, for you are not a real troll. You have been nasty to little children and you must not come back here, ever!" Then all the trolls will chase you away. Is that what you want to happen?'

He shook his head in horror. Her storytelling had left him dumbstruck.

'Do you still want to be nasty to the new baby?'

'No! Never-ever! When do we go to the trolls?'

'First you must grow a little taller. When you reach up to that shield on the wall over there then we shall go, you and I together.'

His eyes were judging the height of the shield and, from his rapid glances around the room, it was clear he was weighing up some alternatives. Perhaps, if he stood on a chair? Would that hasten things along?

'I shall be very good,' he told her, 'to the new baby.'

'I'm pleased. I'm very fond of you, Kolgrim,' she said as she bent to pick him up. 'And you are my very best mischievous friend!'

He threw his arms around her neck and brought his face very close, so that his sulphur-yellow eyes stared directly into hers.

'Have you another friend?' he asked jealously.

Why did he have to remind her about that now?

'No, I have no other friend.' Her words sounded hollow – but she knew that there was now a very strong bond between them. Kolgrim, she knew, needed her.

Dag had been listening to the tale of the trolls without interrupting. Now he said thoughtfully, 'Cecilie, you ought to be telling him about Christian ethics instead of …'

'But that is what I am doing, Papa! I merely turn it

upside down. Don't you see how the boy looks at the world? And today of all days he needs a lot of attention.'

'Yes, we do understand, of course we do.'

'Will witches come too?' wondered Kolgrim.

'Yes! Lots of them – and nymphs and goblins and elves and sprites and pixies …'

'Wizards?'

'Hundreds of them!'

Kolgrim gave a rapturous sigh.

'Now come on, we're going out for a walk! We'll go down to Aunt Meta at Linden Allée. Perhaps she has finished all her Yuletide baking and we can sneak into the kitchen and steal a cake when she's not looking?'

'Yeees!' the boy yelled.

Dag shook his head dejectedly. This was not how he would have wanted it, but as he had never seen Kolgrim so happy before, he decided to ignore Cecilie's lunatic ways of educating the child.

As they left the room he muttered: 'And just how are you going to arrange the Trolls' Great Feast?'

'Oh, he'll have grown out of such fantasies by then,' Cecilie replied, smiling. 'Don't worry about that.'

As Cecilie and Kolgrim walked away from Gråstensholm, they heard a loud cry from the upper part of the house. It was Yrja – her labour had just begun. Liv immediately hurried upstairs to begin the task of tending her.

Chapter 11

In an upstairs chamber, the midwife stood, hands on hips, looking down at Yrja with an indecisive expression on her face. The initial labour pains were continuing at infrequent intervals and Yrja looked at the midwife expectantly, waiting for her to speak.

'It is a child of the Ice People,' she said shaking her head in a worried fashion. 'I *dare not* deliver it on my own – I can never forget the last time!'

'Then what are we to do?' asked Liv, looking enquiringly at Dag and Tarald.

'The young master Tarjei is at home, I believe,' said the midwife firmly. 'I would like to have him here with us.'

'But why Tarjei?' asked Tarald hesitantly. 'He is still so young.'

'Because Master Tengel had such faith in him,' replied the woman.

There was some discussion and a few objections, but they could see the midwife's mind was made up. Eventually they agreed to fetch Tarjei, who by this time was eighteen years old.

When he arrived, he smiled reassuringly at Yrja. An

open-faced young man of medium build, he had distinctive, unusual features and such piercing eyes that those subjected to his inquiring gaze often could not help but scrutinise their consciences. He had done well at university, as they all knew, and over the years had improved his knowledge and practice of medicine, both in college and privately. He was Tengel's worthy heir, but more enlightened and more polished than his grandfather.

During the discussion that preceded his arrival, Yrja had been unable to make up her mind about whether or not she liked the idea of a man as a midwife. She knew Tarjei, of course and had watched him grow up. They had worked together beside Tengel during the plague outbreak and they had both likewise been present at Kolgrim's birth. But since then he had been gone for so long, in a faraway place she knew nothing about, called Württemberg, in a land called Germany. He had returned from there as something of a stranger to her; worldly, confident and intelligent, he seemed so much older and wiser that she was – and to think she used to help Meta swaddle him and change him.

During the latter stages of her pregnancy, Yrja had prayed a lot. In fact she prayed daily to God for help, to grant her strength and to take pity on her. She had seen Kolgrim come into the world so brutally and bloodily – and rob Sunniva of her life. Yet she had still chosen this path and longed to have Tarald's child. But perhaps up to this point she had not fully understood the risks. Only now was it becoming a real prospect that she too might soon suffer the same terrible fate that befell Sunniva. Even Master Tengel had been unable to save Sunniva, she reflected, so how might young Tarjei be able to help her, if misfortune should strike again?

She had spent many nights lying awake in a cold sweat while Tarald slept beside her, but her most fervent prayers had not been for herself. 'Almighty God,' she had whispered repeatedly into the darkness, 'please show pity on us! Let me give Tarald a child that does not bring sorrow with it into the world.'

She knew the time had almost come, but her body felt very weak, seemingly unwilling to make the effort. Her mind also felt woolly, as if it refused to accept what was happening. She did not realise that her reactions were the result of the anxiety and fear that she would not admit, even to herself. 'And this is my fateful hour,' she thought to herself melodramatically. 'I am Yrja, always the unfortunate one …' In truth, she had almost given up the fight before it had begun.

After examining her and doing his best to reassure her that all would be well, Tarjei left her in the company of the midwife and joined the others downstairs in the great hall. Looking very serious, he told them the early labour pains were deceptive and would very likely cease and start again later. The birth, he warned them, might take some time. It was because Yrja was so deformed internally from rickets, he explained. But there was reason to hope that all would be well.

* * * *

And take time it did. There were no normal Yuletide festivities at Gråstensholm that year. Instead every precaution was taken to protect against trolls, magic and other dangers that were believed to be particularly active during Yule. As

219

enlightened as the Ice People and the Meiden family were, even they could not escape the deep-rooted superstitions and prejudices of their national culture.

Liv sat faithfully the whole time at Yrja's bedside, chatting encouragingly to her, while other members of the family were out marking crosses wherever they thought some unseen horror might be lurking and trying to gain entrance. For her part, Yrja just lay in her bed, thinking that this would be her first and last opportunity to have a child. Not only would Tarald be unable to father another since he had suffered ill effects from the mumps – something that she was grateful for – but she felt she could tell from the expression on Tarjei's face that her misshapen body would not be able to carry another child. It would be now or not at all.

Kolgrim was allowed to spend the time at Linden Allée and Cecilie stayed there with him. He seemed overjoyed and would spend a long time looking at the portrait of his grandmother Sol, 'the beautiful witch', as he called her. He was also intrigued by the stained-glass mosaic window that Benedikt the Painter had given to Silje long ago. Kolgrim jumped repeatedly up and down on the coloured patterns it made on the floor, as the sun streamed through, explaining to anybody who asked that he did it 'to kill them'. He tormented Trond and Brand ceaselessly, driving them to distraction by attacking them from the most unlikely hiding places.

Kolgrim seemed to be the only member of the family not affected by the excitement and concern for Yrja. All the preparations for Yule were thrown into chaos. While everybody fretted and waited anxiously for news of the birth, servants were unable to perform their duties, mealtimes were missed and Tarald more than anybody was in a perpetual state of nerves. Once or twice he went outside to walk distractedly around the farm when the tension became too much for him. But he had matured greatly since the last time. He stayed to give Yrja support for as long as he could manage, and he tried to share her pain. He was determined not to disappoint her by his cowardliness and during that Yuletide he gained strength of spirit and grew in stature in everybody's eyes.

Then early on the morning of Yuletide Day, Tarjei descended into the great hall of Gråstensholm and quietly approached Dag, who was nodding, half asleep, in one of the big chairs. He touched him lightly on the shoulder, so as not to shock him into wakefulness.

'Congratulations, Uncle Dag!' he said softly. 'You are a grandfather yet again!'

Dag was taken completely by surprise, as there had been no sounds or commotion from the rooms upstairs.

'What? Is everything all right?'

'Yes, all went very well in the end.'

Dag gasped in relief, 'What is it? A boy or a girl?'

'Yrja has given birth to a fine boy.'

'Another grandson? May I go to her?'

'Please do. But don't stay too long. Yrja is very tired.'

'I can well believe that! But when she has had such a difficult time, she really should not have more children, should she? But that's not something we can easily avoid, of course.'

'She can have no more, so that's not a concern any longer. Tarald was badly affected in his life-giving glands last summer.'

Dag gave him an appraising look. 'You know a lot, young Tarjei,' he said appreciatively, and the young man with the unusual face smiled steadily back at him.

When Dag crept in to see Yrja, he found her room was a place of breathless, joyful silence. All the human figures in the chamber were still and at rest; the true peace of Yuletide Morning seemed to have become tangible.

Yrja lay exhausted on the bed, her face swollen and bright red, with tangles of sweat-drenched hair spread across the pillow. She was not beautiful by any means, but Tarald was beside her, occasionally wiping the sweat from her brow and watching her with the deepest expression of love that Dag had ever seen. As he looked at his son and daughter-in-law, a lump formed in his throat and he felt his eyes dampen with relief and happiness.

The exhausted midwife gave him a tired, blissful smile and pointed to the other end of the room, where Liv stood bending over the cradle. His wife immediately waved him over to her, her eyes shining. On reaching her side, Dag leaned forward, holding his breath, to look into the crib.

The tiny fellow lying there was quiet and still. He had a soft, gentle face and dark copper-coloured hair. A contented smile seemed to play about his lips and his eyes were closed. The face of a newborn child is generally shrivelled and blotched in protest at being thrust so abruptly into the light and this often makes it hard to distinguish its features. That was not the case with this child. He had emerged into the world, it seemed, looking composed, peaceful and at ease.

Seeing this caused the emotional lump in Dag's throat to grow even larger and he now felt warm salty tears coursing down his cheeks. Not until that moment, when it finally lifted, had he fully realised the extent of the deep anxiety with which they had all been living. Unnoticed, he drew a weary hand across his face and wiped away the tears of joy and relief, before turning back towards Tarald and Yrja.

'What name shall the boy have? "Thistledown" perhaps?'

Tarald grinned happily at his father. 'He shall of course be called Dag! But Yrja has asked that he shall have her father's name as well – because this will be our only child, you see. Her father has told her it's his dream to know that a baron will bear his name, if it turned out to be a boy.'

'Quite understandable,' smiled Dag. 'What is your father's name, Yrja?'

'Mattias,' she whispered, her voice almost failing her.

'Mattias, of course!' exclaimed Dag. 'A very lovely name. May I perhaps suggest that we use that in everyday address? It's always so awkward saying "the elder" and "the younger" all the time. We must have him baptised as quickly as we can!'

There was no need for anyone to ask why he was in such haste. They all knew that sorcery hovered close around the baby's cradle – most intensely in the form of his own half-brother.

Liv was standing staring intently down at her new grandson, unaware that her fists were so tightly clenched that her arms were shaking. Inside her mind she was praying silently, repeating the same words over and over again: 'Dear God, do not let me be unfair! Help me, Lord, to look upon them both without prejudice!'

Similar thoughts were also starting to stir in Yrja's exhausted consciousness. 'Thank you! Thank you! Thank you, Almighty God,' she was saying inwardly over and over again. 'Thank you for allowing me to bring this small miracle into the world. What will You ask of me, Lord, since You chose me, your wretched handmaiden, to do this thing? Do not misunderstand me Father, for I do not believe I have found favour, or that there is some mystery about a Yuletide birth or dreams of a Messiah – I mean nothing like that. But are you trying to tell me something – to test me? Am I humble enough in Your sight – not too arrogant? I realise this is a great gift you have given me and I am overjoyed to be able to present my beloved with this little son. Yet there is one more thing I would beg of You – grant me strength, Lord and Father! You know that I shall need it. Yes, this is a test of faith, I can feel it. Then please help me, Dear God, to endure.'

Much of what his wife was thinking was passing through Tarald's mind as well. It was difficult to separate the time of the baby's arrival from the apparent blessing of its safe and joyful birth and he could not stop looking at the baby lying in the cradle.

'A lot of children are born on Yuletide Night,' he said looking around the room in a way that was almost a challenge, 'every year, all over the world – and our son Mattias was born in the morning.'

'Dear me,' said Dag, 'we are not reading anything into it at all!'

'There is no need,' Tarjei told them sombrely. 'There are no grounds for doing so. Yrja has gone far beyond her term. She was not fertile at the Feast of the Annunciation – far from it! For that reason alone, it is by pure chance that the child has been born during Yule.'

'I don't think this is the time to make any presumptuous associations,' said Liv softly. 'What is most remarkable is the look on the little mite's face. What does the Bible say about Our Lord Jesus Christ? That he was meek and mild and good? *That*, I believe, is what will remain in all our minds.'

The others agreed, nodding gravely. No, this was not remotely a likeness of the infant Jesus, by any stretch of the imagination. But indisputably, the newborn baby had already brought an unforgettable glow of warmth and brightness into the world of those who had often experienced much hardship and despair. And one other thought also joined them all: 'If only Silje, Tengel and Charlotte could have seen him – and known him!'

As Yrja began to recover from the worst effects of the birth trauma, she continued to reflect on how precious a treasure she had been given. As a natural reaction, she became very afraid. Like every mother the world over, before or since, she would lie awake in the night and listen for his breathing, almost dying from panic whenever she thought it had stopped. Such is the spectre that haunts all new mothers everywhere.

* * * *

Little Mattias was carried to baptism by his grandmother Liv, one cold day in January. An exceedingly proud grandfather, the crofter from Eikeby, stood among the congregation, surrounded by his many relatives, to hear a baron being named after him. Traditionally Cecilie would have carried the infant, but they decided not to risk an upheaval in the church by making Kolgrim jealous of his new little brother. However, when as godparents, Cecilie and Yrja's eldest brother took their places in the chancel beside Liv, no one could or would prevent Kolgrim from standing close to her, sailing his hand like a boat in the holy water of the font.

Cecilie studied Father Martinius as he read the service of baptism. She had, quite naturally, been watching him throughout the service – that is what a congregation does with its priest. But beyond the formalities, she realised quite quickly that she liked what she saw. The pastor was a handsome young man with sorrowful eyes. His voice was soft and refined, and he reminded her vaguely of somebody. It was not until she had returned home that she realised how like Alexander Paladin he was – and this realisation shocked her. If there was one person she wanted to forget, it was Alexander.

Cecilie could not understand the strange feeling of foreboding she sensed in the young priest. It seemed to her that he might be struggling with private dilemmas. But were they religious by nature? Was he suffering agonising doubts with his faith? No, she thought not – he seemed to be well ensconced with Our Lord. Finding she was becoming preoccupied with her thoughts about him, Cecilie became angry with herself. Why, she wondered, must I always find men with emotional problems?

Many times during his sermon Martinius glanced up and found Cecilie looking at him. Before long he had unwittingly begun to return her gaze. She must be Tarald's little sister, he thought, the one who had left for Copenhagen shortly before he arrived here. For some reason her presence had made this service different to others. How else could he explain this slight feeling of elation, this joyous spirit, he wondered.

He cast a swift glance across to his wife. She sat in her customary place, watching him closely. Her frown was a warning to him. Yes, perhaps he had been speaking a little too freely today, and Julie was such a God-fearing soul. He must pull himself together.

Almost against his will, his eyes sought out Cecilie again – and once more he felt the jumbled emotions of tranquillity and excitement. Cecilie Meiden, he had to admit, was not half the beauty that Julie was, but what charisma, what grace and charm she possessed! During the baptism, by chance they stood very close to each other, almost touching. His hands began to shake, so that he almost dropped his prayer book and the words on the page seemed to dance before his eyes. If the wily young Kolgrim had not pushed between them, Father Martinius would never have been able to finish the ceremony.

Martinius thought Kolgrim's little brother Mattias was unlike any other child he had baptised. He had never before seen such an expression of serenity, of *understanding* – if one could use the word of an infant. He had a trusting gentle smile too and this touched the pastor's heart. How was it, he wondered, that two half-brothers could be so different?

The simple truth, of course, was that baby Mattias had within him all that was good from his ancestors, while his unfortunate brother had inherited all the worst. However, it was fair to say that everyone could also now see that young Kolgrim no longer needed to be ashamed of his appearance – his extraordinary face in fact held a hypnotic attraction – but there was something horribly suggestive about his gleaming eyes. Anyone who gazed into them for too long was liable to find themselves overcome with a feeling of dread that they could not explain.

* * * *

During the weeks following the baptism, Cecilie was a great help to Liv and Yrja. To lighten their load, she would often take Kolgrim with her when she visited Linden Allée. She went mostly to see Tarjei, because they shared so much in common and would talk together for hours at a time.

Life at Linden Allée, she discovered, continued in its usual quiet way as it had always done. Meta did her own chores, scoured and cleaned and prepared food, unlike Silje who had always been happy to leave that to the housemaids and servants. As before, Are worked conscientiously in the forests, fields and outhouses; coming home dirty, worn and taciturn at mealtimes. Brand, an identical though smaller version of his father, and Trond, who chatted incessantly, followed him everywhere. Trond was keen to improve the way Linden Allée was farmed, but because Are considered he had been doing exactly that all his life, he didn't take kindly to the idea of anyone saying they could improve on his work. It wasn't possible to make any more improvements, or so he thought, and all Trond's suggestions fell on deaf ears.

Tarjei often felt sorry for Trond. He had so much energy and great powers of leadership, but precious few opportunities to develop his talents at Linden Allée. Tarjei had discussed this with his brother and Trond agreed. He too wanted to get away, but not to study as Tarjei had. He wanted to be a professional soldier, but Are wouldn't let him go because he was needed on the farm.

'It will all work out, you'll see,' said Tarjei, patting Trond comfortingly on the shoulder. 'A leader will always come to the fore – and you are still young.'

Trond nodded gratefully. It didn't occur to either of them that that there were only a couple of years between them – Tarjei had always seemed much older than his brothers.

* * * *

One day when Cecilie and Tarjei were sitting at Linden Allée, discussing the relative merits of Tübingen and Copenhagen – while also keeping a wary eye on what Kolgrim was doing – they unexpectedly heard the voice of Father Martinius in the hallway. On going out to see what was happening, they found the pastor speaking to Are and Meta. The conversation appeared to be about a collection or some kind of plan to help a family of children that had just lost both their parents.

'Whatever next?' muttered Tarjei under his breath. 'Has he come on his own? It's usually that energetic little doll with the cold stare that arranges this sort of thing.'

'His wife, do you mean?' asked Cecilie.

'Yes.'

'Does she have a cold stare, then?'

'Oh, yes! She's adored throughout the parish. But I can't stand her.'

'Neither can I.'

'Then you've met her?'

'No, not outside a church service.'

When he caught sight of them, the pastor looked a little taken aback. But he nevertheless greeted them very formally, and thanked them again for their contribution to the baptism service.

'What?' asked Cecilie with a smile. 'When my darling forest troll of a nephew splashed around in the holy water, do you mean? It was certainly a lively baptism, I must say. Indeed, it was the most delightful one I've ever attended. Have you been up to Gråstensholm yet?'

'No, I was about to make my way there now.'

'What luck,' said Tarjei at once. 'You'll have company. Cecilie and her bandit were just leaving.'

Cecilie could happily have kicked Tarjei's shins, but with a broad smile she turned to Martinius. 'Unless you are offered a bite to eat here, of course! Are you one of those hungry priests who always call at mealtimes, expecting to be fed?'

'Cecilie!' spluttered Are, shocked and at a loss for words. 'What are you saying?'

In his turn, Tarjei just grinned and the priest also smiled. 'I sincerely hope I'm not one of that kind.'

'No, I can see your legs are well sculptured,' said Cecilie. 'Now give him some money, Uncle Are, and don't keep such a tight grip on your purse! Then we can be gone.'

She was inwardly furious with Tarjei for suggesting she walk home with Martinius, perhaps illogically because she did want to do precisely that. As soon as she had heard his voice in the hall, she had become aware of a vague feeling that she wished to speak further with him.

'You have to forgive her,' laughed Are. 'It's the way she is. She and my son are the two geniuses in the family. That's something they never let us mere mortals forget.'

With Kolgrim rushing around them like an angry stallion, they set off towards Gråstensholm at a brisk pace. The air was cold and clear, and their breath formed clouds of frosty mist around them as they walked. A thin layer of new snow had covered the frozen ground, giving a crisp sound to their footsteps.

'You walk at such a pace,' laughed Cecilie, puffing exaggeratedly. 'Is it my company that disturbs you, Father Martinius?'

She knows my name, he thought excitedly. She knows my name and she speaks it so beguilingly – like nobody else has ever done. Flustered, he stopped and waited for her to catch up.

'No, of course not – your presence doesn't disturb me at all,' he said haltingly. 'It was only …'

He broke off, but Cecilie had already noticed him glancing quickly down the hillside towards the rectory.

'Are you more concerned that your wife might catch sight of you? If she can see you at this distance, then she must have an exceptionally good pair of eyes. Besides, you are with me – and I am no danger!'

'No, of course not! No, I mean …'

'Does she watch your every move?' Cecilie teased him.

'Mistress Cecilie, you must not make a fool of me! My wife is a very fine woman.'

'Indeed,' said Cecilie sombrely. 'Very God-fearing, or so I have heard.'

'Yes.'

'And virtuous.'

'Very.'

'And pretty.'

'As an angel.'

'That does sound incredibly fine! But the good in a person does not always balance out the bad. How are you enjoying this parish?'

'Very much. Yes, very much. I expect you know that Yrja and Tengel and I worked together during the terrible blood pestilence. I felt that made us friends for life.'

'That was just after I left for Copenhagen …' breaking off abruptly, she turned and shouted loudly at her nephew. 'Come down from that tree at once, Kolgrim! I can see you!' She turned apologetically back to Martinius. 'Yes, Grandmama Charlotte and Grandpapa Jacob died at that time. It hurt me so much that I could not be here with them.'

He was astonished. How quickly her mood changes from merriment to solemnity, he thought. It showed him how comfortable she was with her emotions. Then, unbidden, his thoughts turned to his wife. In that instant it was as if the sun had gone behind a dark cloud and he began to ponder what might have been. What if Mistress Cecilie had not travelled to Copenhagen just before he arrived in the parish? What if she too, had helped them to battle against the plague? She would certainly have had the courage, of that he was certain. And how very different, then, his life might have been! Now, however, it seemed as if it was all too late.

* * * *

While he was still at Linden Allée, Tarjei was asked to attend a local crofter who had been stabbed during a drunken brawl; something that occurred all too frequently in those parts. Cecilie offered to go with him and help, and Tarjei was glad to have her company.

The crofter, they found, had already been carried back to his home and, as he busied himself with his task, Tarjei took little notice of the barren and sparsely furnished cottage or the number of small children standing around their father's bed, looking on in horror. He had scant interest in such things, whereas Cecilie saw at once that they must also get help for the family. The sad fact was that it was not very different from almost every other home in the region.

But neither could they let this man die. If he died it would be a catastrophe for his young wife and family. After inspecting the wounds, Tarjei stepped over to one of the men who had brought him home.

'Go and fetch the priest,' he told him quietly, 'just in case he is required.'

The man nodded and left. Cecilie had heard what Tarjei had said and it made her shiver. This was partly because it sounded so ominous for the crofter and partly for other reasons that were only half-formed in her mind and too complicated to explain, even to herself.

The man had been stabbed in the lower part of the stomach and, when Tarjei exposed the wound, Cecilie felt the floor begin to rise and fall dizzyingly beneath her feet. What had she got herself into now?

Thoughtless and over-confident, she had tried to impress Tarjei. 'Let me come and help!' she had insisted. Oh dear, how wrong she had been! If only she could be back at Gråstensholm now, discussing how to bring up children with her dear little Yrja. She really regretted her rashness – and would have regretted it even more if she had been able to see then what disastrous consequences her misguided instinct to play the Good Samaritan were to have for poor Yrja herself.

Through this tumult of thoughts, she realised that Tarjei was speaking to her and she was reminded suddenly of just why she had come.

'Wipe away the blood, Cecilie,' he commanded. 'Now, please!'

He had been holding a cloth out to her, but it fell from her open hand. She swallowed hard, picked it up and tried to soak up the blood, while keeping her eyes tightly closed – but it didn't work.

'Hurry up!'

Tarjei was growing impatient. He could not understand why anyone should feel unwell by just looking inside the flesh of another human body. He glanced up towards the dark rafters of the cottage. The tiny opening in the roof let no light into the room and he gave an irritable sigh.

'No, this is no good; it's too dark and dirty here. We have to get him to Tengel's infirmary. Do you have a sleigh?'

'Only a sled,' replied the man's terrified wife.

'Then bring it – quickly!'

Almost everyone left the room, obviously relieved to have something else to do. A few moments later Father Martinius arrived, but there was no time for his prayers. So Tarjei asked him to helped them load the unfortunate man onto the sled. It was no more than two wooden shafts tied with cross pieces and hung on straps from the horse's harness, so that the ends dragged along the ground. The men who had brought the crofter home helped by leading the horse, whilst Tarjei, Cecile and the priest took care of the wounded man. His wife and children stayed behind in the cottage, because Tarjei told them it was for the best.

The wife's white face stared after them and she called to Tarjei, 'Is he going to ...' and she waved awkwardly at the wretched creature on the sled.

'We shall do all we can to help him survive. But there will be no more children in this house.'

'Oh, thank God,' she sighed, leaving her listeners to decide whether the sigh was one of relief that her husband was still alive or for other reasons.

A sled was obviously not the best way of transporting such a badly wounded man. The path from the smallholding was so strewn with tree stumps and roots that the sled could only be coaxed over and around them with great difficulty. It took all their efforts to keep it from turning over as it bumped through the woods over the hard frozen ground. When at last they drew up at the steps of Linden Allée, Cecilie's back felt as though it had been bent forward for about a hundred years. She straightened her aching spine, piece by piece, moaning loudly as she did so.

Once they had carried him inside, it proved a hard struggle to save the man's life, but most importantly there was enough light to work by in Tengel's infirmary and Tarjei had everything he needed close at hand. He had worked there many times and so felt at ease. Cecilie, however, had no experience of nursing the sick and several times had to fight off an inclination to faint from the sight of it all.

Martinius helped to hold the man still; he had decided effectively to leave his priestly orders at home on this occasion – it was the man's life he was helping to save, not his soul. At first the poor crofter had screamed unceasingly with pain; but after a while he fell quiet. He had lost consciousness – so what good would it do to ask him now if he was prepared to face his maker?

Tarjei also found it far easier to work on the man when he was unconscious. Watching her cousin, Cecilie was very impressed by his skill. She might have been watching her grandfather, Tengel, at his best. Although Tarjei's skills might have been more up to date, and he had greater knowledge as a result of his studies at the university in Tübingen, he was perhaps not as considerate and respectful as Tengel had been.

Cecilie tried not to think how many times her hands had brushed accidentally against the pastor's during the course of their frantic work on the man. But she was very aware of his presence and could not deny that his closeness excited her. He was a very perceptive man, as was the unfortunate Alexander – but she knew instinctively that, unlike Alexander, the priest was a man in every way. These fleeting feelings were also helping Cecilie to realise how starved she had been of what in polite circles was called romance.

Eventually the patient's wounds were all sewn up and he

had at last stopped bleeding. Heaving sighs of relief, they all stood and stretched.

'Thank you for all the help,' Tarjei said to them both. 'Cecilie, I am surprised. You performed splendidly. You seem to have been born to this.'

'Oh, really!' she spluttered, her voice completely incredulous. 'I often feared I would faint away.'

'Now he needs someone to sit with him,' Tarjei continued. 'I have promised Father I will see to the pigs. I have let him down so often of late, I don't suppose …'

Cecilie swallowed and put on a brave face. 'You go! I can stay with him for a while.'

'And so can I,' said the pastor. 'This poor man will need prayers said for him now.'

Cecilie gave a shudder at the thought of how serious his injuries were.

'Excellent,' said Tarjei quite relieved. 'A couple of hours, then?'

They both nodded, but Martinius became very uncomfortable after Tarjei had left the room. It was clear that he felt his offer to remain with Cecilie had been made a little too hastily. Cecilie could not conceal that she also shared his unease. There was not much to sit on in the infirmary apart from a wide couch-like wooden bench covered with a sheepskin. When they sat down awkwardly on it together, both were evidently filled with the same sense of trepidation.

They were unable to sit comfortably with their feet on the floor, because the bench was too wide. It had probably been made as a cot for patients who needed to stay at Linden Allée for some time. So they slid across it and rested their backs against the wall. The silence that ensued in the room was almost unbearably painful.

'He is very clever, young Tarjei,' said the pastor at last, struggling to find words to cover their discomfiture.

'Oh, yes,' replied Cecilie at once, grateful that the slow torture of the silence was over. 'And he has started very young. He has hardly grown up even now.'

'It is a pity we shall not be able to keep him here in our parish. It will seem empty when you both leave us again.'

'But everything is going so well here, Father Martinius. No! I refuse to call you Father Martinius any longer! What was your name before – Martin?'

'Yes.'

'May I call you that?'

He hesitated for a while. 'With pleasure – when no one else can hear.'

Cecilie gave a crooked smile – she had regained her confidence at last.

'I see – is the watchdog looking over your shoulder again?'

'Mistress Cecilie, I beg you …'

'Just Cecilie, please. You are a good friend of the family.'

'Thank you, but Cecilie, I beg you, do not deride Julie! She is so pure and beyond reproach. She towers above me, sinful wretch that I am.'

'Has she said that herself?'

'Oh, please!'

The pastor made a moaning sound and buried his face in his hands. Cecilie sat silent and unmoving beside him for a while. Then she reached out and gently tried to ease one of his hands free. But he refused to move them from his face.

'Martin, I've known for a time that all is not well with you,' she said softly. 'My brother Tarald and Yrja also know. Why don't you tell me what's wrong? You see – I too am in distress. I recently had an unnerving experience, which I must come to terms with. People are not always as they seem to be.'

The sound of her voice weakened his resistance and he let his hands fall into his lap. She could tell from the expression of self-reproach on his agonised face that he was about to reveal his feelings.

'So our pastor's wife is a creature of utter perfection,' she said gently, trying to spur him to speak. 'Everybody says so.'

'Yes,' he replied bitterly. 'Everybody says so – and indeed she is! It is only that I am so weak and unworthy.'

'I can't believe that's true,' she said tenderly. 'It is possible she is perfect for the parish – but not perfect for you.'

Martin leaned his head back against the wall and closed his eyes, as though wishing he could fall asleep. The injured man still lay unconscious on the treatment bench, but the colour of his face and his breathing had not changed in any way since Tarjei had left.

'It is wrong to put it like that,' he said wearily. 'The fault lies with me and my carnal, sinful lust.'

'No, Heaven help me!' she exclaimed, quite shocked. 'What sort of talk is that? It sounds like something your wife would say – although I have never spoken to her. I've hardly even met her.'

Suddenly, to her astonishment, she saw two large tears squeeze out of the pastor's closed eyes and run down his cheeks.

'Cecilie, I can stand it no longer!' he gasped. 'I married my childhood's dream princess, a little angel. So virtuous, so God-fearing, so beautiful! And that is exactly what she was, Cecilie! Compared to her I am a clumsy ignorant elephant!'

'I think you are trying to say something entirely different, Martin,' she said after a moment's thought. 'Although you hardly dare admit it, you are telling yourself that she is virtuous, God-fearing and beautiful – and nothing more!'

He recoiled visibly at her words, as if he felt the sting of their truth, and opened his eyes to look directly at her. 'If only you were not so clear-sighted, Cecilie! You see right through my useless soul and lay it bare in front of me!'

'Sometimes that can be a healthy thing to do. I do not know where all your problems lie, Martin. But I believe you have got things round the wrong way. All my family, including myself, know you as a good, straightforward, spiritual and charitable man of God. There may well be a reason that you are vexing yourself over your wife's highly eminent attributes; it seems to me that she might be over-ambitious.'

'Oh, she is!' he said avidly, his strict sense of loyalty suddenly forgotten. 'Her ambitions are beyond belief! She wishes to be the perfect pastor's wife – she is to be the best and most lauded in all the parishes around. Nobody shall have cause to criticise or challenge her. It is her desire to be the unapproachable saint, while she makes me feel like a worthless insect! In her eyes, all things physical are sinful. We are man and wife, Cecilie, and I may not touch her!'

'What? No, are you mad? Martin, how can you sit here and take the guilt upon yourself? God alone knows how she has been brought up – or whether she has decided this on her own. But it is a very distorted picture of Christianity!'

All at once the floodgates of his pent-up emotions opened and his words gushed out in a verbal tidal wave.

'She says it is dirty, nasty and shocking that I can even

think such thoughts. I must wash out my mouth if I happen to mention that we have a body below the navel. It is almost all she can do to admit that we have legs to walk with. We should be pillars of saintliness, she says. If the saints can refrain from everything then so can we.'

'That's not hard for her to do, if she has no desire,' murmured Cecilie.

'She says that this is the only true Christianity – to deny the flesh utterly and devote oneself completely to good.'

'Then why did she marry you – to climb further up the ladder? Does a priest's wife have greater standing than a priest's daughter?'

Although Martin heard what she said, he was so eager to rid himself of all the misery stored up inside for so long, that he ignored her question and carried on talking.

'You should have witnessed our wedding night, Cecilie! It was the most grotesque experience I have ever known. When I went to her room in good faith, properly and handsomely attired, she stared at me as though I was an outlaw ruffian and gave a piercing scream. When I tried to propose that now we were wed we should, well, be together, she just screamed terrible things at me ...'

'What did she say?'

'She called me a "debaser of whores"! And then she yelled: "Get you gone, you evil swine!" ... I lost my self-confidence completely, for I knew nothing of women. She had always been the only one for me. As prudently as I could, I tried to say that we should have children. But at that point she said she felt sick. She ran to the window and lent out to ... I went away, hurt and disgusted, understanding nothing. She had been my dream, an unattainable dream for so many years. But when I was a boy and later a curate I was as nothing to her – no more

240

than a puff of wind. If ever I addressed her, she turned away and conversed with others as though she had not heard me. But then, when I was ordained priest in this parish, she renewed her acquaintance with me and inquired about my prospects for advancement. She thought I could aspire to bishop! When her father said many people had commended me, and that I might have a good future, she accepted me. I was overjoyed! Now my whole world has fallen down around me. She, the most perfect of wives, doted on by everybody ...'

'Not by my family,' interrupted Cecilie. 'They have seen through her. It's in her cold eyes. But we never thought it was *this* bad!'

The pastor suddenly became consumed with guilt. 'Oh, what am I doing, sitting here telling you all this? I am no better, showing such disloyalty to my wife!'

'I would say Martin, that she has forced you to the end of your tether by her behaviour. It must be dreadful to live with one's beloved for so many years and not be allowed even to touch her.'

He sat up straight with a look of surprise. 'You surely do not think I am drawn to her now? I cannot stand her! And for that reason I have become such easy prey to my worldly needs and feelings ...' He stopped and looked at Cecilie, aghast at his own words.

'What were you going to say, Martin?' she asked gently.

'Nothing! Forget I said it!' He drew a long, deep breath. 'You said just now that you were in distress. Please tell me all about it.'

Cecilie suddenly felt awkward and lost for words. 'It is hard to explain,' she said awkwardly. 'I was alone in Copenhagen for a long time and I found a very good friend in whom I placed my trust. Like you, I had been starved of what is poetically known as "the pleasures of the flesh". When I discovered that he felt no attraction at all to womankind, it came as a big shock; in part because I had not known that such people existed – and also because I lost him and I needed him so much.'

'My dear child,' he said in dismay. 'How difficult for you.'

He reached out unthinkingly to place a comforting priestly arm on her shoulder. Then at once he realised his mistake and pulled it away quickly, as if he had been burned by a hot coal or bitten by a cobra. Cecilie looked away, dispirited and he drew his knees to his chest and rested his head pensively against them.

'Why? Why did you go to Copenhagen when you did, Cecilie?' he whispered. 'Why did we not meet then?'

'But that was when Julie was the centre of all your dreams, wasn't it? Would I have meant anything to you then?'

Martin shook his head. 'You are temporal, wise and very attractive, Cecilie. A misguided dream of an angel pales swiftly by comparison. You mean something to me now.'

They both fell silent again for a time, unsure what to say next.

'What am I to do, Cecilie?' he asked at length in a haunted voice. 'My body burns with passion after so many tormented years of rigorous abstinence.'

Cecilie smiled sadly. 'You are not alone in that, Martin. It's perhaps a good thing that I must leave again in a few days. If that was not the case, it would be so easy to fall into your warm embrace.'

'Yes,' he replied in a low voice. 'I feel that too. There are words I wish to say from my heart that at this moment are perhaps best left unsaid. I shall pray to God to keep us apart until you have left.'

'And I likewise.'

A melancholy smile touched his lips for an instant. 'Strangely, Cecilie, it is comforting to know that we share the same heartache.'

At that moment the door opened. Startled, they both sat bolt upright as Tarjei entered to tell them that he would take over the vigil and that they did not need to watch over the injured man any longer. Both Cecilie and the pastor let out audible sighs of relief. With a curt nod to each other for Tarjei's benefit, they wished each other goodnight and quickly went their separate ways.

Cecilie ran home as fast as she could, feeling an unfamiliar spring in her step. It was exciting and wonderful to know that she was so strongly desired by a physically attractive man of worth and quality. What was more, it seemed destined to be an unrequited love and this was having the effect of spicing up the cauldron of strong emotions simmering and bubbling inside her.

Chapter 12

The homecoming that evening of Pastor Martinius was hardly a pleasant one. After stepping through the front door, he heard the customary angry rustle of starched petticoats, as his wife hurried through the house to meet him. The soft honeyed tones of her voice were not matched by her icy inquisitive glare.

'You are late. Our meal is waiting. What was it that took you so long?'

Honest man that he was, Martin answered truthfully. 'To try to save his life, we had to transport the injured man to Linden Allée for treatment.'

For his wife, the very name of Linden Allée was like a red rag to a bull.

'We? Is manual labour now among the duties of a priest?'

'You know it is, Julie. I had to help. Tarjei and Cecilie had enough to do looking after the injured crofter.' Oh, how wonderful it was to speak her name out loud! As he did so, he felt a warm glow deep inside himself.

Despite her husband's honest innocent face, Julie somehow suspected the existence of a rival. She had loathed and despised the families of Linden Allée and Gråstensholm for a long time. Their lack of reverence for the Church and, even more, their lack of respect for the first lady in the parish had always been a thorn in her side. When she spoke, even the usual gentle tone of her honeyed voice had grown cold.

'Cecilie? Do you mean Cecilie Meiden? That shameless slut, who not only brought that freak of a child into the church, but also allowed him to desecrate Our Lord's font? The one who walked with you recently from Linden Allée to the mansion?'

She knew about the recent walk with Cecilie, because each day Martinius dutifully told her everything that happened to him. He felt obliged to do this by his conscience. It was simply his nature to be totally honest.

'Yes, it was she. But you are unfair to her, Julie. She is a fine young woman.'

He could not have chosen his words less well if he had tried. They had moved through by now into the splendid dining-room of the rectory, furnished by Julie with unadorned sobriety. Her pretty arched eyelids were now closed tight and she listened carefully, to be certain that the servants were out of earshot.

'And what was it, pray, that took so much time?'

'We had to sit and watch over the unfortunate man while Tarjei helped his father.'

'Both of you?'

'Yes.'

'On your own?'

'Of course, what is so strange about that?'

Her lips were pressed together in a thin, bloodless line. 'You ... you vile whoremonger!' she hissed. 'You are despicable!'

'Be assured that nothing untoward took place, Julie. Please calm yourself.'

'And you want me to believe that! You, who stood hammering upon my door every night the first week we were wed! It is clear to me that you have still not overcome your licentious cravings! And she – the little trollop ...'

'Hold your tongue, Julie! Nothing happened.'

His tone and turn of phrase aroused her suspicions still further.

'Perhaps not! But you desired it!'

He sank into a chair, hungry and fatigued from the stress of all that had happened with the crofter. It was perhaps this weariness that caused him to be less careful in his choice of words than usual when he replied.

'Julie, if you are determined to believe the worst of me, regardless of the truth, then I might just as well be unfaithful to you.'

'With Mistress Cecilie?'

In a tired voice he answered, 'With anyone at all. May we eat now?'

'No! Not until you have confessed!'

'Please – you know I always speak the truth. It is not in my nature to be unfaithful. But Julie, I am a man, not a saint. You have denied me everything; above all else you have denied me the right to give you my love. I had so much to offer you, Julie, but it seems we did not take vows of marriage – we took vows of chastity instead, without my knowing. I want our marriage dissolved.'

She gasped, 'Are you mad? Do you want to create a scandal? I shall never agree to it!'

'Then I shall leave you.'

Her chin was quivering and she stared at him, wide-eyed with amazement. She had always taken his adoration for

246

granted, assumed without a second thought that he would always do her bidding. Then her expression changed and she sidled closer to him, murmuring in a sweeter tone: 'I will let you come to me this evening, Martin. And you may touch me … but only a little.'

He gazed at her in sudden disgust. In his mind's eye he saw only Cecilie's pure, wholesome face.

'It is too late, Julie,' he said steadily. 'I do not desire you any more. You make me sick with your hypocrisy.'

The scream that escaped her lips was ear-piercing, 'She will regret this!'

Martinius was alarmed. 'Cecilie has nothing to do with it – besides, she is leaving soon.'

He realised that for the first time in his life he had raised his voice to his wife – but the urge to defend Cecilie had been too strong to resist.

'She will still be sorry,' she squealed. 'Everyone in that insolent pack up at the manor will be sorry they ever crossed me!'

Martin looked at her with a mixture of astonishment and horror. The angelic pastor's wife, adored by everyone, had become an evil figure, burning with a lust for revenge.

Exhausted, sad and fearful for the sake of his friends, he said resignedly: 'Oh, what does it matter. I shall remain with you then. Let us say nothing more and forget all this.'

'Forget? Oh no! You have hurt my deepest feelings.'

'Yes, I know – your deepest feelings are your public prestige and your vanity.'

The pastor could not understand where he had suddenly found such courage. Never before had he spoken to her like this. He knew it would have been wiser to show more restraint.

'Forgive the harshness of my words,' he said in a subdued tone. 'I am simply too tired and hungry.'

'Of course, our food will be served directly,' she told him, reverting instantly to her normal sweet voice.

She had achieved a partial victory at least, she told herself as she hastened out of the room. He had seen sound sense and had decided to stay. But as far as she was concerned, this whole thing was a long way from being over. Then she stopped in her tracks and an evil grin spread slowly across the features of her doll-like face. Cecilie would soon be gone, so she could not take revenge on her, but there were others, weren't there? And perhaps the one she loathed and detested most was that wretched, scrubby crofter's girl who had risen to become Baroness. She was nothing more than a hussy and she had been elevated to the nobility! She was now 'worthy of attending Court' – that deformed clumsy oaf! What was her name – Yrja? Yes Yrja, that was it. Perhaps it was time for her good fortune to come to an end? That should be easy enough to arrange.

* * * *

Meanwhile, Tarjei had begun his journey back to Tübingen, leaving behind family and friends at Linden Allée who had greatly enjoyed his Yuletide visit and who now sorely missed his enlivening presence. But on this occasion, his journey proved to be more difficult than usual. To his surprise he found soldiers taking over almost all forms of transport and big troop concentrations blocked some of the roads. There were even some outbreaks of fighting. Europe's kings and emperors were at war again and, as usual, religion lay at the heart of the matter.

When he was halfway through Germany, on the long

road down to Tübingen, his journey came to a sudden and complete halt. All roads leading south, he found, were blocked and he was suddenly unable to find any further means of transport. By this time he was worn out, confused and quite worried. He tried to retrace his steps and return home, but found he was unable to travel back the way he had come. In a kind of limbo, with the storm clouds of war gathering all around him, he felt very cut off from his beloved family and his homeland.

* * * *

On Sunday, the day after she, Tarjei and the pastor had tended the badly injured crofter, Cecilie decided to go church with her parents. She wanted to see Martin once more before she left for Copenhagen. Yrja came too and it was the first time she had been outside the house since giving birth. For most of the time the new Baroness sat motionless beside the others, silently thanking the Lord for His great gift and begging for His help in the future.

Although Tarald and two housemaids were at home looking after the youngsters, she was not really at ease. Kolgrim could move so swiftly when he made up his mind and he was always so unpredictable. Then halfway through the service, she suddenly realised she had miscalculated. The service was taking too long and her milk was leaking, threatening to stain her clothes. This was something she had not foreseen and the thought of two large, damp patches on her chest was not something she relished.

Beginning to panic, she turned and whispered to her mother-in-law. Liv nodded and slid her white shawl across onto Yrja's lap. Yrja pretended to have dropped something on the floor, and as she bent down, she quickly stuffed the shawl under her blouse, pulling it strategically into shape. Although this made her appearance more buxom, she didn't think that another lump or two on her contorted body would make any difference. She squeezed Liv's hand in gratitude and smiled back.

Cecilie, who had been watching Yrja's activities with amused fascination, did not really grasp what was happening – but she could not fail to see the bond of understanding between the two women. Watching them, she realised just how much deep affection she felt for them both.

Father Martinius had noticed Cecilie as soon as she entered the church. She ought not to have come, he told himself frantically. I have lain awake all night thinking about her. I think I am in love with her. At the very least I know that I desire her – but it is far more than lust alone: I know that we could have been happy together. Yes, I love her – I do – I am sure of it. And that is something that cannot be. I am a married man and a priest. And yet what good would pangs of conscience do? His heart was racing, mad and out of control. He was unable to concentrate and found it hard to deliver his sermon.

Meanwhile, Cecilie had discarded any illusions she might have had that they could have been happily married. She did not share his passion for religion and would never have been a success as the wife of a priest! No, it was Martin, the man himself, who interested her.

She watched him quite candidly during the routines of the service, as would any member of his congregation who was listening attentively. Very little of the wondrous message of the Lord, however, reached her ears. Cecilie instead was thinking how much he was like Alexander –

and each time she thought of Alexander she relived her pain, her turmoil and her sadness. Until now, she had not fully realised the depth of the affection she had harboured for the mystifying aristocrat who had always been so elusive and hard to understand. It was impossible to say for sure what made him and Martin so similar.

Alexander obviously was the more distinguished-looking of the two; he was after all a nobleman. But there was something elusive in the smile and the gaze of each man that echoed the other. Yes, that was it! Every time he smiled there was a touch of sadness in Martin's eyes, and she had noticed the same hint of bitterness and melancholy in Alexander's expression. And of course she knew that each of them had his own cross to bear.

With only a slight turn of her head, she could easily see Martin's 'cross'. Liv had pointed out his wife, the sweet Julie, to her earlier. There was no question; she was certainly very pretty. She had chosen her seat carefully, so that she could easily keep a watchful eye on both the congregation and her husband. Oh, how delightful she looked – blond corkscrew curls beneath a bonnet that set off her heart-shaped face with its big eyes and pert little mouth. Too little and too pert – it would soon become puckered and wrinkled with age, thought Cecilie, who reserved her nasty streak for people she particularly disliked – and she particularly disliked Julie a great deal.

She had cold eyes, Tarjei had said, but as far as Cecilie could see, Julie's gaze was placid enough as she casually surveyed the congregation – then, when her eyes fell upon her husband, they narrowed sharply, glaring at him in undisguised condemnation. As she did this, he stumbled, not for the first time, over the words in his text.

A split second later, his wife's eyes alighted on Cecilie. She could see that they were a pale icy blue and very unforgiving – and the expression in them was unmistakeable.

'She knows!' thought Cecilie, shocked at the realisation. She knows that Martin and I have spoken to one another – that each enjoys the company of the other – but she also obviously suspects there is more. So she has a dirty mind as well, the sanctimonious little trollop, thought Cecilie, beaming innocently back at Julie with such doe-eyed affability that it must have made the woman mad.

In her turn, Julie too was also occupying her mind with less than charitable reflections about Cecilie. So that's her – the immoral slut who is out to steal my husband, she was thinking. But what in Heaven's name does Martin see in her? She is not at all beautiful, and cannot begin to compare with me! Dark auburn hair – that in itself is a sign of sinfulness – and insolent eyes. Oh, yes, they are definitely insolent, no matter that she tries to look so innocent. I know that, well enough! I know that she wants to take my husband from me, make herself the first lady of the parish and lead him into the ways of sin. But she won't have the opportunity to do that before she leaves – such a pity that I shall not have time to take my revenge on her!

But there would be revenge – on the other one sitting in the same pew, who was a different matter. No, not Mistress Liv – she would not tangle with her, she was too powerful. These were not Julie's conscious thoughts. These were subconscious impulses buried deep in the inner reaches of her soul. Had she known Liv better, she would have been aware of just how vulnerable she really was – that she was perhaps the most fragile of them all. But Julie rarely looked at anything in depth.

No, it was the other one she would target – the awful ungainly young mistress. What right had she to be at

Gråstensholm? That was something Julie had never understood. Here was a useless, wretched crofter's daughter rivalling the position in society of a pastor's wife – how galling!

When the service was over, the congregation filed slowly towards the door. Julie had taken her up her customary place at the entrance to say a few words to members of the flock as they left and her husband stood opposite her, out of earshot.

'Good-day, dear Alvilde, and how is your youngest? Such wonderful news! Aah, Peder, did the catskin do any good? Oh, look! It's little Merete – the youngest? Oh, how he's grown!'

There they were – the Meiden family. They were last to leave, because their pew was at the front. Julie had no time for hugging and kissing small children now. As the Meidens approached, she extended her tiny, soft hand – a hand that lacked firmness. It would have been so easy to crush it with just a little more pressure, but Liv shook it gently as they exchanged a few banal but friendly words.

'And this is Mistress Cecilie, I expect?' said Julie, turning to her, while at the same time preparing to greet Yrja. Martin glanced quickly over at them with fear on his face, but he was locked in conversation.

'Yes,' said Cecilie, opening hostilities with a blank stare. 'I don't believe I've had the pleasure …'

'I am the wife of the pastor of this parish,' announced Julie, furious that anyone would be unaware of her and her position in society. 'One may not be big in stature, but one does the best one can,' she concluded with a self-satisfied smile.

'Ah, of course, I remember now. Martin has mentioned you,' cooed Cecilie, with a cat-like spitefulness.

Mentioned? *Mentioned?* How dare she be so blatantly

offensive? 'I believe you mean Father Martinius,' said Julie admonishing her with a frosty glare. 'And here we have the little Eikeby girl, if I'm not mistaken? Are you the one they call "Thistle"? Such a strange name!'

'Baroness Yrja is my sister-in-law,' said Cecilie reprovingly. 'We are overjoyed and privileged to have her as part of our family. We played together as children, she and I. Oh, and by the way, the thistle is a very strong and hardy plant – it is an honour to be named after it!'

Julie glowered back – no longer able to keep up any pretence. Her voice remained soft and gracious, but now her words became vitriolic. 'Yes, I believe the Meidens have always been very close to the people, both in their choice of friends and of spouses.'

'Indeed, how true that is!' said Cecilie, sounding grateful and eager to confide in her. 'And that is our great strength.'

'By joining the lower castes? Do not the Danish nobility have a thing or two to say about that?'

'We live in Norway and count ourselves as Norwegians. Furthermore, the Norwegian nobility does as it chooses, since all our privileges were long since taken from us.'

She has an answer for everything, thought Julie. Then becoming more determined, she took deliberate aim below the belt. 'But that can have unpleasant consequences for the offspring, can't it?'

'Bitch!' thought Cecilie. She would defend Kolgrim with every fibre of her being.

'We haven't seen any signs of that so far,' she replied easily. 'On the contrary, it can sometimes be a very healthy thing to introduce new, vigorous blood to the line. I believe that you have not yet seen Mattias, Yrja's baby son – the most beautiful child born in these parts. But tell me – do you have any children of your own?'

That was too much for Julie. She had been about to say, 'My morals are above such sordid behaviour,' but then thought it best not to stray into the darker sides of marriage. She might have provided this debauched woman with a reason to 'comfort' Father Martinius! With a barely audible 'No' and without taking any formal leave of the Meidens, she turned her attention to her husband.

Cecilie, pleased that she had won the skirmish, looked as satisfied as any well fed cat. As they walked away from the church, she pulled Yrja along with her to catch up with Dag and Liv.

'What a mare!' she said to Yrja. 'You watch out for her!'

But Yrja, who was far simpler by nature and less suspicious of others, thought Cecilie had been unreasonably hard on the sweet little pastor's wife.

* * * *

Cecilie had intended to leave the very next day, but word reached them that her ship was undergoing repairs and her departure would be delayed by twenty-four hours. As the message had arrived in good time, she chose to remain at Gråstensholm instead of wasting time in Oslo.

Having been presented by chance with the unexpected extra day at home, Cecilie decided she would make good use of it. During the afternoon, she visited the churchyard to place candles on the graves. With her head bowed, she stood in sad and silent tribute before the last resting places of all those loved ones who were no longer with her.

To her in that moment, the future seemed forlorn. In many ways she was looking forward to the prospect of returning to Court in Denmark. She found it generally stimulating trying to equip the King's children for an enlightened future and was professionally pleased with her life, but socially and emotionally there seemed to be little to look forward to. And what about Alexander, the Marquis – would she ever be able to see him face to face again? She had no real wish to go calling on him and hoped they didn't meet by chance. And what too of Martin? He was so much like Alexander and she realised that she had also grown very fond of the priest, although he was living in such a rancorous, unhappy marriage – so perhaps little could become of that either.

Engrossed in these thoughts, which seemed to lead nowhere, she stayed at the churchyard for longer than she had planned. A calm mysterious aura of serenity grew around her as she watched the tiny flickering flames of the candles on the graves. She found it easy to imagine they were the souls of the departed welcoming her. Oh, how much she wanted to speak to those older, wiser souls now – Grandpapa Tengel or Grandmama Charlotte, or dear Silje, who intuitively knew so many things.

Cecilie was still standing there as dusk began to close in around her. She cleared away some dead flowers and some empty pots; then carried them down to the little shed by the stream behind the church. The shed was used to store spades and pails and other objects that should not be left to litter a place of peace and tranquillity.

As she came out and turned to close the door, she caught sight of a figure between the trees, up near the churchyard wall. Cecilie was not superstitious or afraid of the dark and didn't for one second believe in the resurrection of the dead. No, it was a human being, a man, nothing more or less. But where had he come from, and so

256

swiftly? There had previously been no sign of anybody either on the road or in the pastures surrounding the churchyard.

It was difficult to identify the shadowy figure in the fast fading light, but as soon as the man climbed over the low wall and walked towards her, she saw it was the pastor. She felt no sense of surprise – in some strange way she had been expecting him – neither could she stop the wave of mixed emotions that quickly engulfed her. Part of her wanted to meet him again, yet another part of her did not. As he came up to her, she took a step back into the shed and he came in, pulling the door shut behind him.

'Where did you spring from?' she asked in a light tone. 'I had no idea you were near.'

When he spoke, his voice was shaky. 'I've been watching you for a long time – from inside the church. I waited until you came down here.'

'And Julie?'

'She was so sure that you had left, she decided to visit her parents, who live near Oslo. I too, was certain you were on your way to Denmark.'

'The ship has been delayed for twenty-four hours,' she said shortly. She was feeling uncomfortable and not fully in control of the situation. She knew she could just leave, but made no move to do so. Something – a stirring excitement, a forbidden expectation – held her there.

'I have asked Julie to release me from my marriage vows.'

That was unexpected. At least he didn't beat about the bush.

'Not on my account, I hope?'

'No, no. I simply could not constrain myself any longer.'

'I fully understand. But a priest seeking to annul his marriage – that's not possible, is it?'

'No, but I am desperate.'

'And she – what does she say?'

'Of course, she did not agree to it – but worse than that, she threatened retaliation. She does have the power to exact her revenge and because I had no wish to see you harmed, I have promised to remain with her.'

'Yes, it was the only thing you could do. A divorce would be very damaging for you, especially since she is so adored by the people. So she knows about me, then?'

'She guessed – but it wasn't difficult for her.' He paused in confusion; then rushed on impulsively, 'I believe you are my whole life, Cecilie!'

Cecilie felt a glow of excitement flaring deep inside her, but she did not want to do anything underhand. She wanted to keep herself true to Alexander, didn't she? To Alexander – oh God, no! He would not be there for her any more. In truth she had nobody.

It suddenly dawned on her that the other young noblemen in Denmark – those who had only courted her out of civility – had kept their distance because of Alexander. They were unsure of him, uncertain whether or not she was his intended. That was what Alexander had meant when he said that he had used her! She had been a shield to hide behind, proof of his innocence when those accusations were levelled at him. Poor Alexander! He had believed that she understood all this and had played her part in the game willingly. But all the time she had known nothing at all.

There was precious little room in the tiny darkened shed. Cecilie was standing with her back pressed against the wall, but even so Martin could not help standing very close to her. Indeed he was so close that she could feel his warmth and it came as no surprise when she felt his hand on her cheek.

At first she instinctively shied away, trembling – her mind in turmoil. She was afraid to give in to the desire growing inside her, to commit an unclean muddled deed. Then she pictured the icy Julie in front of her. She saw that sanctimonious smile and heard the barbed taunts against the innocent Yrja and Kolgrim. Cecilie was very able to look after herself, but they had no defence.

Martin's hand was still on her cheek and he was tenderly moving his thumb back and forth against her soft skin, lost in thought. Suddenly, in an instinctive gesture of affection, she placed her hand on his. Her trembling immediately stopped – her uncertainty had gone, and been replaced with a calm insight. If Julie had been a proper wife, then this would never have happened. But now, at this moment, Martin needed her – Cecilie. He desperately yearned for tenderness and compassion and she was there.

Once she had surrendered to her feelings, she was relaxed and it all felt so right. When at last he moved closer and put his arms around her, there was only a feeling of warmth and sanctuary.

He was aflame with passion and fear. She was a glowing ember, pulsating and burning with vivid intensity. He began kissing her inexpertly, but her unhurried response boosted his confidence and his lips pressed against her mouth, her neck, her face, again and again. When she felt his hand reach down impetuously to touch her lower body, she helped him lift her heavy skirts and find his way.

At once the thrill of his touch aroused her – the glowing embers within her burst into all-consuming flames. With an animal mewing sound, she drew him tightly to her, returning his fiery kisses. She knew her legs would no longer have supported her, if she had not been driven back against the wall by his thrusting rhythm. But very strangely, the name she kept repeating in her head was 'Alexander! Alexander!' and, no matter how hard she tried, the name would not go away.

Cecilie was one of those few women who lose their maidenhead without any pain. It was a wonderful, indescribably exciting experience – to be desired by a man who found joy and release in her! Their passion flared and burned to its climax very quickly for them both and they clung to each other in an amazed and breathless silence when it was over.

Afterwards, as she hurried home through that dark winter evening, she thought it had all been rough, dirty and unnecessary – but by then it was too late.

* * * *

Father Martinius, on the other hand, walked very slowly as he returned to the rectory. The magnitude of his sinful deed seemed to overwhelm him. He was lost: an impenitent – a man no longer worthy to be a priest and stand in the pulpit preaching words of condemnation to an innocent congregation. After arriving home, he spent the whole night on his knees in prayer, pleading for help, understanding and forgiveness.

Unfortunately Martin was far too pure in spirit to be able to keep quiet about his crime. The following day, when Julie returned, he told her the whole sorry saga. What she said to him need not be retold here, but it was exactly what a reproachful Julie, when faced with such ignominy, would be expected to say. She then locked herself in her room and punished him by not joining him for two successive mealtimes. When at last she re-emerged, her expression was severe.

'Martin!' she demanded in an icy tone. 'What had you thought to say about all this in church on Sunday?'

He looked at her with surprise. 'Naturally I shall confess my sin and then allow the congregation to judge me.'

Julie paled at the thought and told him curtly: 'I have spoken to God ... and He forgives you. I, therefore, shall not be less generous. This event never occurred, Martin – remember that! Yesterday I spoke to my father about several other matters. You will be given a deanery – in a larger town.'

Martin was terrified. 'But I cannot accept that now – surely you must see that? I have sinned, Julie! Nor do I desire such a living. I have always enjoyed being here. And it is my intention to resign the priesthood to be an itinerant preacher: a penitent sinner among the unfortunate of the parish, doing good works to the glory of Christ – just as you have done for so long. Now you and I can be together as friends and ... '

'That's entirely out of the question,' she snapped. 'And there's another thing – what had you thought to do with her? The bitch who seduced you?'

'Cecilie did not seduce me, Julie,' he repeated for the tenth time, if not more. 'It was my body that was too weak to repel my desire any longer. But I shall not see her again. She lives in Denmark and it will be many years before she returns home.'

Julie had been fighting a hard-won battle with herself. She was not so foolish that she didn't understand her own guilty role in all this. It was that thought which had tormented her so fiercely during the time she had locked herself in her room – and finally she found her voice.

'Whether it is her or anyone else, it will be the same – you men can never control your lust! But Martin – there is one thing I would beg of you.'

'You have only to ask!' he said contritely.

'I do not want us to separate – I cannot! The shame would be too much to bear. So two things I would ask of you. First that you seriously consider my father's offer of a deanery … and … and …'

'And what else, Julie?' he asked in a mystified voice.

'Well, secondly that you show me … how … to love.'

He could only stare at her open-mouthed.

'Not now! Not at once!' she added hastily. 'But slowly, slowly.'

Words were beyond him. He thought of Cecilie, whom he would never see again. He thought, too, of his long and enduring love for Julie, which she had never returned; and he thought how sadly that had faded and died. Could the same damaged love now be revived?

'I shall try,' he promised, attempting not to notice her long drawn-out shiver of distaste. 'I shall do my best.'

* * * *

When Julie returned to her room, she felt half-satisfied with the outcome. She had averted one catastrophe – she had stopped him blurting out her disgrace in church. And he had almost committed himself to the position of dean in a town parish. Yet her victory had cost her dear.

Martin was a handsome and attractive man, and it was not him personally she despised. No, it was her warped view of love and sin that distorted her attitude to all men.

262

Julie could never have tolerated the idea of living her life as an unwed virgin – *that* would have been an affront to her vanity. Martin had been the most pleasant man she had met – and the easiest to manipulate. She had been guided by her ambitions for his career, and her own.

Now she would have to suffer his declarations of love! He would *touch* her with eager, greedy fingers – the same ones that had touched that aristocratic slut. No, she still could not really bring herself to contemplate it. She had never been able to enjoy physical contact, not even as a child, long before she ever took any notice of Martin.

He had placed her on the horns of this dilemma, and it was all too difficult. She must find some release for her feelings in vengeance. She could not avenge herself on Martin directly, because he would leave. And Cecilie had already left. But there still remained Yrja, Gråstensholm's little upstart – she was still here. And she, the pastor's wife, would make sure that Yrja paid heavily for all their sins!

Chapter 13

The day after Cecilie left to return to Copenhagen, Kolgrim's apathy and lack of interest in everything around him returned once more. He was moody and irritable, and it seemed that only her story of the Great Troll, who chased any youngster who was unkind to smaller children, kept him from attacking his little brother Mattias. Yrja felt very sorry for him and tried hard to compensate for Cecilie's absence, but she could not replace her.

'When's she coming back?' he asked truculently.

'As fast as she can, Kolgrim. She wants so much to see you again. In one year, maybe two.'

With that he gave a heavy sigh. So did Yrja, silently. Cecilie had been a blessing for them all, despite putting strange ideas in the boy's head. Anyway, no harm seemed to have come of them, just the opposite in fact. No matter how grotesque they had been, he had obviously been enchanted by all her talk about trolls and witches and the Ice People's secret crafts.

As soon as she had dressed him, the boy decided to start beating angrily on the bed with a stick. He went on doing it unceasingly and Yrja hadn't got it in her to make him stop. At least, she sighed, it would keep him occupied for a while.

While this continued, the friendly and innocent eyes of baby Mattias gazed up gently at her from his crib. There were times when she broke out in a cold sweat at the mere thought of what Kolgrim might be capable of doing, if he took it into his head to harm the baby. For that reason alone, she made sure that she always showed the older boy all the love she could, while being very careful not to let him see how deeply she cherished the infant Mattias.

Yrja knew that Dag and Liv were very puzzled by Kolgrim. Despite having all the outward attributes of one of the accursed Ice People, he had never shown any signs of having inherited their strange powers. She had heard all the stories, of course: how Sol was able to kill somebody without ever touching them; how Hanna knew the Satanic secrets of the whole world and worshipped the Horned One; how Tengel was capable of terrible wrath.

Yrja shuddered at these thoughts and told herself that she had at least been lucky with Kolgrim. He was apparently nothing more than an unfortunate little child. Overcome with compassion, she once again pulled him close and gave him a hug, but as he had done so many times before, he pushed her indifferently away from him. She bit her lip and said nothing. It was on occasions like this that she felt desperately inadequate.

On this particular day she also had another worry on her mind. Her beloved Tarald had been nervous and distraught for some time and that morning she had found him sitting lost in thought, biting his thumbnail and swinging one leg abstractedly over the arm of a chair. She had to speak to him several times before he looked up and acknowledged her, with a startled expression in his eyes.

This had made her feel useless and afraid. Had he tired of her? Did he have regrets? She had not, however, been able to glean anything about his inner thoughts and he had gone off to his work without another word.

A chambermaid entered the room at that moment and Yrja managed to relieve Kolgrim of the stick, but not without a struggle.

'Baroness, you have a visitor,' said the maid politely.

Although they were both born into the same social class, there was no trace of disrespect in the maid's tone of voice. With her placid manner, Yrja was liked and respected by all the staff on the estate. They may also have felt a certain affection for her, perhaps even pride because the young Master had chosen a bride from among the common people.

'A visitor – me?' This was unexpected. 'Is it someone from home? From Eikeby?'

'No, Baroness. It is the pastor's wife.'

'Oh, my goodness! Will you be kind enough to see to the boys?'

'Of course.'

The chambermaid was well aware of the great responsibility she had been given. The two boys were never to be left alone together without someone to watch them and, although she was less than happy at the thought of keeping an eye on the uncontrollable Kolgrim, the maid knew very well how important it was. He immediately began kicking her chair to see if it would make her angry, but she was wise to his tricks and stayed calm.

Puzzled about the reasons for the visit, Yrja walked slowly down to the great hall, where Julie had been waiting. At the last moment she stopped herself from curtseying to the pastor's wife. For the visit, Mistress Julie had deliberately chosen simple clothes, but she looked even prettier than usual – if such a thing were possible.

However, even after her guest began speaking, Yrja remained unable to fathom the reason for her visit. She was inquiring about old Ma Augustine, who lived far off at the other end of the parish. Why had she come to Yrja about something like that? She could tell her nothing whatsoever about old Ma Augustine!

The beautiful woman did not stay long. With a saintly expression, she politely declined all refreshment and got up to leave. While she drew on her gloves, as though it was an afterthought, she added with a melancholy smile, 'Oh, by the way, my dear Baroness, please tell your husband, that I am no longer displeased with him. I have decided to forget the entire matter.'

Yrja looked at her quizzically. 'I'm afraid I don't understand – what matter are you speaking of?'

'Oh, we all know how difficult it can be for men when their wives are in a state of grace. It came as a shock, naturally – but I shall not hold a grudge.'

She turned away and started to walk to the door and Yrja remained standing in the middle of the room – ungainly, her hands hanging like large red sledgehammers at her side.

'Tarald?' she asked hopelessly. 'Has he ... I don't understand.'

Little Julie, looking smaller and more fragile than usual when compared with Yrja, clasped her hand to her mouth in a horrified gesture.

'Oh! Oh, dear me. Has he not told you? Aah! It was nothing – you must forget what I said. Please, my dear sweet child ... Oh, how terrible! But I thought ... His wife and ... everything! Oh, forget it all!'

Yrja stared at her, wide-eyed and defenceless.

'And say nothing of this to your husband, I beg you,' the pastor's wife added, unhappily. 'I have forgiven him, so it is not necessary to drag it all up again. Men find it so hard to control their lustful urges, and it would grieve him to be reminded of such an insignificant matter. I feel sure he has got over his little infatuation, merely a little foolishness on his part, nothing more. Please, spare his feelings and let the past stay in the past! Farewell, Mistress Yrja, and thank you for all your invaluable help!'

She hurried out without looking back, the clatter of her heels resounding across the hall floor.

After she had gone, Yrja found she could not move. Her body felt like a dead weight. What was this? Tarald – her Tarald. He had been so edgy and nervous these past days. What had the pastor's wife meant by referring to 'his wife being in a state of grace'? What had he done? When was he supposed to have become involved in this 'insignificant matter'? This 'little infatuation'?

Feeling downhearted and deserted, Yrja swallowed over and over again. With ponderous steps she made her way back upstairs to the children and thanked the maid for her help, then sank into a heap on the bed.

'What's wrong, Mistress?' asked the maid. 'You look pale and troubled.'

'No, I … I just feel a little unwell.'

The chambermaid looked at her with a worried frown. 'Lie down and rest, Mistress, and I will take Kolgrim downstairs. He can stay with me while I work.'

'Thank you,' Yrja whispered, leaning back on the pillow. 'Thank you.' And she lay there, in a stupor fuelled by doubt and sorrow, until it was time for Mattias' feed.

Later Tarald returned at the normal time from his day's work in the forest. Fully occupied with thoughts of his own, he didn't notice Yrja's uncomfortable silence at first. It did not dawn on him until the boys had been put to bed and Yrja climbed into bed in her night-clothes, seemingly indifferent to him.

'What's the matter with you, Yrja?' he enquired in a concerned voice. 'You haven't said a word all evening.'

It was a few moments before she could whisper her reply, 'I can't, Tarald. I am so afraid.'

He came over and sat with her. 'Afraid? You? Why would that be?'

Yrja swallowed hard and asked, 'Are you in trouble, Tarald?'

He was instantly on his guard. 'Me – in trouble? What makes you ask?'

'You have been so distant of late. It scares me.'

He was silent for a while. 'And is that why you are afraid?'

'Yes.' She remained silent for a moment then added haltingly: 'And I received … a visitor today … it came as a shock.'

Tarald jumped to his feet. There was trepidation in his voice. 'A visitor – who?'

'The … the pastor's wife.'

'The *pastor*'s wife! What has she got to do with all this?'

Her face muffled deep in the pillow, Yrja asked: 'What is *all this*?'

When he didn't reply, she stretched out her hand towards him. He took it in his and sat down again. She was trying to stay calm, but was close to tears.

'Tarald dearest, tell me what is troubling you! I could not bear the thought of losing ...' She broke off, having been about to say 'you', but changed it hurriedly to 'your confidence'.

Tarald stared at her, mystified. 'You will always have my confidence, Yrja,' he said softly. 'I only want to spare you sadness and worry, that's all.'

So it was true! She hid her face in her hands.

'I can move back to Eikeby whenever you want me to,' she said, brimming with tears.

'What foolishness is this?' he bellowed. 'Why would you move back there?'

She could not hold back the tears any longer and began to weep, 'Because of what the pastor's wife told me, of course!'

'And what does that damned pastor's wife know about Ole Olesen? Nothing!'

Yrja stopped crying. 'Ole Olesen? Who is he?'

Tarald gave up. 'No, it's time to sort this out – this is becoming a game of guessing and asking back and forth. What did the pastor's wife say?'

'I was not supposed to remind you of it. It would grieve you.'

'Now you're talking in riddles. Remind me of what?'

She began sobbing again. She curled up and turned away from him.

'I don't know, Tarald. I didn't understand what she was trying to hint at.'

'Tell me what she said!'

'It hurts me to speak of this, Tarald. My whole being is in pain. But I understood it like this ... that you had made some crude, lustful advances towards her while I was pregnant with Mattias. You could not "control your lustful urges" was how she put it.'

Tarald felt as if some giant hand had squeezed all the air out of his lungs. He listened dumbstruck as Yrja, sniffing and hiccoughing, repeated all of Julie's words as closely as she could, just as she had uttered them. When she had finished, he lay perplexed and unmoving beside her on the bed.

'What a fiendish bitch!' he said slowly. 'A witch of such infamy! What in God's name was she trying to do with such a cowardly attack?' He threw his arms around Yrja. 'My beloved girl, I can place my hand on the Bible and swear to you that I have never been infatuated with that wax doll – far less touched her. And not once in my life have I lusted after her either! She must be mad!'

Yrja nodded in silence, still struggling with her tears.

'But this is terrible – she might easily have poisoned our life together. She could have broken you with suspicion and doubt.'

'She almost did.' Yrja wiped her eyes again, gradually regaining her composure. 'But I have remembered something, Tarald – something Cecilie said just before she left. How could I have forgotten?'

'What was it?'

'She said: "Keep a close watch on sweet little Julie at the rectory, Yrja. She is out to get us now!" Because it made no real sense to me, I forgot it all. But now I'm starting to wonder.'

'Cecilie?' murmured Tarald thoughtfully. 'What on earth does it all mean?'

'Anyway, now it's your turn,' said Yrja, blowing her nose loudly. 'Who is Ole Olesen?'

Tarald sighed. 'Yes, it's only right and proper that I take you into my confidence, even though I am loathe to worry you. This is something that took place in Sunniva's time.

And I know how easily things to do with her hurt you –
that's why I have said nothing to you before. Do you recall
the week that she and I stayed at the house in Oslo?'

Yrja nodded. 'Yes?'

'Well, we lived the wild life briefly. We played at being
worldly – partying and buying so many expensive things. I
gambled, although it is forbidden, on secret games of
hazard. Drunk and too sure of myself, I soon incurred a
large debt. Ever since then I have been trying to repay what
I owe …'

'To Ole Olesen?'

'Yes, but as you know I have no money readily to hand;
everything is bound up in the estates. So I have been in
great difficulty. Now the man has lost all patience and is
demanding repayment in full – and I have nothing to give
him!'

Finally Yrja realised that, for some unknown reason,
the pastor's wife had been lying. Ole Olesen and the
gambling debt were of no importance. In fact they were
almost a welcome relief for her.

'When does his debt fall due?'

'On Friday – if I fail to pay, he will seek surety in
Gråstensholm.'

'How much is it?'

'I still owe him 500 daler.'

Yrja's heart sank. This was no small amount! She had
hoped her life's savings – of eighteen daler – might have
helped!

'If only I could help you,' she said fervently, intent on
demonstrating her loyalty. 'But what I have is no more than
a drop in the ocean. What about your parents?'

'No! No, they must not know of this. I have been the
cause of too much sorrow in their lives. I would rather not

drag them into this. I am a new person since you came into my life.'

'Is he coming here?' she asked.

'No, I am to meet him at the inn. He is there most evenings – it is his business to travel all over Akershus county.'

'I see. Well, then we have a few days' grace. Tarald, please, do nothing reckless!'

'No, I promise I won't,' he paused and his gaze softened. 'I am very grateful that you said "we" just now. You are such a good person, Yrja,' he paused again, shaking his head, 'but how could you have believed I would deceive you?'

'I admit it was horrid of me – but she is the pastor's wife and I thought more than anyone else here in the parish, she must be pious, beyond reproach. What was I supposed to think?'

Tarald nodded understandingly and lay back on the bed. Now he had told Yrja all about the gaming debt, it seemed to have become less important and he started to realise just how great an affront Julie's behaviour had been to his wife. He felt his fury growing and he jumped to his feet with a resolute expression on his face.

'We will not allow her to get away with this unpunished! We shall go to Mama and Papa. They must hear of this! Can you get someone to sit with the children?'

'Of course, but isn't it a little late?'

Tarald was in no mood to hear any objections. As soon as Yrja had arranged for a servant to watch the boys, he took her by the hand and they went down to where his parents were sitting. Liv was sewing, while Dag was perusing some papers in front of a warming fire.

'Oh,' exclaimed Liv. 'I thought you had gone to your beds. But what's the matter, Tarald? You look incensed.'

'Indeed we are!' Tarald told her. 'You are about to hear the most ridiculous story!'

Once again Yrja retold every detail of Julie's visit, word for word – and did not forget to add Cecilie's mysterious farewell warning.

'But this is quite scandalous – absolutely shameful!' Dag declared when she had finished. 'I find it hard to believe.'

'But she was here today,' said Liv, alarmed. 'We ought to speak to her – but how can we manage it? Father Martinius is our friend.'

'I happen to know he is in the next parish this evening,' Dag told them, getting to his feet. 'Come children, we shall go at once to the rectory! I will not tolerate such things in my house. She could have caused us irreparable harm.'

With utmost urgency, all four of them put on their outdoor clothes and informed the servants where they would be going. Yrja's hands were shaking as she pulled on her fur mittens. She had no great yearning to meet the pastor's sanctimonious wife again. When they reached the rectory, Mistress Julie received them in the parlour, her starched skirts rustling furiously. She had turned slightly pale at the site of her visitors, but managed to keep her composure.

'How charming it is to receive guests so late in the evening,' she smiled, with her usual ability to deliver a gibe under the guise of a well articulated pleasantry. 'To what do I owe this honour?'

Dag, with the practised air of a Public Notary, spoke first. 'Mistress Julie, you have today made very serious allegations regarding my son to my daughter-in-law. Be so good as to explain yourself!'

Julie was taken aback. Because her own marriage was no more than a formal sham, she had no experience of the trust and confidence that many spouses shared. She would never have believed that stupid and clumsy-looking Yrja would dare to go and tell her husband the things Julie had implied. But she immediately assumed she had screamed the accusations at Tarald during a furious quarrel.

'I do not know what Mistress Yrja has accused her husband of doing. But I should say that whatever it was they argued about, I distinctly begged her to show him mercy. She has apparently not done that – which is very disloyal of her.'

Tarald exploded. 'Yrja has neither quarrelled with me nor made any accusations against me, Mistress Julie! She simply found herself at a loss to comprehend the things you had said and came to discuss them with me. She was sad, but calm.'

Julie suddenly felt extremely uncomfortable; she had never expected anything like this. Even the Notary himself had come too. What was this ridiculous attachment they all had to one another – that snotty-nosed tribe from Gråstensholm? At least it was a good thing Martin wasn't at home!

'And what am I supposed to have implied about you, Herr Tarald?' she asked icily when she found her voice. 'Please be precise.'

'That I made advances to you while Yrja was with child – that I was unable to control my lust and desire for you. The idea is absurd! I love Yrja and would never lay a hand on you – not only because you are the wife of my best friend, but also because you are unattractive to me!'

Tarald's anger was making him disrespectful and Dag waved his hand in warning.

In her turn Julie laughed, but the laughter was somewhat forced and uneasy.

275

'Listen please, all of you!' she said in a tight voice. 'You have completely misunderstood me! I have never said that Herr Tarald molested me personally! It was a girl in the village who became the object of your lechery, Herr Tarald – as you well know! She came to me in a sorry state, and I felt disgust that you could behave in such a way to your wife.'

In that moment, Yrja's doubts started to surface again – but Tarald instantly made it plain he had none.

'What lies are these!' he yelled. 'Who is this girl supposed to be?'

'You will not make me reveal her name. You know perfectly well who she is.'

'Oh, no, I do not! Nor do I sleepwalk or drink myself senseless since I wed Yrja. What on earth is the matter with you?'

Liv, who had stood and said nothing until now, went over to Julie and placed her arm around her shoulders.

'My poor dear woman, I think you are unwell,' she said gently and led her over to the couch. 'Sit down, my dear. You are such a lonely and unhappy soul, plagued with troubles that are beyond our understanding.'

Furious and humiliated, it took the pastor's wife several moments to regain her power of speech. 'Unwell? I am not unwell. It is you! Your souls are all warped and awry! It is all as I have told you. A girl from the village came to me – came to me and confided in me – but of course she must have been sick. Yes that was it!'

The visitors from Gråstensholm watched Julie in astonishment as their hostess quickly brought her temper under control. Very soon she had reverted to her calm and gentle self.

'So perhaps we can just forget this whole sorry episode,'

she said with feigned sweetness. 'It has obviously been the result of a misunderstanding. The girl must have been whimsical and imagined things.'

Yrja shook her head determinedly. 'I distinctly understood you to mean that it was you that Tarald had molested – and I am sure that he did not.'

'No, it was not me,' insisted the pastor's wife. 'I can also swear to that. It was indeed this girl.'

Liv looked at her calculatingly. 'Tell me, Mistress Julie, when was all this supposed to have taken place?'

'It was … let me see … yes, it was in August!'

'And you are sure of that?'

'Yes … let me think! Yes, the girl came to me at the end of August. It must have occurred shortly before that.'

'Thank you,' Liv said placidly. 'At that time Tarald was very sick with the mumps. He lay in his sickbed for a whole month. I hardly believe he was in any condition to violate defenceless women.'

Julie rose unsteadily from the couch, willing the situation to end. 'It all happened as I said – the girl must have made it all up!'

Their collective expressions of disbelief angered her more than she could bear and her manner became haughty again. 'Will you doubt the word of a priest's wife? Will you instead believe your lecherous son, who has deceived his ugly "thistle" of a wife – and who now tells lies to her face?'

They stared at her in disbelief. Too late, she realised that this time she had gone too far. By then they were already on their way out of the house.

'For your husband's sake we shall not continue this inquiry, Mistress Julie,' Dag told her harshly as he opened the door. 'We shall let the matter rest now.'

At his side, Liv nodded her agreement. 'We have long

understood that your marriage is not a happy one, Mistress Julie. And we all wondered why that should be. But now we know! We feel sorry for poor dear Martin! And for you too Mistress Julie, hapless creature! You are the more pitiable, for you are a prisoner of your own vanity and prestige – and your own untold inhibitions.'

As they walked away, Julie threw the door wide open and screamed so loudly that her words could be heard in every corner of the rectory: 'You have nothing to be so proud about, believe you me! I know things about your daughter that will soon bring you down to earth again!' With that she slammed the door with such force that the horseshoe hanging above it loosened and fell to the ground.

Like a cat, the God-fearing wife of the priest was docile and amenable as long as she was admired and indulged. But when things went against her, it brought out all that was immature, childish, repressed and distorted in her. Before that day, she had never allowed her parishioners to see the darker side of her character.

Outside in the snow, the four members of the Meiden family exchanged baffled glances. Dag wanted to go back and demand to know what Julie had meant by her insinuation about Cecilie, but Tarald held him back.

'No, Papa,' he said quietly. 'I think it best that we do not inquire too deeply into Cecilie's affairs. That is where the root of this problem lies. Can't you see that?'

Liv agreed with him and after a moment's reflection, Dag too gave a curt nod. With that they climbed into the sleigh – and the apprehension they all felt began to turn to a deeper anxiety.

Chapter 14

That night, after returning home, Yrja lay wide awake for a long time with Tarald's head resting on her breast. They had caressed with deep affection, showing each other that their bond of trust had not been broken. They pledged solemnly to each other that nobody in their parish would ever come between them – neither angel nor false god.

Tarald lay fast asleep now. Without waking him, Yrja eased her arm from behind her head and began to fondle his dark wavy hair. I love you, she thought to herself. I love you for the weakness you had once and for the strength you have now. You and I travelled a long road before we found each other. There were many pitfalls. But now, tonight, for the first time I feel really sure of you. My clumsiness and my looks have always stopped me from believing that you truly loved me. But at last I am sure. You really need me – and you need to love me.

Feeling deeply gladdened by the way things had turned out, she turned her mind to his other problem. How would they pay off the debt he owed without upsetting his parents? She knew there was nothing she alone could do.

Eikeby had precious little of everything, except people

who needed money. If only Master Tengel had lived! That was her constant plea, whenever things were bad. He was a wizard and had power over anything and everything. Then in a flash, the solution came to her – and it had come from thinking about Tengel. A little while later, feeling quite relaxed, she fell asleep.

The following day she left little Mattias in Liv's care and took Kolgrim down to Linden Allée. She already knew she would find Are at home, caring for a sick cow, not working in the forest as usual. On arrival, she released Kolgrim into the hands of Trond and Brand. They were energetic enough to be able to satisfy his need for heavy-handed play. Well, Trond definitely would and Brand was strong enough to tame him if things went too far.

She found Are in the barn, just as she had expected. Inside, despite being bigger than most barns, it was dark and the ceiling was low. The warm air had turned to a steamy haze.

'Hello, Yrja!' he called with a cheery grin. 'It's nice to see you!'

'And you,' she replied, feeling embarrassed at the unstated reason for her visit. 'How is the cow?'

'Better. She will survive.'

'That's good news …' she hesitated for another second or two. 'Master Are, I have a favour to ask of you.'

'Do tell, then!'

She bit her bottom lip in a last moment of hesitation. She found it hard to look directly at Tengel's son and focused instead on the cow that now lay peacefully chewing the cud.

'My Tarald has got himself into difficulties. I miss not having Master Tengel to talk to so much, but then I thought I could come to you because there is so much that you have taken over from him.'

Although Are was starting to show signs of going grey, his body was still well toned. There was a gentle tranquil air about him and he waited patiently for her to say more.

'I could not approach his parents … he did not want that. But you are head of the family – the Ice People – and I hoped that you could tell me what I should do.'

Are still said nothing and she didn't realise how honoured he felt to be thought of as the head of the family. So Yrja related the story of Tarald's gaming debt at breakneck speed, and how, even after his marriage to her, he had tried to deal with it on his own.

'So what am I to do, Master Are? I want so much to help him. If there is a way out of this then please show me!'

Are stood up and placed a heavy hand on her shoulder. 'That good-for-nothing nephew of mine! Still, I suppose it was in Sunniva's time – and he has matured a lot since then.' Are's voice was stern, but his face indicated it was a warm-hearted grumble. 'I can see that he wouldn't want to go to Dag and Liv, even though they would have soon helped him. Perhaps Dag would have been able to put a stop to that bloodsucker Olesen at the same time – I know of him by reputation! Mind you, it stands Tarald in good stead that he did not want to burden his parents. Five hundred daler you say? Not exactly a trifle, is it? We must get this sorted out!'

'Yes, but how? I have eighteen daler that I have saved over the years, but they are as nothing!'

'No, you are not to touch them. I want you to know that my parents, Silje and Tengel were enormously wealthy. We, Liv and I, have money in the bottom of the chest that they left to us.'

Yrja's voice trembled. 'Would you lend it to me?' Her eyes implored him. 'I will pay you back, even if it takes 100 years!'

Are smiled. 'You will borrow nothing from us. This is Tarald's doing. But I suppose you are here without his knowledge?'

'I am. He did not want to seek help from anyone. He wants to take care of it himself.'

'Yes and how had he thought to do that? We had better make haste before he does anything untoward.' Are paused and thought hard for a moment. 'Now I know that Mama Silje held you in the highest regard, Yrja. She often said that your help was invaluable. I want you to take the money you need as a gift from her and Tengel – it is yours to use on that wastrel of a husband! If you do not, you will never again be happy. And we must of course save Gråstensholm as well.'

'But that is your inheritance!'

'A bagatelle – I have enough left for all my children and any grandchildren. Besides, Tarald is their grandchild too. Anyway, I'll no doubt be able to lure the money back from Dag and Liv one day! First and foremost we must rid ourselves of this Olesen. Did you want me to go and pay him off?'

She hesitated. 'Perhaps it is better that Tarald goes by himself?'

'Yes, it is, but how had you thought to explain where the money has come from?'

She was crestfallen. 'I don't know. I hadn't thought of that!'

Are was unruffled. 'Let me take care of it! I shall come up to see you this evening with the money. I will say that I have heard about the debt from an acquaintance, outside the family. Then I shall say exactly what I have just told you, that Mama Silje was very fond of you and had always hoped Tarald would marry you instead of Sunniva. And I am telling you that because I know that is what she had wished for.'

Yrja nodded. She knew it too.

'So this is a gift to you, Yrja, from Silje. But, so that Tarald will not refuse to take your money, I will bring you 600 daler. That way you can keep 100 for yourself and he will not feel so bad. Then, later, if he wishes, he can pay back the 500 to you.'

'I could not ask him to do that!'

'You must not prevent it, Yrja. It is not for you to sacrifice yourself for sins he committed in Sunniva's time.'

She nodded. She knew what he said was true.

'Oh! Thank you, Uncle Are!' she said. Her warm eyes held a grateful smile. 'Thank you a thousand times!'

'That's too much – I only need 500 thankyous,' he replied with a broad grin.

* * * *

The year 1625 was to be a fateful one for the Ice People. When Cecilie set off from Norway for Copenhagen, shortly after they had ushered in the New Year, she had no way of knowing that the Yuletide they had celebrated so recently was to be the last that they would all share at Gråstensholm and Linden Allée. Her kin would soon be scattered again, some by choice and some not, leaving only a very small group behind at home.

Neither did she know that she was taking with her to Denmark the seed of a new life, planted by an unhappy young priest in the parish of Gråstensholm. Because of the position she held at Court, this was likely to prove a disaster for her. As yet unaware of any such change, she still shuddered at the thought of meeting Alexander Paladin once again.

She did feel she was a lot older and wiser than when they had last met, but she still had no idea how she would conduct herself in his presence. Would she even be able to face meeting him at all? No man had meant so much to her as the tall, outwardly strong and confident marquis – that was something of which she was more and more certain. But she was anything but confident that she could successfully handle the complications of these little-understood feelings.

Whatever else the year that lay ahead held in store, one other thing was certain: in 1625 it would be revealed which grandchild of Tengel had inherited the yellow glimmer of evil in its eyes. This was likely to have an important bearing on the future lives of all the surviving members of the dwindling Ice People clan. It would also lead to other unwelcome events. But predominantly 1625 was to be a year of separation.

Tarjei was already lost to the family, hopelessly ensnared in a war in Germany. That particular war had begun in Bohemia in 1618, and spread in the most predictable directions, fuelled by the avarice of a number of princes with greater and lesser importance and influence. It would rage back and forth across Europe for some thirty years and this was only the seventh of those years.

King Christian IV had long been eager to join the fray. Whether his motives were entirely of a religious nature, or not, is open to debate. The territorial gains he could make, and the consequent boost this might give to his personal prestige, were probably equally attractive objectives. Unfortunately, the current Danish Council of Ministers was so petty-minded that it refused to sanction anything – neither money nor the use of the army.

The Swedish king, Gustav II Adolf, who was a renowned warrior and devout Christian, was also a dangerous antagonist. If King Christian waited too long, then Gustav Adolf would put himself at the head of the Protestant march against the advancing Catholic armies in Germany. Both kings had been asked to lead the campaign by the Lutheran Protestants, but the Swedish king's terms were less acceptable.

For that reason Christian decided to act on his own, without the blessing of his Council of Ministers. He promised his Protestant allies that he would field an army of several thousand foot soldiers and mounted knights. Fired with enthusiasm, he began to recruit his men – apart from Danes, most of them were European mercenaries. He also tried to enlist Norwegian peasants, although Denmark had not had great success with them in the past. He judged this was because they seemed to have no real fighting spirit. But this was of course quite unfair. Why would Danish kings have expected them to rush to heed the call to arms? Norwegians would fight for Norway, sure enough. But it was not surprising that they had little interest in Denmark's predicament.

So, like his forebears, Christian IV soon gave up his efforts to recruit Norwegians to his war. But before this happened, one shipload of very reluctant soldiers had been dragged from the countryside surrounding Oslo, in the shires of Akershus. Indeed the Danish pressgangs arrived unannounced in the parish of Gråstensholm one fine sunny day in early spring. Families there were immediately horrified and alarmed to find their strong able-bodied young sons and husbands being taken by force and led away.

The news soon spread and men left their homes to hide wherever they could. That day Tarald was in the forest. Liv sent Yrja to find him and tell him to stay in one of the forester's huts until the recruiting troops had left the area. Yrja ran off at once, her heart pounding, petrified at the thought of losing her beloved husband in a senseless war. With her heart in her mouth, she searched frantically back and forth to be able to warn him in time.

Klaus, the former Gråstensholm stable lad, and his wife Rosa were not so lucky. They were suddenly confronted by soldiers ordering their young son Jesper to go with them. Klaus, now a man in his fifties, stared at them in despair.

'Go to war! Fight? Against who?'

'The Catholics, of course – down in Germany.'

'Who are they? Trolls or spirits or what?'

'Are you a fool? Don't you know that we must defend our faith against those Papists?'

Klaus looked at them helplessly. The word 'Papist' meant nothing to him. Rosa and their little girl were sobbing uncontrollably. Young Jesper tried to tear himself free.

'Where is … Germany?' asked Klaus.

The recruiting troops were growing impatient.

'Aah! It lies to the south of us.'

'South of Akershus, do you mean?'

'Yes! Good God man, it's south of Denmark!'

Klaus yelled angrily at them: 'I will not let you take my boy from me to fight for something we know nothing about in a place so far away. You cannot take him. I shall speak to the Baron!'

'These are the orders of the King,' barked one of the recruiters. 'Everyone, even barons, must obey them. Come on lad!'

'Papa!' Jesper screamed heartrendingly, as they dragged him away, 'Papa, help me!' Klaus ran after them, tears streaming down his face. When he desperately tried to wrench his son from their grasp, the troops beat him off with musket butts and left him lying injured on the ground, gasping for breath.

Meanwhile at Linden Allée, Are was staring horrified at the recruiters who stood menacingly in front of him. 'You want both my sons? I have one who has already left to make his way in the world – and the others are needed here on the farm. We cannot manage without them!'

'You are still a young and healthy man – you can work the farm on your own. His Majesty needs your sons and it is a great honour to fight for your homeland.'

'Which homeland is that?' hissed Are.

'For Denmark of course, and the true faith.'

'We care nothing for either of those things! We shall not send our sons to an unknown war that does not concern us.'

Trond interrupted. 'Let me go, Papa! I have always dreamt of becoming a soldier – to be an officer and win my spurs.'

'But Trond! We cannot afford to lose you!'

'I will come home again,' his son told him confidently. 'Maybe I shall return as a captain, Father.'

'But you are so young – and Brand is only sixteen years!'

'The canons never ask how old their fodder is!' said the Danish soldier brutally. 'Your sons are big and strong, so get ready and come with us.'

Meta, who was standing watching in alarm, let out a cry of anguish.

'Hold your noise, old woman!' said the soldier. 'We have grown sick and tired of the sound of women's screams.'

The King would probably have been shocked if he had

known of the ways in which his men went about recruiting his army. He did not demand that they display quite so much zealous enthusiasm for their work and, as we know, he soon gave up on the obstinate Norwegians after this first and only shipload had been dispatched to the battlefields of Europe. From then on he concentrated on attracting experienced mercenaries, whose only purpose in life was to kill enemies, regardless of who they might be.

Meantime up at Gråstensholm, Dag was also confronting the recruiting sergeants. Yrja had already returned with the reassuring news that Tarald and a couple of the stable hands were safe. She had found them in time and they had taken refuge in a remote woodland hut.

'No, I shall not allow my son to go with you under any circumstances,' Dag told them, with his customary air of authority. 'He is the only one here who can work the estate. Besides, he is not actually here at present. He has left to purchase some unusually good seed-corn that is on offer for the spring planting.'

'Where is he?'

'That I cannot say. He is travelling to several places in the shire.'

'When will he be back?'

'He left yesterday and thought the journey might take several days.'

The soldiers looked around them. Baron, landowner and Public Notary, Dag Meiden was clearly a man of influence. So they decided it was best not to pursue the matter further and with a sullen nodding of their heads, they turned and left.

A short while later, Liv and Kolgrim watched from a window, as the wagon carrying the young men of the parish ground its way down the road toward the church. In front and behind it marched the King's knights. Liv was heartbroken at what she saw. The desperate screams and cries of the young men's families could be heard from Gråstensholm. She did not want Yrja to witness this – many had been taken from Eikeby.

'Where is your Mama?' she asked Kolgrim.

'In with that stupid baby again – she's always there.'

'But he must be fed often, and he still pees himself, so she must change him. You know this, Kolgrim. And Mattias is not a stupid baby. He is your very own little brother. He smiles nicely at you, doesn't he? He likes you – you can see that he does. He thinks you are big and strong.'

Oh, it's no good, she thought; she didn't have Cecilie's way with words.

Kolgrim muttered to himself: 'Don't need to kill him – not really. Not be nasty to him either. The Head Troll won't like that. But I can get rid of him other ways.'

Catching the gist of what he was murmuring, Liv felt icy fingers of fear take hold of her heart. Did he mean magic? Did he possess those undisclosed, preordained powers that were secretly evolving to get rid of his unwanted half-brother – or did he mean something else?

'Dear God,' she whispered to herself, 'Dear God – help us! Keep me from striking him; teach me to control my urge. For were I to beat him, his hatred for his gentle brother would grow a thousand times. Make me gentle too, oh Lord! And thanks be to You, Lord, that Tarald is still with us – with Yrja! We would have found the load too much to bear on our own.'

Putting the thought out of her mind, she turned her attention again to the macabre scene playing itself out on the road below. Look, there was Meta! Oh, God, yes it was Meta, and as Liv watched, she gave up chasing the wagon and fell to her knees at the side of the road. Unable to rise, she sat curled up in a heap of utter despair. From this, she knew that one of the young boys from Linden Allée must be amongst the unfortunate creatures in the wagon! Maybe even both of them?

'Dag!' she cried out in a distraught voice. 'Dag where are you?'

But her husband did not hear her. She could see that the soldiers were beating off assaults from women and older men running after the wagon. And look – there was Klaus! He was too slow and too heavy to keep up with the rapidly disappearing procession. So they had taken his son Jesper as well!

Liv would never forget the sounds of the cries and the tumult down on that road; or the sight of their loyal former stable hand, his wail of anguish echoing despondently in the wake of the waggon. She watched him as he staggered along, all hope gone of trying to prevent his son from being killed in some strange incomprehensible war.

Turning her eyes away from the distressing scene, she gripped Kolgrim's shoulder tight and wiped away her tears. Of the six grandchildren of Silje and Tengel, only Tarald was still at home and that was thanks to luck and a timely warning. Sunniva was dead; Cecilie was in Copenhagen; Tarjei on his way back to Tübingen; and now Trond and Brand were disappearing to an unknown fate. Liv's heart felt as it was about to break from all this sorrow.

Like everybody else on the estate, she remained completely ignorant of the desperate and forlorn circumstances under which her nephew Tarjei was existing, caught without food or help in the middle of an increasingly fierce war. She was equally unaware that her daughter Cecilie had a personal crisis to overcome in the

Danish capital. Nor did she know that among Tengel's surviving grandchildren, one was already carrying forward the evil curse of the Ice People – and the terrible moment when that would be revealed was not far away.

A remarkable epoch that had, by and large, been peaceful and happy, was over. The door to a new and unknown age was about to open.

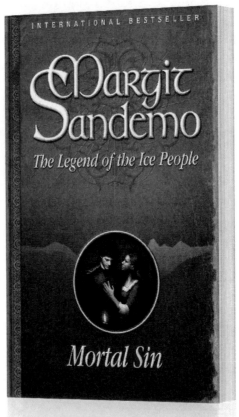

ISBN: 978-1-903571-85-9

Book 5 of The Legend of the Ice People series, Mortal Sin, *is to be published on 6 November 2008*

Further Information

Publication for the first time in the English language of the novels of Margit Sandemo began with *Spellbound*. The first six novels of *The Legend of the Ice People* are being published monthly up to Christmas 2008 and further editions will appear throughout the following year.

The latest information about the new writing of Margit Sandemo and worldwide publication and other media plans are posted and updated on her new English-language website at www.margitsandemo.co.uk along with details of her public appearances and special reader offers and forums.

All current Tagman fiction titles are listed on our website www.tagmanpress.co.uk and can be ordered online. Tagman publications are also available direct by post from: The Tagman Press, Media House, Burrel Road, St Ives, Huntingdon, Cambridgeshire, United Kingdom PE27 3LE.

For details of prices and special discounts for multiple orders, phone 0845 644 4186, fax 0845 644 4187 or e-mail sales@tagmanpress.co.uk